Stephen Havard

The Duel

Copyright © 2020 Stephen Havard All rights reserved.

The characters and events portrayed in this book are fictitious. Any similarity to real persons, living or dead, is coincidental and not intended by the author.

No part of this book may be reproduced, or stored in a retrieval system, or transmitted in any form or by any means, electronic, mechanical, photocopying, recording, or otherwise, without express written permission of the publisher.

ISBN: 9798553881160
Imprint: Independently published

Cover design by: Author/Getty Images

For Cathy. Thanks for always believing in me.

Chapter 1

My skin felt clammy despite the apparent coolness of the room I had now been incarcerated in for the last thirty minutes, although it felt much longer. The young woman who had escorted me here had been pleasant enough, but I was glad when she had left so I could compose my thoughts and think of the task that lay ahead of me.

Looking into the mirror that faced me I could see the make-up was losing its magic and the red blotches on my cheeks were already starting to show again. The sight of this reminded me of the discussion I had an hour or so ago, in another room a few doors down the corridor.

'Have you ever thought of moisturising?' said the woman as she applied the foundation skilfully around my face, whilst I sat nervously in the chair facing the dressing room mirror with the fancy lights around it, like you saw famous actors' facing before they go on stage.

'No' I said rather gingerly as she moved behind me to style my hair into something reassembling fashionable.

'I know a brilliant face cream that could help' she said. 'I can write it down for you if it's easier, as it's a bit tricky to remember.'

Not wanting to cause offence, the only sentence I could utter was, *'Yes, that would be lovely'* as my face reddened even more. All I wanted was for this ordeal to finish so I could leap off the chair.

Recalling this incident my hand moved slowly to my trouser pocket as I removed the small piece of paper. Unfolding it, I then proceeded to crumple it into a ball, before throwing it expertly into the waste bin around 10 feet away.

'That is what I think of your advice' I shouted rather too loudly, as my anger at the comment grew.

Yes, I knew my skin was not as radiant as it should be for a 42-year-old man, which I had put this down to my over fondness of alcohol and fast food. A jumped-up make-up artist was not going to wind me up now, of all days. I reached for the glass of water on the table before me with trembling hands as I desperately tried to calm my anger and nerves.

The sweat was by now dripping off me and I could see marks starting to show on my expensive silk shirt that I had bought a week earlier from that posh shop that 'never knowingly undersold', although I couldn't quite get that slogan considering the extortionate prices they charged. This was an incredibly special occasion for me, and I wanted to look my best, so paying over £200 for this shirt was well worth it, especially if the night ended on a successful note. Remembering that afternoon over a week ago made me smile, as I pictured the sales assistant fussing over me whilst being oblivious to other customers in the store who also wanted his attention. He even wanted a selfie with me at the end which made me laugh, as he wished me all the best for the following week. To be honest, although this incident amused me, it also filled me with enormous pride. I was now being recognised and complimented on for my achievements. The last few months had made me famous and it felt so good.

Since a young age I had always craved this recognition, as growing up I had always felt like an invisible soul who was never really part of the cool crowd. Even my own parents never really pushed me, or complimented me on many things, so as an adult I was determined to prove them all wrong and make that 'invisible kid' the most famous person in the country.

I stared at the clock in the room as it slowly crept towards 19.45, the time when the woman said she would return. I took one final look at my phone as I would not be allowed to take it to my destination within this vast building. It had been pinging all day from family and friends wishing me luck for this evening and I re-read some of them as I waited.

'Good luck mate, we knew you could do it' said one from my colleague in the office, with most of the other messages also being of the same ilk. I looked again at the message from my wife which read 'Good Luck babe, we are all so proud of what you have done and know that you will smash it tonight. I cannot wait to see you later. Love you loads. xxx'

She always had faith in me, and I loved her for that. Whilst my mother would dismiss my ambitions and dreams, she would listen and encourage, even if sometimes I thought she was just doing it to please me. She was truly the 'Love of my life' and had really made me the man I was today, and for that I would always be entirely grateful.

It was the last message I had received before entering this room that had really spooked me though, and which had been playing on my mind ever since. Looking at it again brought a chill to my bones, and I just stared at it for a few minutes as I tried to process the repercussions of what it could mean for me and my future.

It was short and to the point, 'I know what you did Ashley. I will be in touch soon. Good luck for tonight!'

I had been so careful in my planning and execution, even impressing myself I was therefore utterly amazed that anyone had found out what I did. I could not allow this message to interfere with tonight though. This would have to be dealt with later because now I had work to do, and nothing could get in the way of that.

Suddenly there was a knock on the door, and I looked at the clock to see what it was bang on 19:45.

'Come in' I said as the door opened, and the young woman reappeared as bright and breezy as she had left me earlier. She was typical of the people that worked in this industry with her cheery and chatty manner, in the hope that one day she would make it to the top of the career ladder. She had told me her name was Lauren and she enjoyed cooking, especially Thai food, and loved travelling.

'We all set?' she said.

'As ready as I will ever be' I said as I rose from the chair and took one final look at myself in the mirror.

Leaving my phone on the table, I followed the young woman out of the room and into the corridor outside. Whilst she locked the door, I took a moment to compose myself for the task that was now only minutes away from starting.

As she led me down the corridor, I looked at the walls that were adorned with pictures of celebrities that had made this place their home throughout their careers. The people I had watched on the TV as I grew up, and now I was going to perform on the very stage they had stood on in years gone by, and in some cases were still performing on.

It might seem very strange but at this point I was not at all nervous. Do not get me wrong, on my first visit here over two months earlier, I was so nervous I had been sick in the bathroom literally minutes before the young woman had called for me. This evening was different though. I had proved myself already and tonight was going to be the night all that hard work came to fruition. Or so I hoped.

The young woman stopped me behind a curtain as that make-up woman hovered around me with last minute touch-ups. No mention of my skin deficiencies this time from her, and I smiled insincerely as she did her job.

'Good luck' the woman said as the curtain opened, and my name was announced. I walked onto the stage, towards the host, with a roar of the audience's clapping and screaming ringing in my ears.

As I did, I thought of the many bad things I had done to get to this point, trying in some way to justify what I had did.

I told myself that I was desperate for this opportunity, but in the end that did not excuse what I had done. I had lied and cheated to get to this point. I had even committed MURDER!

Chapter 2

1 year earlier...
Click...
Click...
Click...
That bloody noise was driving me crazy and I was awfully close to jumping out of my chair and shouting as loud as I could in her face to stop.
Click...
Click...
Click...
How could I be so unfortunate to sit here all day next to the 'Usain Bolt' of the typing world, where it seemed every word and character needed to be typed in record speed. I was not even sure if she knew what she was typing half the time, with the delete key being used far more often than needed.
Rising from my seat, I left the woman to her typing and made my way to the coffee machine.
'Morning matey, how are things?' I heard a voice behind me say as I waited for my synthetic coffee to be dispensed from the machine.
'Not too bad Elliot' I said, as I sat down in one of the fancy pods that my firm had recently installed, a move that was designed to be more like the IT firms that littered the trendy parts of London.
Elliot Ross was an acquired taste and most people in the office couldn't stand him, but I had a bit of a soft spot for the old fella and he did make me laugh, which was definitely needed at times in this god-awful place!
'Family all good' he said as he clambered into the pod opposite me.
'Yes, all good' I said, 'although Sadie is still waiting for that Hernia to be fixed.'

'Hernias can be bloody awful things to get sorted. I remember the wife going in for one a few years ago, and it was a month before we saw her home again after she caught that bloody MRSA in the hospital.'

'Thanks for those pearls of wisdom Elliot' I said, closing my eyes, hoping that this would show him I was not in the mood for his nonsense this morning.

Still, he wittered on, it being another 10 minutes more of listening to his inane chatter before he suddenly remembered he needed to be in an important meeting.

I just sat there for a few more minutes with my eyes closed, thinking I was somewhere a hell of a lot better than here.

I was lying on my sun trenched lounger sipping a cocktail, the sun beating down on my bronzed body.

'Would you like another massage Mr White?' the woman asked as I sipped more of the cocktail, slightly light-headed as the temperature neared unbearable levels.

As tempted as I was, I thought this might be chancing my luck. Sadie would be back soon from spending my hard-earned money down the local Bazaar, and I did not think she would take kindly to find me having a massage from the delectable Luciana when she go back.

'I'm fine for now, Luciana' I said, as she gave me that wistful smile of hers and returned to the bar area.

I was suddenly taken from these lovely images by the words 'Penny for your thoughts Ashley?'

Sitting before me was Charlie Roe, my manager here. Dressed immaculately as ever in a white shirt and blue tie, a dress code he stubbornly refused to ditch even though the company now advocated a more casual attire.

'Hope I didn't wake you from paradise' Charlie said as I took a gulp of my now cold coffee.

'No Charlie, I was just dreaming of spreadsheets as usual' I joked.

'I was just going to remind you that we have your performance review this afternoon' he said, fiddling with the pass around this neck.

This was the meeting I had been waiting all week for, with Christmas only a month away I was hoping for good news from it so I could spoil the wife and kids.

'No, I hadn't forgotten about that' I said, as I rose from my seat to throw the reminder of my cold coffee down the sink.

'Good stuff Ashley. Will see you later then.'

Left to my own devices again, I thought about what to have for lunch, a lunch that was still a couple of hours away.

I know I should have eaten more healthily and bringing my own food in everyday would have saved me so much money, but my daily visit to the supermarket was more about getting out of this hellhole, more than anything.

I could hear my wife in my head saying, 'You know if you made your own lunch, you could save over £20 a week, and that equates to nearly £1000 a year!'

Yes, I knew all that, and had tried the 'Packed Lunch' a few times, but soon got bored, and was back to my old ways within a few days. The thought of preparing it every evening did not appeal, and there was no way I was going to get Sadie to do it for me every night.

God I was even boring myself with these tedious thoughts, and it made me realise even more that I needed to follow my dreams, leaving this world that made me so unhappy and lifeless. I really did feel like that 'hamster on the wheel', desperately trying to jump off, only to find I did not know how to.

Walking back to my desk I could see Linda was not at her seat, hopefully allowing me a few minutes peace from her clicking. I had things to do, and a few minutes alone is just what I needed.

Logging back onto my computer I quickly brought up Google and typed the following: 'Applying for quiz shows.'

After clicking on the search results, I was disappointed to see no new shows were being returned. Looking back over the emails I had received over the past few months I wondered if my dream of appearing on a TV quiz show was ever going to materialise. The emails had the same depressing opening sentence in them.

'Thank you for applying for our show, unfortunately you have been unsuccessful this time.'

I had not even got a telephone call back, yet alone an audition. Was I that boring? Did I need to make myself more interesting, even if it meant lying?

I decided it was time for a new approach, if I was going to make my dream come true.

Chapter 3

Patrick Reed looked out of the window of his office, to the large expanse of garden that overlooked his Georgian mansion in the heart of the Kent countryside.

Patrick loved this garden and had personally planned its transformation into one of the most envied and admired landscapes in the whole of the country. He particularly loved this time of year when he thought the garden looked its absolute best, with the dazzling yellow beds of Chrysanthemums being one of his favourite areas to admire. The more recognisable plants and flowers of an English garden were also mixed with more exotic ones from around the world, with the Joe Pye Weed and Japanese anemone being his particular favourites here.

Yes, this was definitely his pride and joy, a place to relax after work, a place he could be himself. A place he was finding himself increasingly in as work became non-existent, and his life spiralled into a world of darkness and despair.

Walking away from the window, he sunk into the leather chair of his large study and opened the drawer of his desk. Lifting the newspaper out he read the front-page article for about the millionth time.

TV PRESENTER HAS SEXUAL ASSAULT AND RAPE ALLEGATIONS THROWN OUT BY COURT

Today, the TV presenter Patrick Reed sensationally had all the alleged sexual offences against him thrown out by a judge.

In a packed Court 1 at the Central Criminal Court in London, there were loud cheers as the judge threw out all the charges and said that Mr Reed could leave the court as an innocent man. During the trial, it was discovered that Mr Reed had not even been alone with two of the women

who had accused him, this revelation causing the case for the prosecution to lack credibility early in the proceedings, and in the end led to the trial being stopped.

Mr Reed, 58, was arrested last year, and later charged with 4 sexual assaults and 1 rape, said to have been carried out between 1992 and 2012.

The presenter who started his career in local radio, came to national attention in 1989 when he presented the hit Saturday night show 'Make me a Star.' He vehemently denied all the charges against him and had been supported by several showbiz pals during the trial. He is currently suspended from his presenting duties on shows 'May the Best Chef Win' and 'A&E with Patrick Reed', and it remains to be seen if he will now be reinstated to these shows.

Speaking outside court an emotional Mr Reed who was supported by his wife Maria said, 'I always knew I had done nothing wrong or anything to hide. I'm so grateful that during the proceedings the judge agreed with this and I now hope I can put this awful experience behind me.'

Patrick thought the nightmare would have ended on that day six months ago, unfortunately that had not been the case though. The hope that his bosses would welcome him back with open arms had not materialised, and instead of resuming his TV career, his shows had been quietly cancelled.

Reaching for the phone he dialled a familiar number and waited for it to be answered.

He was just about to hang up when the recognisable voice boomed down the line.

'Hi Patrick, sorry about the time I've taken to answer. I'm currently playing a round at the club. How are things with you? Maria ok?'

I was fuming to be honest but did not let that show. 'I'm ok thanks Lance. I was hoping we could meet up as it's been a while. Maybe have a chat about my career.'

'Yes, I am really sorry about, been rather busy with other clients I'm afraid. I can pencil in a meeting for next Wednesday if that's suits you?'

God his agent Lance Poole was a complete waste of space at the moment, his friend and agent for over 30 years, the one who had made him a star if he was being honest, was now next to useless as he tried to resurrect his career. Since the court case had ended Lance had been slightly distant, and he got the impression he was not really making much effort to reignite his career.

'I was hoping to meet a bit earlier to be honest. I know you are busy, but I'm still paying you good money to find me work.'

'I'm sorry Patrick, I've been hitting a brick wall when it comes to getting you back on the box. The execs are just not interested, even when I say you are willing to take a pay cut. I am still looking at a few options though, so hopefully we can go through these on Wednesday. Sorry, my shot next, so must run. See you next week.'

And with that the phone went dead, and Patrick was again alone with his thoughts.

He really thought this career would pick up from where he had left it, when the court case had ended, it seemed that was not going to happen, not quickly at any rate.

Mud really did stick, especially when it came to the TV industry.

Whilst many of his showbiz pals had stood by him during the trial, many others did not, and he still felt sad that had been the case.

He reached for the bottle of Brandy on his desk and poured himself a large measure. Never a big drinker, the allegations and the subsequent court case had taken its toll and his consumption of alcohol had grown considerably in that time.

Taking a large swallow, he was suddenly aware of a figure standing behind him.

He was not sure how long his wife had been there; he had been so consumed by his thoughts that a pride of lions could have entered the room and he probably would not have noticed.

Maria Reed was ten years his junior, and they had been happily married for over fifteen years now. She had been a junior assistant on one of his shows and against the advice from friends and colleagues they had begun a relationship. 'She's only after your money', 'she's a gold-digger who will bleed you try' were their protestations at the time, warnings he blindly ignored, and to this day was awfully glad he did.

Standing there now in her tight jeans, a low-cut top, her auburn hair flowing down over her shoulders, Patrick remembered why he had fallen in love with her all those years earlier.

'Bit early for one of those isn't it darling' she said, pointing to the glass of brandy he was holding.

'Maybe, I think I need the whole bottle after the chat I've just had with Lance though.'

'Still no joy then?' she said as she started to massage his shoulders.

'That's nice babe' he said as he poured himself another glass. 'Yes, still nothing. Looks like the industry has well and truly thrown me to the wolves, even being cleared has not made a blind bit of difference.

I'm sure things will come good soon, and it's not like we are destitute, is it?' she said, as her hands continued to work their magic on my shoulders.

Whilst Maria may have said that in jest, it was closer to the truth than she may have thought. The subsequent court case had been costly, with him hiring the best legal brains in the country to defend him, and the money they had would not last forever, especially if they wanted to continue the lifestyle they currently enjoyed. It was imperative that he found work quickly.

Maria opened the top couple of buttons of his shirt and rubbed the hairs on his chest.

Moving around to face him, she gently kissed him on the lips.

'Everything will be ok' she said.

Patrick sincerely hoped she was right.

Chapter 4

'Which female British tennis player won the 1976 French Open?' said the rather overweight middle-aged man into the microphone he was holding.

'Bloody hell Brian, how many more tennis questions do we have to hear tonight?' said one of the regulars from a nearby table.

Brian Archer was the local quizmaster at the 'Cricketers', a role he had done for the last five years. A divorced father of two, he had recently started a relationship with a tennis coach, and it had seemed his recent quizzes had been influenced by this new relationship.

'Don't know what you mean Hugh, this has been only the second one tonight, I do have a squash one coming up in the second half though.'

'Pull the other one' shouted Hugh. 'I've counted at least three tonight, and who the hell knows anything about bloody squash?'

The whole pub laughed at that one, and a rather embarrassed Brian quickly finished the last few questions, calling a halt to the first half of proceedings.

Sitting in our usual seat near the window, I sat with my wife Sadie and our two friends, Paul, and Jenny.

Sadie had met Jenny at the local playgroup when our youngest child was small, and they had been best friends ever since. To be honest, I was not that keen on Paul, who worked as a social worker and whose opinions differed wildly from mine. I had to admit his knowledge of Opera and Formula One was useful for the weekly pub quiz though.

'Same again?' Paul said, as he got up from his seat.

Everybody nodded in confirmation, and I followed him to the bar.

Waiting for our drinks to be served I said, 'So, how are things in work. Still having issues with all the druggies down there?'

To be fair Paul did have a stressful job, and I really felt for him at times when he told me of all the families he had seen torn apart from drink, drugs, and sexual abuse.

'You know what it's like on some of those estates mate. Parents who are druggies or alcoholics, or more likely both. Kids neglected, so they end up in a life of crime, with the same addictions as their folks, and then to top it all off, the girls likely to be pregnant by fourteen, with a life of benefits to look forward to.'

He was right of course; I was not going to give him the satisfaction of letting him know that though. Instead, I stayed quiet.

Handing a twenty-pound note to the barmaid, he continued, 'Like I have told you before, we need a revolution in this country, and I'm not talking about a bloody socialist revolution.'

I laughed as it really did tickle me that Paul was such a right-wing revolutionist. Before I met him, I always though social workers were left wing nutters. Judging from the man next to me, that was clearly not the case though.

'So how are things in the world of IT? Still as boring as you make it out to be?' he said, taking his change.

'Yes, still as boring as watching a boxset of Mrs Brown's Boys' I said, taking a sip of my beer.

I was still seething about the meeting earlier in the day with my manager, a meeting that had once again dashed my hopes of a pay rise this year.

'Another great performance this year Ashely, it's just unfortunate that the company has not hit their targets again. This means no money in the pot I am afraid. Please be assured we really appreciate all you hard work and hope we have better news next year.'

Praise and disingenuous pity did not solve the problems I had though. I needed money badly, and now I would have to find another way to get it.

We carried the drinks back to the girls and settled back in our seats ready for the quiz to resume.

The Cricketers had been our local since we moved to the area 15 years earlier, and we both loved coming here, especially for the quiz every Friday night. It was one of those traditional pubs that had stayed true to its roots despite the chain that had owned it for the last couple of years trying to turn it into one of those trendy gastropubs with modern decor. In spite of this, it had retained its original oak beams and rustic charm, something I was extremely glad of.

'So, are we going to win this tonight? Sadie said, 'Despite the dodgy questions from Brian.'

'I certainly hope so' said Paul, 'I could certainly do with some extra beer money this weekend.'

Reaching for the bag of crisps that were open in the middle of our table, I said, 'So, all ready for Christmas both? Sadie said you were looking at hitting the slopes again this year?'

'Yes, all booked up' said Paul.

'The boys loved it there last year, so we couldn't really say no, and it's a great way to unwind' Jenny said, taking a sip of her white wine.

I liked Jenny; I really did. It was just unfortunate that she was married to a complete wanker like Paul.

The sound of the microphone being turned back on reverberated around the room, and the booming voice of Brian could once again be heard.

'Right folks, a bit of quiet please. I can confirm that all the answers from the first half of proceedings have been marked and verified. The current standings are as follows: In first place we have The Buccaneers with 25 points, in second place are the Lost Souls with 23 points, followed closely in third by the Village Idiots with 22 points.'

'Amazed we are still in the hunt after that first half' I said, hoping that we could claw back the 2-point deficit in the second half.

'I think we have a good chance as long as we start getting some decent questions from Brian' said Paul, as the room fell silent again.

'So, to kick off the next half, we will begin with a film question. Which sport was the basis of the 2004 film starring Paul Bethany and Kirsten Dunst?'

'Not bloody tennis again Brian' shouted a man in the far corner, as the rest of the room just formed a collective groan.

An hour later the four members of 'The Lost Souls' stood outside the front entrance of the pub, where a light drizzle had started to form.

'Can't believe we lost on the tie break' said Jenny as she put her umbrella up.

'I know' said Sadie 'Bit of a stinker if you ask me. How on earth will anyone know how many words are in Harry Potter and the Chambers of Secrets?'

'Well, the other team had a better idea then we did' I said, taking a drag on my cigarette.

The funny thing was, I had never smoked a cigarette in my whole life, unless you counted a few drags behind the bike shed when I was at school. After watching my Dad smoke sixty a day for most of his adult life, an addiction which led to his untimely death a long time ago, it was not a path I wanted to go down as well.

The stress of the last few months had seen me being drawn to them though, after a colleague had offered me one during a night out. The cigarettes and the alcohol seemed to make my worries go away, albeit for a short time. Problems I could not face without them.

'So, same time again next week?' Paul said, as we offered our goodbyes.

As Jenny and I embraced for a little longer than was necessary, I remembered the foolish mistake we had both made months earlier.

Chapter 5

His legs and arms felt like they were literally on fire, and the perspiration was running down his face and chest as he powered down the last 500 meters.

It was not yet eight in the morning, but Patrick was already in the state-of-the-art gym that he had installed not long after purchasing the house years earlier. With its array of exercise machines and weightlifting equipment, this was the place that he could truly relax, and for a brief couple of hours forget the worries that were currently plaguing his life.

Patrick had always loved exercise from a young age, when his prolific aptitude for cricket had attracted the attention of several professional clubs in the English game. Unfortunately, a nasty knee injury when he was sixteen curtailed his cricket career, and from then on, all his sporting endeavours had been purely for pleasure.

He did always wonder what might have been though if his knee had not given way when he was bowling on that fateful summer's day over forty years ago. He could still remember the noise as his patella shattered in the middle of his delivery stride. He heard later that spectators on the boundary could even hear the shattering noise, and said it sounded like a 'pistol shot.'

After twelve months of recuperation, he tried to make a comeback, unfortunately it was not to be. With his dream of winning the 'Ashes' with England over, he had to turn his attention to other things in life.

Finally, the screen hit zero and Patrick leant forward on the rowing machine, bathed in sweat, pleased with the time he had achieved.

He always liked to get this exercise regime over before Maria got up, so they could enjoy breakfast and a leisurely morning together. He had plenty of time on his hands at the moment, after all.

He had to make the trip to London later for this meeting with Lance, not that he was expecting much to come out of it. He had seriously been considering moving on from Lance, but it was hard to fire a man that had done so much for him, both in his personal and professional life.

He would see what he had to say today, hoping that these openings that Lance talked about were really there. Yes, he could do with the money that work would bring in, but he also needed the public back on side, to forgive him for everything that had happened. That was just as important to Patrick.

And so, three hours later he found himself travelling up the escalator of Charing Cross station towards the exit into Central London. He knew much of the country complained about the rail system, but he had always found the journey into London from Sevenoaks very pleasant, especially at this time in the early afternoon.

After exiting the ticketing area Patrick found himself standing in the mad hustle and bustle of the centre of London. Being in the industry he was, Patrick always loved being here. This was the city where he had mostly worked, the place where his dreams had come true and the place where he felt he truly belonged.

He had not been back here since the trial had ended and it had been over a year since he had last worked here before. A long year without being Patrick Reed, TV personality.

In some ways this city and the celebrity circus that inhabited it should now have terrified him, should have made him wary. Instead, he found himself desperate to return here, desperate to be loved in this city again.

It was about a 5-minute walk from the station to Lance's office in Covent Garden, he could have got the tube there but fancied the walk to clear his head.

Covent Garden always had a special place in his heart, as it was here in the world-famous Drury Lane Theatre that he hosted a variety show in the early 90s. The TV industry in those days had largely given up on variety, this show breathing new fire into the format, and he had spent many happy years hosting it before the arrival of reality TV had finally killed off the format.

He could still remember standing on that stage in front of almost 2000 people every Sunday night as they, and millions at home watched singers, comedians, and a host of other variety acts.

Before he knew it, he was standing outside the rather grand red brick building that housed the office of his agent. Situated next to a Thai restaurant, the four storey Victorian building was on a little side street in the heart of Covent Garden. The 'Lance Poole Talent Agency' only took up half of the third floor and Patrick really did wonder if Lance needed an office in this expensive area of London. When he once challenged him on it, Lance replied rather firmly that he needed to be based in the heart of the entrainment district in order to serve his clients' needs.

Walking up to the rather nondescript front door, he looked at the intercom and pressed the button for the office of his agent.

'Good Afternoon. How can I help you?' came a metallic female voice through the intercom.

'Hi Louise. Patrick Reed here. I've got an appointment with Lance.'

'Hi Lance, come straight up' she said, as the door was clicked open.

The ground floor of this building always impressed him, with its marble floor and elaborate winding staircase to the upper floors, but it was the lift in the centre that always fascinated him no matter how many times he had been here. It has one of those old cage lifts that you often saw in the grand old hotels around Britain and he marvelled at how well it ran after well over a century of use. It was just a great shame that this once great country had forgotten how to build things like this anymore.

A couple of minutes later he found himself in the rather cramped reception area where he was greeted by Lance's receptionist, Louise

Preston. She had been with Lance for over 20 years and Patrick considered her as close a friend as Lance was.

'Hi Patrick, it's great to see you again. Been way too long since the end of the...' Her voice trailed off as she stopped herself mentioning the word that now hung in the air.

'It's ok Louise, you can mention the word 'trial' without fearing that I might burst into tears.'

'I'm sorry Patrick, it was just awful what happened to you, and so bloody unfair on how you have been treated since it ended' she said as she lifted the phone to let Lance know I was there.

Seconds later his agent opened the door of his office and hugged his client with the ferocity of some long lost relative. In his early fifties, Lance was a few years younger than Patrick, and like himself he kept in good shape with golf and cricket being passions of his.

'It's so good to see you again' he said as he pulled away. 'I'm really sorry it's been so long, I've just been stupidly busy, you know how it is?'

To be honest he did not know how it was and was still rightly pissed off with Lance but didn't want to get into all of that now, especially in front of Louise.

'Coffee, tea, or would you prefer something stronger?' Lance said.

'Coffee will be fine thanks' Lance replied, even though he was tempted by having something stronger.

'Two coffees please Louise' Lance said, leading me into his office and closing the door behind us.

The office was much more spacious than the small reception area outside it and Lance ushered him to a seat before a large curved walnut desk. The room was adorned with pictures of famous celebrities and acts that Lance was proud to call his clients, and Patrick was relieved to see that his picture was still amongst them.

'I was actually going to call you yesterday with some good news Patrick, then I remembered our meeting today so thought it would be good to say face to face' Lance said, taking a seat in the leather chair in front of him.

'Good news?' I said, turning to the sound of a knock at the office door.

'Come in' said Lance, as Louise entered with the two coffees and a plate of biscuits.

As she left, Patrick turned once again towards his agent, who now had a broad grin on his face in anticipation of the news he was about to reveal.

'So, don't keep me in suspense Lance, good news is something that has been in short supply for me since the trial ended.'

'Well, I had a call yesterday afternoon from a production company that specialises in quiz shows' Lance said, with a smile still on his face, a smile that was starting to irritate Patrick.

'Bloody hell Lance, I come all the way here and all you can come up with is a crappy little quiz show.'

'Look Patrick, I'm talking here as much as your friend as your agent, but do you really think we can be fussy in the circumstances?'

Patrick leant back in his chair and stared past Lance towards the window and the London skyline beyond. Of course, he knew Lance was right in that regard, though he did not think a quiz show was the answer.

'I know you want to go back to the shows you did before, but that's just not possible right now, so at least hear me out and then you can decide what to do?'

'Go on then, hit me with all the gory details' he said with a feeble laugh.

'Well, yesterday afternoon I was called up 'out of the blue' by a producer at a production company that specialises in the quiz show genre. Seems this guy is a big fan of yours, judging by the gushing words he was using on the phone.'

'Well, I'm glad someone still is' Patrick said.

Ignoring the interruption Lance continued 'He was saying that they had pitched this big primetime quiz to the channels, which they all loved, and it seems after a bit of a bidding war it has been picked up by one of the big commercial ones.'

'At least it's not daytime I suppose' Patrick said. 'I really couldn't bear being stuck in the afternoon schedules, with only students, pensioners and the workshy watching.'

'Let us not count our chickens yet, they want to see you in their office for a run-through, but I don't think they would have got in touch unless they were really keen on getting you on-board.'

'So, when do they need to know by?' Patrick said.

'Well, like I just said, they would like you in for a run-through first, that depends on whether you want to do it though' Lance said, looking intently at Patrick. 'So, what's the answer?'

With a sigh and knowing he had no real other options, Patrick said, 'Of course it's a yes.'

Chapter 6

God my head was banging, and it did not help that I had forgot to turn the alarm on my phone off.

Waking up at 6:45 on a Saturday morning was not my idea of fun.

In fact, it was hard to remember the last time I had a decent night's sleep.

Reaching across the bedside table for my phone, I quickly turned the alarm off before it woke the whole house.

Looking at the sleeping form next to me, I was relieved to see that Sadie had not stirred despite the noise. I often liked just staring at her when she was sleeping, thinking how beautiful she looked in that natural state, with not a care in the world. Sleeping without worry, unlike myself.

Sadie did not know the half of it, and that was the way I wanted it to stay.

Slipping quietly out of bed I checked my phone as I walked slowly towards the bathroom. I berated the kids for checking their phones as soon as they got up, and now here I was doing exactly the same thing. After a quick check on the news websites to see if any Royals or Celebrities had died overnight, I was looking through my emails and bank accounts to check for any good news. As always, there was none. There had been no good news since the day I made the biggest mistake of my life.

Looking in the bathroom mirror I could see the physical effects of the last few months etched on my face. Bags under my eyes and noticeable reddish skin from one too many of the drinks, the drinks that had become my faithful companion over these last few months.

Walking downstairs I was greeted by the friendly face of our dog Riley.

'Morning Riley old boy' I said as I knelt beside him and gave him a good rub behind the ears, which he loved.

I had never been an animal lover since childhood, with dogs being a particular phobia of mine. Thinking back to that incident when I was seven, as our neighbour's Labrador escaped their back garden, my terrified bewilderment as it would not stop jumping on me. The incident still sent shivers down me after all these years. There was nothing really aggressive in what the dog did, he just wanted some love and attention I guessed, but for some reason the incident had traumatised me ever since.

My determination not to have animals had stayed firmed until the kids had arrived, and now the house was alive with fish, rabbits, a cat called Marty and our latest addition Riley.

Riley was a Cavachon breed, who with his soft coat, droopy ears and big brown eyes had immediately melted our hearts as soon as we had seen him. A cross between a Cavalier King Charles Spaniel and a Bichon Frise, Riley had not been cheap, and considering my current predicament it was a purchase that probably should have been avoided.

After putting the kettle on and giving Riley his breakfast, I went into the living room and switched on the TV. A committed news junkie I could sit down for most of the day watching the 24-hour news channels that now dominated the schedules.

The news was its usual diet of doom and gloom which seemed to accurately reflect the way my life was going now. The only light relief was news that a reality TV couple had split up, although the entertainment correspondent assured the worried public that they would remain best friends.

My head still felt like I had gone ten rounds with Mike Tyson and the black coffee I now nursed in my hand was not really helping. The whiskeys at the end of the night had seemed a good idea at the time, boy was I now regretting it now though. Being up so early, I decided that maybe a walk with Riley might shake the cobwebs off and take the edge off my throbbing head.

Never the most active person you could meet, that had all changed since we had got a dog, and now his twice daily walks had at least made me feel healthier, though my waistline was not quite showing that yet.

Quickly dressing into a pair of jeans and a sweatshirt, I gently tapped Sadie on the shoulder as I sat on the edge of our bed.

'Morning babe' I said, watching as she slowly opened her eyes.

'I'm just going to take Riley out for a quick walk to try and shake off this bloody headache.'

Rubbing her eyes as she got accustomed to the early morning sun, Sadie said, 'Why don't you take some paracetamol for it.'

'You know I don't like taking tablets. I'm sure the walk will take the edge off it.'

'What time is it anyway?' she said as she let out a big yawn.

'It's early. Go back to sleep and I'll see you later' I said as I gave her a quick kiss, before disappearing out of the bedroom and returning downstairs.

Riley could already sense that a walk was on the cards and was whimpering by the front door as I descended the stairs.

'Be with you in a sec old boy' I said as I put my trainers on and got my coat.

I put his lead on, and then opened the front door, both of us then venturing out into the winter sunshine.

I really loved living in this small village in the heart of the Gower peninsula. The rolling countryside behind us contrasted with the white sandy beach that I and Riley now headed towards. It really was hard to believe sometimes that we were so close to the busy city of Swansea.

As we reached the beach, I let Riley off the lead to run up and down the beach, something which he loved to do. Finding a spot on the rocks where I could keep an eye on him, I sat down.

The walk here had indeed eased my head, with that came back the worries though.

What would Aunt Joan have said if she had been alive to see the mess, I now found myself in?

Thinking about her, and what she had done for me brought tears to my eyes. Aunt Joan was married to my uncle from my mother's side, with both her and my uncle being my godparents as well. Childless throughout their marriage, it had been their wish to bequeath me something in their will when that time came. Sadly, that time came sooner than we all expected with both dying of cancer within a year of each other.

I can still remember the letter arriving from the solicitor detailing the money I had been left. It was not a life changing amount and I certainly could not quit work, but it was enough to clear my debts and put a small amount into my savings.

And that was of course what I should have done, so why the hell did I change the habit of a lifetime and take the stupid risk I had?

Of course, I could blame it all on Martin for getting me involved in the first place, that would be so unfair though. I went into it with my eyes fully open, and Martin had been conned just like me, although he had much deeper pockets to absorb the losses than me.

Martin Burgess and I had been good friends since meeting at work five years earlier, the investment scam had soured that friendship though and we now barely talked.

Cryptocurrency had been my downfall, and what a downfall it had been. Usually so careful with money, I had been seduced by the passion and excitement of Martin for this virtual currency, which he assured would make us both a lot of money.

I could not believe how stupid I had been, believing the bogus promise of a 200% return on my investment. Not only had I invested all of Aunt Joan's inheritance, but I had also added to my stupidity by chucking my small amount of savings into the fraudster's pockets.

I had thought Martin and I had done all the right things before investing, unfortunately we did not realise we were dealing with some very clever bastards who had covered their tracks very well. We had gone to the relevant authorities when our investment had disappeared into the ether, the chances of us ever seeing that money again was slim though. We were told thousands had been scammed, not only here but in America and Canada to. The fact there were thousands of other gullible fools out there did not make us feel any better.

Deciding that was enough exercise for Riley today, I rose to get up and called the dog towards me.

Feeling my phone vibrate in my pocket I pulled it out and read the text message that now showed on the screen.

It simply read 'Ashley, we need to talk ASAP.'

With everything else going on in my life right now, this was all I needed.

As Riley bounded up towards me from the sandy beach, I sat down again on the rocks and cried my eyes out.

Chapter 7

'For god's sake Patrick, will you please calm down' said Lance, who was sat beside him on the leather sofa in the plush offices of Gem productions.

'I'm sorry Lance, I just can't help it, I haven't done this sort of thing in such a long time.'

'You will be fine, and remember they approached us for this, so unless you totally cock it up, I'm sure it's yours.'

'Thanks for that uplifting pep talk. I'm sure I will nail it after those words of wisdom' Patrick said, taking a sip of the glass of water that had been offered on their arrival.

The truth was Patrick was shaking like a leaf and the sweat was dripping off him despite the coolness of the office. Yes, he had done plenty of screen tests and interviews during his long career, but this one felt different in so many ways.

He sensed this wasn't going to be a walk-over despite the reassurances from Lance, and he knew he would have to be on top of his game in order to impress the TV bosses that awaited him behind the closed door on the opposite side of the room.

'So, how's your rival to Kew Gardens coming on?' Lance said.

Before Patrick could answer, the door opposite opened and out stepped a middle-aged man and a younger woman, Patrick guessed she was in her early thirties.

'Good morning both' said the man, extending a hand to greet them both.

'I'm Mike Phelps, the CEO of Gem productions and this is Sarah Mills, a senior producer with us.'

Sarah gave them both a radiant smile, shaking both their hands as she did so.

'Really great that you could both make it here today and apologises for the short notice, they joys of TV I'm afraid' Mike laughed. 'You hear nothing from a channel for months, and then suddenly they want the programme you pitched to them on air ASAP.'

Mike Phelps had a slim masculine build, that clearly showed he worked out regularly. Dressed in jeans and a denim shirt he had a confident and cheery manner that made you feel at ease as soon as you met him.

'Would you guys like a tea or coffee before we get down to business?' Mike said, turning to the young woman behind the reception desk.

'I'm fine thanks Mike, what about you Patrick?' said Lance.

'I'm good thanks' Patrick said, thinking that he needed a clear head for this, and coffee always made him lethargic.

'Excellent, so I thought we would start off by running you through the show' Mike said, leading them both into the room that he and Sarah had emerged from a few minutes before.

The modern conference room contained a large oval table with a large projector screen on one side and a whiteboard on the other. Mike and Sarah sat on one side of the table whilst offering Patrick and Lance the seats opposite them.

'Please just relax guys' said Mike as he connected his top of the range MacBook to the projector screen. 'We have a very informal approach here and want you to enjoy the experience as much as possible.'

Mike could say all he liked, but this felt very much like a job interview and that was the way Patrick was going to treat it. He really needed this job, and he was going to make sure that by the end of this process, both Mike and Sarah would be begging him to take it.

The projector fired up and two words lit up the screen. 'The Duel.'

Patrick thought he was going to present a quiz show, with the title that just appeared on the screen he was not too sure about that now.

Noticing his puzzlement Mike said, 'Don't worry Patrick we haven't brought you here to commentate on fencing if that's what you think. It really is a quiz show, and if I say so myself, a bloody good one.'

'Before I move on, I probably should give you a little background on the history of Gem Productions and what we actually do. Well, I started the company in 2012 with my business partner after working for several years at ITV and then latterly at independent producers. We were so lucky in that first year that a lot of our work came through working with the London Olympics on promotional videos, work which really helped raise our profile and brought in major clients pretty quickly.'

Patrick was certainly impressed with the spiel that Mike was spouting and judging by the clients and productions he had spotted on the walls in the reception area it was all justified.

'The early years were mainly spent on factual programming until we brought Sarah on board with her experience on quiz shows and our focus changed to bringing formats to this genre of programming. Sarah has done some amazing work here and we have made successful quiz shows for both the terrestrial channels and satellite.'

As interesting as all this background on his company was, Patrick was beginning to get restless and wished Mike would get to the point. He was here to hear about this quiz show and his hopeful participation on it and nothing else. He could sense Lance was also wanting the conversation to move onto the real matter they had come here for.

Clearly sensing their restless mood, Mike finally moved onto the matter in hand, 'So what is The Duel all about, I hear you say' as he moved the presentation along to the next slide.

The heading on the next slide said 'The Concept and Rules of The Duel (working title for the quiz show, devised by Gem Productions).

'So, I'll let Sarah take over here to explain what the show is all about, as she helped devise it and will also be the producer.'

This was the first time Patrick had really focussed on Sarah Mills, as Mike had done all the talking so far. She was certainly an attractive woman, with dark brown hair that was cropped to just above her shoulder and wearing a mustard-coloured t-shirt that had the words 'Be kind' emblazed on it.

'Morning again guys, so as you can see on the screen our new show is provisionally titled 'The Duel.'

'Not sure I'm too keen on the name myself' said Lance. 'Feels like the audience will be expecting a joust between Henry VIII and one of his knights, not a quiz show.'

'We think the name works and the channel execs love it based on what the show is about. We've also done some audience research on the same basis and the feedback we have received has been incredibly positive on both the name and the format.'

Lance just shrugged; he was not entirely convinced but said nothing more on the matter.

Returning to the items on the screen, Sarah continued, 'As you can see on the screen our show will feature thirty-two quizzers who will compete in head-to-head contests until only two remain for a live grand finale.'

It all sounded a bit dull to Patrick, but he would let her continue before he passed a final judgement.

'Now here's the bit we think the audience will love and keep them coming back week after week. Instead of us awarding points for correct answers, it will be up to the contestants themselves to award their opponents points for correct answers. The points they can award are 5, 3, 2, 1 or 0. If the contestant believes their opponent will easily get the correct answer, then they can award zero points to disadvantage their rival. Similarly, if they believe they will not get the correct answer they can award the full 5 points, knowing their opponent will lose the chance of maximum points.'

Noticing the blank and seemingly confused expressions on the faces of Patrick and Lance she continued with a knowing smile 'Don't worry both it's not as confusing as it sounds and will all become much clearer when we film a portion of the quiz downstairs later.'

'We want to make this a TV event all the country will watch and talk about the next day' chipped in Mike. 'The biggest thing since Millionaire we hope, with all the tension that went with that show as well. Contestants facing each other over five rounds, with the lights down and a hushed studio audience watching this ultimate game of quiz chess. Even I can't wait to tune in.'

It was hard not to get caught up in Mike and Sarah's enthusiasm for their show, and despite his initial misgivings Patrick was beginning to hope he was the only candidate for the hosting duties.

'Any questions before we go downstairs for a run-through?' Mike said as he got up from his seat.

'And this is definitely not going to be on daytime is it?' Patrick said.

'My god Patrick this is not a show for daytime, especially as the winner gets two million pounds.'

'You have both gone very pale' Mike laughed as we both sat there in stunned silence.

Two hours later, Patrick and Lance were sitting in a relevant quiet corner of a pub, situated just around the corner from Gem Productions.

'Well, that seemed to go really well, even I may watch it after seeing you do that run-through' Lance grinned.

'I'm still reeling on that prize money to be honest. Two million quid is just insane!' Patrick said, picking up his pint of Guinness.

'A major sponsorship deal with a multinational IT company helps' Lance said, 'saying that it's still crazy money.'

Looking out of the window at the busy life of Shoreditch passing them by, Patrick turned back to Lance 'Yes, the run-through went well, still not sure it's a definite though.'

'I think it's in the bag myself, could be wrong though.'

'Do you think they just want me to boost their ratings? Patrick said, 'The shamed TV host accused of sexual offences who is now trying to get his life and career back on track. It won't do their new show any harm with me at the helm, don't you think?'

'I'm sure that's one of the reasons for approaching us, but I also think they know you are a bloody good presenter and can hold together a show of that magnitude with your eyes closed. You are a people person Patrick, and that show will all be about getting the best out of the contestants.'

'I hope your right' said Patrick, draining the last of his drink.

'Well, we will soon know, and then hopefully we can have a proper celebration to toast your return to primetime.'

Both men had failed to notice the woman watching them intently from a nearby table. The woman that had been following them ever since they had left the offices of Gem Productions.

Chapter 8

'Did you always feel loved?'
'Yes, I did. I did not always feel wanted though.'
'What do you mean by that Ashley?'
'I'm not sure what I mean by it really. Like I said I felt nothing but love from both my parents, though there were times when I did not always feel wanted or appreciated, especially by my father.'

I had been attending these sessions with Dr Sharma for two months now, only now feeling comfortable enough to open-up, especially when it came to talking about my childhood. I really did not want to discuss these things especially with a total stranger, but Dr Sharma said it would help to understand what lay behind the depression that was engulfing me now.

'Did you have a good relationship with your father?'
'We loved each other; the relationship was difficult if I'm being honest though.'
'And why would you say that?' Dr Sharma said, making notes, like she often did in the sessions we had.
'I always felt second best. It was my older brother who he took to the football, who he encouraged, and I hate myself for saying this, who I believed he loved the most.'

I could start to feel the tears swelling in my eyes, I was determined not to let the floodgates open though, especially here. I was never one to show my full emotions even to Sadie, and I was surprised as anyone that I was even attending these sessions, let alone letting myself open-up so much.

'Look Dr Sharma is this really all necessary?' I said, regaining my composure. 'I thought the antidepressants I'm on would be enough.'
'Medication can only take you so far Ashley. We need to understand the deeper reasons for your depression if we are to manage it in the long term.'

I looked at the clock on the wall and could thankfully see our session had only a few minutes left. The truth was I was only coming here to please Sadie, who two months earlier had demanded I see our GP as the mild depression I had suffered since my early twenties had manifested into a dangerous issue. Of course, Sadie did not know the reasons for my decline and that was the way I intended it to stay. How could I tell her that our whole life was on the line unless I got some serious money together quickly.

'I've been feeling much better since I've been on them anyway. Sadie and the kids have said how much calmer I am, and my tendency to fly off the handle at the smallest of things is thankfully diminishing.'

'That's really good to hear' said Dr Sharma as she looked at her watch. 'But we really still need to get to the root cause. In our next session I would like to continue to explore your childhood, if that's ok with you?'

'If we must' I shrugged, reaching behind the chair for my coat.

'It will help I promise' she said, as I said goodbye and left the room with still doubts very much in my head.

I was meant to feel better after my sessions with Dr Sharma, the truth was I always felt a hell of a lot worse every time I left her practice though.

What was her obsession with getting me to talk about my childhood and my relationship with my parents?

Then again, the more I thought about it, wasn't that what most shrinks did? Get you to open-up about your early years in the hope that they could connect your depression to a long-forgotten incident from your childhood.

Wasn't this what they did to Serial Killers? I knew I had problems but surely Dr Sharma did not think I was capable of murder!

Chapter 9

The woman closed the door of her small flat.

It had been a long day, not the sort of day she had expected when she had left early this morning.

Seeing him again so unexpectedly had really shook her up and she was still shaking as she took off her coat and entered the kitchen.

Putting the kettle on she recalled the last time she had seen him. He looked like the victim sitting there with false tears swelling in his eyes as he listened to proceedings, but she knew the truth.

He and his legal team may have duped the jury, but she knew the bastard for what he was. She knew most of those women had been victims of that monster and it still felt raw that a small minority had wrecked the case with their lies.

She had just frozen when she had seen him laughing and joking with that obnoxious agent of his. He looked like he did not have a care in the world unlike herself.

That man had ruined her life. A life that had promised so much as she graduated from university with a first-class law degree. A bright career beckoned as she started work at a law practice in Croydon which specialised in criminal law.

Months after starting this dream job she met the man who would go on to destroy her life. The suave TV host who mingled with the law profession in his role on a show that exposed miscarriages of justices, and the pretty young law graduate who he took a shine to instantly as he visited her firm as part of an investigation.

She was flattered by his interest at first, as the weeks passed his over- familiarity was beginning to freak her out though. She begged her boss to take her off the case his show was investigating, desperate to be away from this man.

'Just make sure you are never alone with him' they had said, in a feeble attempt at advice.

She should have listened, should never have gone for that drink with him that evening.

An evening she would never forget.

Chapter 10

The Italian restaurant was busy, Lance managing to book his favourite table in a quiet area near the back.

'I'll like to make a toast' Lance said raising from his seat. 'To Patrick Reed, and his return to primetime TV.'

'To the return of Patrick Reed' the other occupants of the table joined Lance in saying, all of them clinking their glasses.

As well as Patrick, Lance, and Maria, they were also joined by Lance's current partner Cindy. A petite blond in her early thirties, who Patrick had only met on a handful of occasions since they had started dating a year earlier. Cindy was not the sharpest when it came to intellect, she was great company though and seemed to make Lance happy.

'I still can't believe the amount of money on offer' said Maria, taking a large sip of the expensive champagne Lance had ordered.

'You better believe it Maria, and your husband's pay cheque isn't to be sniffed at either. He will be the face of primetime TV again on what will be the biggest quiz show the UK has ever seen, indeed the world has ever seen. Your lives will never be the same again.'

Sensing the anxious look on her face, Patrick gently put his hand over hers and gave her a reassuring smile.

'Sounds ridiculous to me anyway. 2 million pounds for answering a few silly questions' Cindy chirped in.

'Quizzing is big business these days my love. Just look how many people go to pub quizzes every week in this country. The illusion that quizzes are for geeks and middle-aged white men is well and truly over. Millionaire changed all that and now this show will do the same all over again.'

Cindy did not argue the point.

'And by the way this is just between us now. The guys do not want any details leaking out before they launch the show to the press.'

Both Cindy and Maria nodded in agreement.

Patrick had been uncharacteristically quiet throughout the evening preferring to let Lance and the others do most of the talking. The truth was for the first time in his life he was really scared of the job that lay before him. The euphoria of being offered the job a few days ago had turned to sheer terror at the magnitude of what he was taking on. Yes, he had done loads of TV throughout his long career, but this felt so different to all the other shows he had done. The money on offer, the live element of the final stages and the predicted public interest was just overwhelming, and the show had not even started yet.

'Your pretty quiet tonight Patrick?' Lance said, struggling with the stupidly expensive lobster he had ordered. 'You should be on top of the world now. I know I certainly am.'

Yes, I bet you are thought Patrick, especially with that 30 percent commission coming your way.

'Sorry for my lack of conversation folks. I'm just feeling a bit apprehensive about all this still.'

'Don't be silly. You have done this countless times before. Yes, I know it is a slightly bigger gig than usual but remember they wanted you. You will be simply fine.'

Despite the supportive words from his friend, Patrick still had major doubts swirling in his head.

Just after one in the morning, Patrick and Maria returned to their hotel. Realising it was going to be a late night and not fancying the journey back to Kent at this late hour, Patrick had decided to book them into this fancy Knightsbridge hotel for the night.

They had not had a night out, let alone a night away since his trial and it felt good to be in new surroundings, even for a brief period.

'I thought Lance was on top from tonight' Maria said, climbing into bed next to him.

'Isn't he always? I do think being with Cindy does bring the best out of him though, and I know he's really excited about me getting this show.'

'I sense you don't feel the same?'

Putting the book down he was reading, Patrick let out a sigh before responding.

'I don't know what's wrong with me love. I should be just as excited as Lance about this, after all that's happened my self-confidence has taken more of a hit than I realised though.'

'You heard what Lance said tonight. They wanted you for this. They headhunted you. They wouldn't have done all that if they weren't confident you could do a great job.'

'I know that, and I also know I can do this sort of job with my eyes closed, for some reason these doubts won't leave my head though. I'm also wondering why they are so keen on getting me, after most of the industry shunning me after the trial.'

'I think your reading too much into this. They wanted you because your one of the best presenters out there, and like you said, you can do this type of show with your eyes closed.'

Reaching across to turn the bedside lamp off, Maria leaned in to give Patrick a lingering kiss.

'Now, let us take advantage of this king-size bed while we can' she said, her hand slowly moving towards Patrick's groin.

Chapter 11

As I drove through the wrought iron gates and up the sweeping driving towards the large Victorian house, I got the same feeling of dread I always got when I visited here.

Parking in a visitor's bay I sat in the car for a moment to compose myself as I always did before entering the building. Looking out of the windscreen at the large house before me, with its three acres of beautifully landscaped garden still took my breath away, even though I had been here so many times in the last few months.

The house was an imposing sight with its three stories and stone exterior, a house that I always imagined would be a good setting for a gothic horror movie. Whilst the exterior of the house had kept its original Victorian architecture; the inside had been totally modernised in most aspects to reflect its current use. New wiring, central heating and even a large modern extension had been added to the rear so more residents could be accommodated in this attractive and peaceful setting.

A place where my mother resided, the progression of her dementia making it impossible for her to stay in her own home now.

I still found it hard to see her here and felt failure in the fact that me and my brother could not keep her in the home that she had lived in for over forty years. The house we had grown up in and a house my mother adored. We had tried our absolute best to care for her there, the task in the end becoming impossible as her illness progressed, and her living alone had not been an option anymore.

Making my way up towards the front entrance I could hear singing and laughter as I often did when I visited.

This was a happy environment for all its residents, with wonderful staff who made sure that each one of them had every day filled with laughter and joy. Most of the residents here had dementia in various stages of progression, and it was through the dedication of the staff that their lives were as happy and contented as they could be in the circumstances.

The trouble was this place cost a bomb and it was money me and my brother just did not have. We were currently using Mum's savings to cover the cost, that could never be a solution in the long term though. That was why it was imperative that the house was sold and then the burden of finding this monthly cost would be eradicated.

Making my way towards the reception desk I smiled at the young lady sitting there.

'Good Afternoon Mr White' she said, returning my smile. 'Your Mum is watching some TV in her room if you would like to go down.'

'Thanks Amy' I said, making my way down the now familiar corridor towards the room my Mum resided in.

Standing outside, I gently knocked the door before entering.

My Mum was seated in the beige armchair that was seated next to her bed watching an episode of Countdown, a vacant expression on her face, and expression that was normal to see as her condition worsened.

'Hi Mum' I said, leaning down to give her a light kiss on the cheek.

Without acknowledging my presence, she just kept staring blankly at the TV in front of her.

Taking her hand, I said 'So are you winning today?'

Mum loved watching this show, and many of the other quiz shows that seemed to litter the daytime schedules these days, often playing along in an effort to outscore the contestants.

Now this competitive edge and thirst for knowledge had all but disappeared as the dementia slowly ravaged her brain.

'I don't like this new woman' she suddenly said. 'Showing far too much flesh for my liking. They should never have sacked that nice Carol. She and Richard were so lovely together.'

And it was that kind of words that gave me hope that the illness was not as bad as the doctors said, and that the Mum we all knew and loved would come back to us.

Her next words shattered that illusion though.

'Isn't it about time you had a shave and haircut?' she said as she continued to stare at the TV. 'You know your father would hate to see you looking so scruffy. I hope he has remembered to feed the cat whilst I am here. When is he coming to visit anyway'?

Taking a chair near the door, I moved it to face Mum and sat down.

I clutched both her hands, the tears already beginning to form in my eyes.

'Dad died three years ago Mum; don't you remember?'

'Died? Do not joke about things like that please. He was only here yesterday telling me how well I looked.'

I could only guess that she meant my brother Marcus, who bore a much more striking resemblance to Dad than I did.

'Mum, that was probably Marcus.'

'Marcus?'

'Yes Marcus, remember he popped in with the boys yesterday.'

I could see the confusion in her eyes as she tried to register what I was trying to tell her.

'I'm scared here, please can you take me home to your Father please. I need him to tell me it's all going to be alright' she said, gripping my hand tightly, so tightly I could feel my circulation going.

It was at that point we both burst into tears.

An hour later, I was sat with the senior staff nurse in her office.

'I know it's difficult Mr White, but I can assure you we are looking after your Mum very well. I really do think she has settled in well here.'

'I'm not in any way saying she isn't being looked after really well here, and I'm sorry if what I've said as come across like that.'

The nurse opened the drawer of her desk and handed me a leaflet.

'Have a look through this Mr White. I know we have talked about support groups before but this one is local and I'm sure you and your brother will find what they offer a great help.'

Looking down I could see an image of an elderly man smiling as he played the piano, and a woman of about the same age laughing with a Christmas hat on.

I was not convinced that everything would suddenly be better after chatting to these.

Sensing my apprehension, the nurse said, 'Just give them a try Mr White, it will make things easier, I'm sure.'

Chapter 12

'Wow, they have certainly splashed the boat out here' Lance said, looking out of the window, at the River Thames below them.

Patrick had to agree that this was a magnificent setting to launch the show.

Standing forty-two meters on this bridge, above the river that meandered through the capital like a slippery snake, Patrick was probably the most nervous he had ever been in his entire professional life.

Launching here from the stunning east walkway between the north and south towers of the majestic Tower Bridge showed how important this show was to everyone involved in it.

Patrick still felt a great buzz coming to London, and the view from here confirmed his belief that this was the greatest city on earth. From here he could see the all the magnificent landmarks that the city possessed, the Tower of London and St Paul's represented the old, whilst the Shard with its 95 stories of glass represented the modern city.

The selected press would be here in a few hours, Patrick being needed earlier to meet the TV execs and the main sponsor of the show.

Bang on cue, Patrick and Lance were interrupted from their sightseeing by a voice behind them.

'Afternoon gentlemen, great view isn't it' said a smartly dressed man in his early fifties.

Patrick had not seen James Pullman since the day he had suspended him from all his shows. A man he had once considered a true friend, the Director of Programmes had literally blanked him since that day.

'It's great to see you again Patrick' James said, extending his hand out with the warm charm Patrick had always remembered.

James was one of those old school TV executives who could still remember the golden age of TV in the seventies and eighties. He had worked for most of the major channels on British TV and knew the industry like the back of his hand. A man who could exude charm when needed, he was also ruthless if the situation required, a ruthless streak Patrick had personally seen in action.

'So how does it feel to be the host of the biggest TV show this country has ever witnessed?' James asked me.

To be honest Patrick still did not know how he felt. Just a few weeks ago he was sitting in his study wondering where his life was heading and trying to come to terms with the fact that maybe his career was over. Now he was here awaiting press scrutiny again, thankfully this was for a much happier event though.

'Still a bit shell-shocked if I'm being honest. All this has happened so quickly and to be frank I had thought the industry was happy to leave me on the scrapheap.'

He had said it. He had let the 'Genie out of the bottle' and it felt good to see James squirm at the words he had just uttered.

'Patrick, I'm sorry you felt that way, nothing could have been further from the truth though. It was hard to re-instate the shows you had been presenting before, but I can assure you we have been working hard to find the right vehicle for you after all that nasty business had been sorted out.'

Patrick really did not believe all this bullshit James was spouting, and the look on the face of Lance confirmed to him that it was indeed a load of bollocks.

But did it really matter how all this came about?

He was here now preparing to host the biggest show of his life and what occurred behind the scenes to get him here did not really matter. All that mattered was he was back at the top, and if that meant sharing pleasantries with the likes of James Pullman again, then so be it.

'Water under the bridge now James. Clean slate and new beginnings for all of us now' Patrick said, through gritted teeth.

'That's the spirit Patrick. Now let me introduce you to everyone else before the press arrive. Big night for us all, so best we all sing from the same hymn sheet and avoid any misunderstandings.

As James led them towards a group of people at the end of the walkway, Lance muttered 'What a smug bastard' under this breath.

Chapter 13

There was no Cyber Crime Unit as such at South Wales Police. Instead, our case had been forwarded to Action Fraud which was the UK's national reporting centre for fraud and internet crime, from where it was being investigated by the City of London Economic Crime Directorate, the recognised national police lead for fraud.

DCI Huw Evans was our liaison with the City of London police, and it was in his cramped office at Swansea Central police station that myself and Martin now found ourselves for his latest update.

'Good Afternoon Gentlemen, thanks again for coming in at such short notice. I know this can't be an easy time for you and appreciate your patience whilst my colleagues in London look into this matter.'

Martin and I had both taken the day off for this meeting and waited anxiously for what the DCI had to say.

The DCI was a tall man, whose large frame looked uncomfortable in the small seat he occupied in this cramped space. On my previous visit here, I had at first been intimidated by this giant man in front of me, his genial and relaxed manner had soon put me at ease though.

'Well, it's not great news I'm afraid' he said, looking down at the notes on his desk. 'We believe that the Boiler Room that initiated this scan is based in China, with substantial help from British and American individuals.'

The word Boiler Room scam was something we had both heard numerous times since we had both been fleeced, and it was a word that still brought shivers down my spine.

A Boiler Room scam we had been told is a scam that uses cold calling and high-pressure sales techniques to entice in its unsuspecting victim. Think of it like a 'spider's web' Huw had told us when we first met. The spider in the middle is the scammer and the victim is the insect trapped on the outside of the web. The spider/scammer then slowly brings the insect/victim to them until that fateful moment it catches them and BOOM, there is nothing left to devour!

A bit over the top I thought at the time, that allergy was pretty much spot on though. In our case Martin had been cold called, initially being very wary of the investment he was being asked for. He was not a stupid man and had done his research after that call. The company website, the testimonials from previous investors and a swanky office in the square mile of London all looked legit so there was no reason for Martin to suspect anything was wrong after all that research.

Maybe I should have checked as well, instead of taking Martin's word as a good friend and trusted colleague. Maybe I should have stayed cautious and kept far away from the scheme, after all there is nothing like free money, is there?

'So, what are you exactly saying here Ian? Are we going to get our money back or not?' Martin said, with far too much aggression than was strictly necessary.

'Like I have said before Mr Burgess, these scams are difficult enough to stamp out when they have originated out of Europe, let alone China. Authorities here are working closely with law enforcement in the US, Canada and Australia, but it's a thankful task with over five thousand people affected by the scam worldwide.'

'So, we just say goodbye to the thousands of pounds we were conned out of and let those bastards off the hook. Is that what you are saying?'

'Of course, that is not what I am saying, I'm just trying to be realistic with you both. These scammers are very clever and work from countries with let us say, much less moral authority and regulation than we do here in the UK. We are trying to follow the trail, but these things take time, and I'm afraid to say often lead to a dead end.'

I felt so deflated by all this. I was not expecting a breakthrough here and now, the news from the DCI was even bleaker than I had expected though.

'I'm really sorry I couldn't bring better news; I just don't want to give you any false hopes that we will catch these guys and you will get all your money back.'

Martin looked like he was about to say something, then thought better of it. I think this meeting had finally hit home what a forlorn task all this was and the fight he had shown to right the situation for both of us had finally drained away.

The DCI's next question hit us both for six, although in some way it felt good that the question, a question we had both been asking ourselves had finally been asked directly to both of us.

Clearing his throat, the DCI said, 'Please don't take this the wrong way both, and it's not in any way meant to be a criticism, but working in the industry you do, couldn't you see this coming?'

It was at that point Martin stormed out of the office leaving me with a shellshocked Huw Evans. It was a question I was trying to answer myself.

Chapter 14

The camera flashes were constant, the memories they brought back to Patrick were as unwanted as watching Arsenal beat this beloved Spurs.

All he wanted was for them to stop, the sweat trickling down the white shirt of his dinner jacket.

All he could think about was that daily walk out of the Old Bailey. The camera flashes as he made his way through a scrum of reporters towards his waiting taxi after another tortuous day in court.

The feeling Patrick was experiencing now was the same as then. Seeing those camera flashes now transformed him back to those dark days he had never wanted to experience again. The sweats, the tightening in his chest and the panic attacks that enveloped him then were in real danger of returning, and this was the night those demons had no place in.

Patrick had to pull himself together. There was too much at stake here, not only for himself, but also for the others that were seated with him in front of the gathered press.

Snap out of this Patrick, said the voice inside his head. *You have done this many times before so relax and enjoy the ride.*

Taking deep breaths, he started to relax slightly, the camera flashes now suddenly diminishing as James Pullman rose to his feet and the room hushed.

'Good Evening Ladies and Gentlemen, and first may I extend my thanks to you all for coming here tonight. For those that do not know me, I am James Pullman, the head of programming here at Channel 3.'

Patrick could still feel the eyes of most of the press on him, the feeling he was finding rather disconcerting. They had not been given any details of the show before this event, though seeing him seated before them obviously gave them a noticeable hint he was going to be the host.

'As was mentioned in the press release, the quiz show we are about to launch here tonight will be the biggest event British TV has ever seen.

And with that, James ran through the format and rules of *The Duel* whilst the press listened intently.

Patrick had heard this all many times in the last few weeks and began to zone out whilst James droned on. To be honest, he was incredibly surprised that Mike or Sarah had not done this, but it was typical of James Pullman to take control.

Shaking himself back into focus, Patrick heard James finishing his opening spiel and it was hard to tell what the press felt about what they had just heard. Judging from their expressions, he felt it had not set their world alight.

'So now you know what *The Duel* is all about, I would like to introduce Mike Phelps and Sarah Mills of Gem Productions, who have created the format and will produce the show for the network.'

Mike and Sarah both smiled in acknowledgment.

'And I am sure you all know our host' he said, turning towards Patrick. 'It is my great pleasure to introduce Patrick Reed.'

The cameras began to flash again at this point, with Patrick suddenly being bombarded with questions.

'How does it feel to be back on the box Patrick?'

'Does this mean the industry has forgiven you?'

Patrick was taken aback and was relieved to see James put his hand out to hush the audience.

'Please everyone, we will take questions at the end, first let me finish the introductions and then I will let you all ask questions to everyone here.

The journalists were desperate to carry on with their line of questioning, only reluctantly stopping to let James finish.

Turning to a middle-aged man with a neatly trimmed beard next to him James said, 'So finally, I would like to introduce Stephen Howard, who is the CEO and founder of SMH Data Solutions.'

The audience turned to look as the CEO as he gave a cheery smile in greeting.

'As you know most TV programmes rely on sponsorship, and quiz shows are no exception to this rule.'

Patrick felt his heart thumping, and he knew what was coming next.

'We are incredibly grateful that Stephen and SMH Data Solutions have decided to sponsor *The Duel* and cover the considerable prize money that is on offer.'

Patrick could see Lance at the back of the room grinning like a Cheshire Cat as James continued.

'We are all here immensely proud of the show we have, and that is reflected on what is on offer to the winner. We want the whole country and indeed the world to be talking about *The Duel* over the coming months, and that is why the winner will receive the largest ever single prize seen on a quiz show anywhere in the world. We are incredibly pleased to announce that the winner of the show will receive 2 million pounds, the largest prize money ever offered on a quiz show.'

The audience gasped in unison as they took in what they had just heard.

Chapter 15

In all his years in the entertainment business, Patrick had never quite seen members of the press look so stunned at the piece of news they had just heard.

They just sat in stunned silence as they took it all in.

Patrick could see the big grin on James as he also took in the reaction. This was clearly what he wanted to see from the press in front of him, and he was probably already seeing this as a major story on all the nightly news bulletins tonight.

Resuming his seat James said, 'So if you have any questions and I'm sure you do, we would love to take them now.'

Suddenly a sea of hands rose, and the cameras resumed their incessant flashing.

'Lady in the front with the red jacket' James said, pointing to the young lady.

Rising to her feet, a microphone was thrust before her by a camera technician.

'Michelle Doherty from the London Post' she said, as the room became silence again.

'With the country going through very tough times and austerity still affecting many millions, don't you think a quiz show offering 2 million pounds to the winner, quite frankly a bit obscene?'

Another left-wing journalist Patrick thought, a woman whose high moral judgements probably did not quite correlate with the way she lived her own life.

'Quite the opposite actually' James replied, as Michelle Doherty resumed her seat with a smug grin.

'We believe this show will create much-needed positivity throughout the country and allow that one lucky member of the public to change their life forever. I will let Stephen explain more about the prize money on offer though.'

James turned to the CEO of SMH Data Solutions, with Stephen Howard picking up the question in his cheerful Yorkshire accent.

'Thank you, James, and firstly can I say how delighted I am to be here tonight launching *The Duel* with you all. SMH Data Solutions are delighted to be the sponsor of this show and hope over the coming months the whole country gets as excited as myself about this great opportunity for someone.'

Patrick had really enjoyed the company of Stephen Howard when he had met him earlier, their mutual love of cricket and gardening helping to break the ice.

'I understand the concern you have brought up; however, I do believe the life changing prize money on offer will lift the spirits of a country fed up with austerity and politics. I appreciate it is a lot of money though, and to mitigate the concern you have addressed I will also be donating 2 million pounds to charities here in the UK and Africa.'

There was yet another gasp from the audience at this revelation, and Patrick was pleased to see the smug grin had been wiped off the face of Michelle Docherty.

Then Patrick witnessed something he had never seen at a programme launch before. The whole audience of journalists rose to their feet and clapped in admiration for what Stephen had just told them.

James rose to his feet and struggled to contain the unscheduled appreciation that had suddenly descended from the media in front of him.

Eventually the room quietened, and James could continue.

'Thank you, Stephen, for that wonderful gesture from your company.'

Stephen did indeed look pleased by the reaction of his news. It was a job well done, with his desire to make the company he had founded twenty years ago a global player certainly taking a major step forward today.

The questioning after that mainly concerned more detail of what the show was about, and how logistically it would work.

Both Mike and Sarah explained that from tomorrow morning applications would open for a period of two weeks. This would then lead to four weeks of auditions before the final thirty-two contestants were selected. James also confirmed the show would start airing in early spring on the network.

It had been a long day and Patrick was beginning to feel jaded. Just a few more minutes of this Q&A hopefully and then back to the hotel for a few drinks, which he felt he deserved.

Patrick had escaped the questions so far, he knew that could not last though, given the earlier interest about his involvement.

'Yes, the gentleman in the blue shirt' James said, pointing to a man in the middle row.

'Sebastian Porter, entertainment correspondent for the Daily Chronicle' he announced in a rather posh Home Counties accent.

'Just a couple of questions for Patrick if I may?' Sebastian said, as Patrick nodded in confirmation.

'How does it feel to be back on the TV after such a long absence, and how do you think the audience will react, especially after what you had been accused of?'

Lance had told Patrick to expect this type of questioning, and they had prepared themselves as well as could be expected.

Taking a sip of water to compose himself, Patrick said, 'It feels great to be back and I'm delighted it's on a show like *The Duel*. This will be the first quiz show I have done, and I am looking forward to the challenge as we prepare to give away such a large amount of money to the winner. Regarding your second question, I am hoping the audience will react positively to my return to television. The awful things I was accused of were untrue and this was proven in a court of law. I am grateful to James and the guys at Gem Productions for this opportunity and hope the public really enjoy the show we are going to make.

Sebastian Porter was about to respond to those answers before James raised a hand to stop him in his tracks.

'I'm sorry everyone, our time is up unfortunately. I am incredibly grateful to you all for coming tonight for this launch event and hope you are as excited as us about the show we have planned. I would also like to thank Mike and Sarah from Gem Productions, Stephen from SMH Data Solutions and Patrick for their input this evening. With that, I bid you a very goodnight and hope to see you all again soon.'

And with that the launch night for *The Duel* was over, and boy did Patrick need a stiff drink after all this.

Chapter 16

It was just after eight that I opened the front door of our small semi-detached house and wearily closed the door behind me.

I could have been home hours ago, instead of diverting myself to the nearest pub after the visit to the police station. The need to unwind was paramount in my mind though, and I just could not do that in the house.

Sadie had thought I had been in work all day, and due to my current workload and commute it had been easy to tell her I would be late home tonight.

Sitting in the pub had given me time to think, and boy did I have a lot to think about.

To be honest I was not expecting much from the investigation into our case and certainly was not expecting my money to be recovered. The update from the police had depressed me though, seeing the futility of it all in black and white. The only hope was that this scamming operation would be closed down and some of the scammers arrested.

I had tried ringing Martin a few times since he had stormed out of the police station, all I got was his voicemail speaking back to me though. I did not blame Martin for all this, though I could understand why he blamed himself. The jibe from the DCI had hit a nerve, the accusation that it was our own stupidity that had lost us all that money. The stupidity of Martin, which I blindly followed.

How could highly intelligent IT professionals be duped so easily?

Martin had the funds to mitigate his losses though. A wife with a high-powered job as a manager of an NHS Trust, and of course he was not as stupid as to put all his savings into the scheme.

Just one stupid idiot did that, didn't they?

And then there was Mum.

Seeing her today just broke my heart, the deterioration in her condition being plain to see today. I lost my old Mum, she had now been replaced by someone else, a person who I did not know anymore.

We had to sell her house as fast as we could, so at least she could stay in that nursing home. It was an environment she liked, and it was close enough to me and my brother so we could continue to be regular visitors.

'How was your day love?' Sadie shouted from the front room.

'Same old shit, different day' I said, plonking myself down on the settee next to her.

Sadie was engrossed on the laptop with several Open University books around her. After years in a retail job she hated, she had finally plucked up the courage to enrol herself onto a History degree.

'I'm sure it will get better, and it could be worse you know?'

'How?'

'You could be serving members of the public every day.'

We both laughed at that.

'Kids in bed yet?' I said kicking my shoes off.

'What do you think?' Sadie said, turning the laptop off and closing the lid.

'I'll go up in a minute and remind them that it's still a school night' I said, watching as Riley suddenly bounded in and started sniffing around my feet.

'Hello Riley, and how has your day been? Better than mine I hope?'

With that the dog barked, as if to say it had been a good day for himself.

'That's my boy' I said, giving his coat a good ruffle, wishing some days that I could swap places with him.

Chapter 17

'I really needed that' Patrick said, putting his empty glass down onto the table. A few seconds ago, it had contained a double brandy which Patrick had gratefully downed as soon as Lance had given it to him.

'Steady on Patrick, the night is young as they say.'

Patrick had been glad to get back to the hotel after hours at Tower Bridge, glad to ditch the bloody dinner jacket he had been forced to wear. Now sitting here in the hotel bar, wearing jeans and a sweater, he could finally relax.

'I thought that went very well, and did you see the reaction on those journalists when that businessman said he was giving two million pounds to charity as well' Lance said.

'Yes, I was there Lance.'

'I really loved seeing that smirk wiped off that *leftie*. She really had nowhere else to go after he said that.'

'Well, I'm glad it's all over if I'm honest.'

'Come on Patrick, it wasn't that bad, and I thought you got off quite lightly.

Patrick did have to agree with that particular statement. James shutting off the Q&A really helping before anyone else could ask an awkward question. He would have to thank him the next time he saw him, with gritted teeth of course.

'Another?' Lance said, picking up both of their empty glasses.

'Why not' Patrick said, watching Lance make his way towards the bar.

Patrick was glad to have him here tonight. He was not sure how well he would have coped if he had been on his own. Yes, Maria was a great strength to him, and he could always lean on her when needed, his relationship with Lance was different though. Lance was the glue that held him together and they had been through so much together. He could rely on him for anything, he would never let him down.

Lance returned with the drinks and stifled a yawn.

'Age catching up with you?' Patrick said, with a grin on his face.

'It's been a long day and I didn't get a lot of sleep last night if you know what I mean.'

Patrick could well believe that with Cindy.

'I was thinking a holiday with for the four of us would be nice. A bit of Winter sun will do us a world of good.'

'I'm not too sure Lance. Shouldn't we be here with the show just being launched?'

'A week will not matter, and you won't be needed for a couple of months anyway, the priority will be getting the contestants together.

The idea of a holiday certainly did sound good and it had been years since he and Maria had been aboard. Work, and then the trial had got in the way.

'Maybe a holiday would do us good' Patrick said, turning to look at the barmaid that was collecting empty glasses from the table nearby.

'Be a good boy please' Lance said, noticing his friend's wandering eye. 'We don't want any mishaps, especially with things looking so good now.

Chapter 18

'Not bloody Masterchef again' I said, entering the living room after saying goodnight to the kids upstairs.

'I like it and it's better than that Australian version you love to watch. At least they can cook on our version.'

'That's a bit harsh love' I said, sitting next to her. 'At least the Aussies have a bit of fun on theirs. All we get are the same old boring contestants, bringing up the same old dishes, to the same old boring judges, hardly ground-breaking TV.'

'You are such a grump' Sadie said, grabbing my arm and pulling me close to her, planting a playful kiss on my lips as she did.

'Old before your time, that's what you are. You moan about everything now, so imagine what you will be like when you are an old man!'

I could not really argue with her on that one. I had always been a *glass half empty* type of person. Moaning about a TV show might seem like a trivial thing, to me it probably masked a deeper problem though. I was a distant person, someone who found it hard to express my feelings, someone who was far more negative than I was positive. I was good at masking it most of the time, it was hard to trick Sadie though, she knew me far too well.

She was the one that pushed me to see the doctor as my depression worsened over the last few months, and the reason I was now attending those sessions with Dr Sharma.

Sadie could never find out why I had got so much worse these past few months. She could never find out about the financial cliff edge we were now teetering on. A cliff edge that I desperately needed to step back from, before it all came crashing down into the choppy sea below me.

I desperately needed to find a lifeline quickly, or Sadie finding out would be the least of my troubles. Our home being repossessed, followed by bankruptcy was the only logical conclusion I could think of, unless I got my hands on some serious cash quickly.

'Did Ellie tell you she needs some money for a Geography trip next week?' Sadie said, the Masterchef credits now rolling by on the TV.

'Yes, she did mention something. Got to be in by the end of the week, yes?'

'Think so, and Elliot needs new football boots too.'

I nodded my head. More money I did not have, I thought.

'Coffee?' Sadie said, rising from the settee.

'Yes, that would be great thanks' I said, as the nightly 10 o clock news began.

It was the same depressing headlines as ever that flashed up on the screen. Threat of war in the Middle East, that small little guy in North Korea playing with more nuclear weapons and the US President tweeting nonsense yet again.

It was the next headline that caught my attention and made me sit up.

'Tonight, there was excitement as the biggest quiz show prize ever was announced at a lavish launch at Tower Bridge' said the newsreader.

Biggest quiz show prize ever, what was all that about, I wondered.

The newsreader came back into vision with the main story of the night about the tension that was increasing in the Middle East. My mind was not focussed on that story though. It was this quiz show story I was now waiting anxiously to see.

Sadie came back into the room just as the third story of the night about the US President tweeting derogatory comments about one of his democratic rivals came up.

'Anything interesting on the news or is it the usual doom and gloom?' she said handing me my coffee.

'The usual, the next story seems interesting though' I said, as the President came into vision complaining that the tweets he sent and the reporting of them was yet another example of *Fake News*.

'What's so interesting about it then?'

'You'll see, it's the next item after this I think.'

And sure enough, as the Washington correspondent returned to the studio, the newsreader began to read the item I was most interested about.

'Tonight, the biggest prize money ever offered on a TV quiz show was announced. *The Duel*, as it will be known, will offer a staggering two million pounds to the eventual winner. With more details from the launch at Tower Bridge, here is our entertainment correspondent Anita Lang.'

'Bloody hell. Two million pounds!' gasped Sadie, nearly spitting out the coffee she had been drinking.

'Shush a minute love' I said.

The screen cut to the inside of Tower Bridge, where a young woman was standing in front of the camera.

'Tonight, here in a lavish launch at Tower Bridge, the biggest prize money ever seen on a TV quiz show was announced. The show called *The Duel* will award the winner a staggering two million pounds, an amount which is possible due to a lucrative sponsorship deal.'

Snippets were then shown of James Pullman announcing the show to the media with brief segments of the Q&A that followed, with interest focussing greatly on Patrick Reed, the host.

The reporter then finished her piece and returned to the newsreader in the studio.

'So, Anita, what has the reaction been to what was announced tonight?'

'Well, as you can image Peter the reaction has been one of astonishment at the prize being offered. Social media tonight has been awash with the news coming from here tonight, with many thousands expected to apply when applications for the show open tomorrow.

'Has all the reaction been positive though'?

'Mostly positive, although as you can imagine there has also been some concern about such a large prize. There has also been some criticism that Patrick Reed has been chosen as the host, due to the recent court case he went through. A trail that I should add, found him innocent of the charges against him.'

'Thanks Anita. That was Anita Lang, our entertainment correspondent reporting live from Tower Bridge this evening.'

The news then moved onto a badger culling programme that was being vigorously opposed by animal rights groups.

'Wow that is some prize. Surely my clever and handsome quiz genius husband is going to apply?'

All I could do was stare at the TV, dumfounded about what I had just seen and heard.

'Earth to Ashley' Sadie was shouting.

Shaking myself back to reality I said, 'Of course I will apply, what have I got to lose.'

Was this the moment I had been waiting for? Was this the moment my life was about to change?

Chapter 19

The woman could not believe what she had just seen.

That monster grinning on the TV screen, as if he did not have a care in the world.

The monster that had destroyed her life.

She had friends, a career, and a wonderful life in front of her before that night.

Since then, she had lost contact with many of her friends and her promising law career had been replaced by an assortment of retail jobs. She hated staying anywhere long in case she grew close to any of her colleagues, and they started to ask awkward questions about her past.

She could not allow that to happen.

And now Patrick Reed was returning to our screens in the biggest quiz show the world had ever seen according to the news report.

How could they allow that?

Could they not see what a lying bastard he was?

He may have tricked a jury, partly due to lies from other women. Surely that did not give him the right to walk back into TV though, and surely not in such a high-profile way.

Is this what he had be planning when she saw him a few weeks ago? His comeback?

She picked up her glass of red wine, taking a large swallow of it.

It had taken all the courage she had to go to the police, the process being easier once other women had come forward. Not that it had done any good in the end.

You can sit there grinning all you like Patrick Reed.

You will face justice eventually. Even if that justice is not in a court of law. I will make sure of that.

Chapter 20

Stop. Start.
Stop. Start.
The journey was just like that film Groundhog Day.
Surely there were better things to do with the limited amount of time we had on this earth than this. Spending three hours a day sitting in this metal box to an office where I would then spend another eight hours sitting on my arse was not my idea of fun.

As I sat stationary in the traffic I often wondered where my fellow motorists were headed as we all endured this hell together every morning. Were they all going to exciting jobs which would at least fulfil their day or were most of them just like me?

I moved the car into first gear as we moved a few yards, before stuttering to a complete halt again.

Looming into view in was the sprawling mass that was Port Talbot steelworks, with fumes and water vapour spewing from its many coke oven furnaces and cooling towers. The smell of sulphur was quite pungent as you passed so I had learnt never to have the window down or the air con on as I passed. An ugly sight in daylight, the steelworks became a light show at night, with the furnaces and towers lit up like a magical winter wonderland. It was a sight I always loved seeing.

Sitting there all I could think about was the news last night. Two million pounds for winning a quiz show still seemed unreal, and I still not sure if I was dreaming it all.

All the talk radio stations were talking about *The Duel* and now I was listening to a fascinating debate on the morality of offering such a large amount of money for answering a few quiz questions.

'I quite frankly think it's immoral to be offering two million pounds on a quiz show when so many people are struggling financially in this country', said a well-known Labour MP.

'I really have to disagree with that argument' said the well-known TV producer who had worked on many TV quizzes in his long career. *'This show will create a much-needed boost to this country and provide a public weary of austerity the hope that maybe one of them could take home this amazing prize.'*

Of course, the MP furiously disagreed with his argument and a good slanging match was about to develop before the host abruptly shut down the debate before it really got started.

'Shame I was starting to enjoy that', I said, as I inched the car along a few more yards.

It was just after three, and I could not barely keep my eyes open as I stared at the screen in front of me. Taking my glasses off I rubbed my eyes with the now familiar squelching sound emanating from them. The optician on my last visit had said it was trapped air escaping and nothing to worry about. I had to admit it was quite a party trick though, one for the application form I thought.

I deliberately had not even gone on the web yet to check out the application process, I guessed there would be a section on *unusual party tricks*, most did, and I presumed this one would be no different. I also had a ton of work to get through and knew even a sneak peek would have been a distraction. Best to look tomorrow with a clear head and hopefully some peace and quiet.

At least Linda had the day off, so I could get on with things without her constant typing distracting me.

Martin had called in sick and still was not answering my phone calls. I had managed to get a curt reply of *'I'm fine'* from one of my texts though.

It was beginning to amuse me that Martin was now beginning to make me out as the guilty party. Why was I feeling bad for Martin when in truth he was to blame for the mess we were both in. Was it my fault that his integrity and judgment had been put into question at the police station? No, it was not and my sympathy for him was beginning to wane with his current attitude. He was not the one facing financial ruin because of this, was he.

I put my glasses on and returned to work, grateful that they were only another couple of hours left of my day.

Chapter 21

Mike Phelps had never seen anything like it during his twenty years in the TV industry. Three hours since the application process had opened and already his staff here at Gem Productions had received over 50,000 applications.

'Are you sure we can cope with all this?' Sarah Phelps said.

'I really hope so, and hopefully we can filter out a lot of these applications pretty quickly.'

In truth, Mike was beginning to have some doubts about whether his company could cope with the flood of applications that were coming. At this rate they would be seeing hundreds of thousands of people applying before the two weeks were out. His staff would certainly be busy in this period, he just hoped they could get through it all.

'Yes, I've already got the researchers on to that. We are discarding all applicants who have been on TV in the last year and any persons known to have lied about any appearances on previous applications. These only scratch the surface though, and we will still need to read through most of the applications unfortunately.'

Although the TV industry had no real rule on blacklisting, it was really frowned upon to lie about previous TV appearances on an application. The TV quiz community was small and tight knit, and any known offenders were routinely passed around between production companies. Here at Gem Productions, they had a database of these individuals which could be cross checked against applications coming in. Any matches would automatically have that application discarded.

'At least we only probably need to find half of the contestants through this process' Mike said, taking a bite out of his ham sandwich. 'Hopefully, we cover the rest by out targeting of the quiz community.'

That was the plan anyway. Both Mike and Sarah knew *The Duel* was being marketed as a high-end quiz show which meant that it needed to attract a mixture of top-class quizzers and novices.

'Yes, I've already contacted the UK Quiz Association on that score. Keen interest from their best quizzers which you would expect considering the prize money. I'm off to their Grand Prix event on Sunday where hopefully I can tap up the absolute best there.'

'Thanks Sarah. Be good if we can so it takes a bit of pressure off us going through all these applications.'

'Well, at least it keeps us busy' Sarah said, getting up to leave.

'Yes, it's going to be a busy few months for all of us.'

'I'll better get back out there then and rally the troops' Sarah said with a grin.

Chapter 22

'Well, let us hope the second half is better. We were dreadful in that first half' said Pau, finishing what was left of his drink.

'You can say that again' Sadie said.

'I blame Ashley if I'm being honest. He has been useless all night. Isn't that right mate?'

With total silence coming back to him Paul said, 'You still with us or are you still daydreaming about that bloody new quiz show?'

Suddenly I could feel Sadie nudging me, bringing me back into the real world.

'Paul is talking to you love.'

'Sorry, what were you saying? Was in a world of my own there for a minute.'

'You're telling me. I was saying how useless you have been tonight and wondered if it had anything to do with your preoccupation with this new quiz show.'

Paul was dead right to be honest. I had been useless tonight and it showed in the lowly position we currently held.

'Yes, I'm sorry about that. Think I'm coming down with a bit of a cold so not firing on all cylinders.'

'Pull the other one. The only thing you are coming down with is a boring obsession with that show. It's all you talked about before the quiz started.'

'I apologise for being so boring tonight' I said. 'I promise to be much more interesting from now on.'

'Well, I wouldn't say you were ever interesting, less talk about that show from now on might be a good start.' Paul said, with that annoying laugh of his.

Sadie laughed at his poor sense of humour, me and Jenny did not really see the funny side.

'So same again for everyone?' Paul said, getting to his feet.

'Think I will go out for a quick cigarette before the second half. You don't mind giving Paul a hand, do you love?'

Sadie gave me a look that said whilst she did not mind helping with the drinks, she was not really happy with me nipping out for a cigarette. A habit she definitely wanted me to kick.

Walking slowly across the room towards the smoking shelter at the rear exit, I could hear many tables talking about *The Duel*. I wondered how many of them would be applying, most I guessed.

Standing outside in the chilly night air I soon regretted my need for a cigarette and resolved this would be a very quick excursion outside.

Suddenly I heard a voice behind me.

'You can't ignore me forever you know?'

Turning around I found myself starting at the slender figure of Jenny.

'I didn't realise I was.'

'I've been sending you text messages all week and still haven't received a single reply' she said, coming to stand next to me.

'I'm sorry, I'm just so busy in work right now. I'm talking to you now, aren't I?'

'Probably not the right time. Can we meet one-night next week please Ashley?'

'I'm not sure that is such a good idea.'

Jenny took out her own pack of cigarettes and lit one, 'I really think we do.'

She touched my right arm as she said it.

I pulled away instantly and said, 'Jenny please not here, what if Paul or Sadie came out.'

'They won't. Paul is boring her too much with the delights of social working.'

'Still, I don't think this is the right time or place.'

'Your right' Jenny said, stubbing out her cigarette in the bin next to her. 'Next Wednesday at seven sounds a much better time. Shall we say The Harp in Bridgend. Far enough away from here so we can avoid prying eyes.'

'I can't. What am I meant to say to Sadie if I come home that late?'

'You will find an excuse Ashley, you always do' she said, before making her way back inside.

An hour later we were all commiserating a miserable fifth place.

'That went well' Paul said.

'We can't win them all' I said, mock disappointment in my voice.

Usually, I was so competitive when it came to this, tonight I just did not care though. I was too hyped up about getting my application out tomorrow and then there was all that business outside with Jenny.

'Well, a fat lot of good you were anyway. Better get swotting up if you want to get on that show.'

'Don't say that Paul' Sadie said, 'You know Ashley is the star of this team most weeks.'

'Fair point. I do apologise, your star was definitely not shining quite as brightly tonight though.'

'Apologise accepted' I said, putting my hands together and bowing with insincere forgiveness, all whilst trying hard not to start laughing.

'Very funny, and anyway where were the tennis questions this week. I learnt all the Wimbledon Champions and then there was nothing on the subject.'

'I heard she's left him' Jenny said.

'Well, I least we won't hear anymore bloody tennis questions. Let us just hope he doesn't hitch up with a netball player next.'

We all laughed at that one.

Chapter 23

Miles Harrison had never seen such a buzz for a grand prix event in all his five years as chairman of the UK Quizzing Association.

With a membership of just over one thousand, the association had been inundated with enquiries in the last twenty-four hours, enquiries that had seen its membership increase to over two thousand for next season. The reason for this sudden interest was down to one thing, and that thing was *The Due.'*

The new quiz show was all his members were talking about since they had first arrived over an hour ago, and it was the reason his secretary was still struggling through all the new applications for next year.

Miles was certainly not complaining though, and anything that brought more public attention to the hobby he had enjoyed for the last thirty years was most welcome.

Miles had always splashed the boat out for the last Grand Prix of the year and this year was no exception. The overall champion would be decided today after eleven tough events since the turn of the year and there was high anticipation with three competitors still bidding for the title.

The setting of the stunning Albert Ballroom at the majestic Grand hotel on the Brighton seafront was the perfect backdrop for this end-of-season event where the country's best quizzing talent were assembled. The Albert was the original ballroom of the hotel and the most prestigious of all the meeting rooms that it had to offer. With its exceptionally high ceilings, which were complimented by an array of ornate chandeliers, Miles could well understand why this meeting room was so sought after.

Sarah Mills had been sitting with him for the last two hours, meticulously going over the membership details he had shared with her since she had asked for his assistance over a month earlier.

Miles had often helped quiz shows in the past to find contestants and he was more than happy to help Sarah with this new show when the request had come in. It did unfortunately mean he could not apply for shows himself, and in most cases, he did not mind that. This show was different though, and he did have a pang of disappointment that he could not go for the two million pounds prize himself.

'Still a distinct lack of female quizzers I see' Sarah said, closing the file Miles had prepared for her.

'Yes, I know. It has been a bugbear of mind for years and still something I'm trying to resolve. We have seen a slight increase in female participation in this last year, though still nowhere near a level I am happy with.'

'Still far too middle aged and white as well Miles. We need a diverse line-up of contestants as you know, and it's hard to get that from this list.'

'Like I said we are trying really hard to attract females and different ethnic backgrounds, it's just taking far longer than I would like.'

'Unfortunately, time is something we don't have. We need all the contestants lined-up before the end of January, so we are ready for filming in early Spring.'

Miles picked up the file and opened it again, turning to look at Sarah. 'Look Sarah, there is plenty of talent you can use in here and whilst not as many as I would like, there are females and different ethnicities in there.'

To be fair, Sarah had seen plenty in there that she could use to fill half of the contestant quota they would need, she still felt most of the female and ethnicity mix would need to be found mainly from the general auditions.

'I've highlighted some names in there that are probably no-no's due to working as question setters on other shows, and others who actively work as professional quizzers, either on TV or radio.'

Yes, Sarah had recognised some of those names and Miles was right that none of these individuals could appear on the show as they were making a living from their quiz activities.

'Thanks Miles, I'm sure we can use people on this list' Sarah said, rising from her seat. 'I'm going to grab a bite to eat whilst you lot get on with the quiz. I'll be back in an hour if that's ok, I can then chat with potential contestants I've identified.'

'That's fine. We should be all done in about ninety minutes and then the buffet will open, you are more than welcome to join us for that?'

'OK you've twisted my arm. Will just nip out for a small latte and save the company some expenses!'

Chapter 24

This was bliss, absolute bliss.

Sadie had taken the kids to their usual Saturday morning activities, Ellie to dance, and Rhys to football. Then it was a trip to the cinema, so I could have peace and quiet for the important job in hand.

Yes, it might sound ridiculous, but this was like an important job to me. An application that could literally change my life.

Who was I kidding though?

Even if I did manage to get an audition this time, what were my chances of even getting on the show? And then of course winning the whole thing?

Pretty slim if I was being honest with myself. I had to at least try though, didn't I?

Numerous times I had gone through this same process over the last year or so without success. It was then the same depressing outcome each time, application sent off and then the complete silence as my dreams of competing on a TV quiz show were dashed yet again.

I remembered the last show I had applied for. It was one of the established teatime quizzes that seemed to dominate the TV schedules now, and which was looking for yet more contestants to fill its all-year-round broadcast.

I thought I was a prime candidate for at least an audition as I had not been on TV before and they were looking for hundreds of contestants, so felt reasonably optimistic as I sent my application in. As the days turned into weeks, I heard nothing as usual and realised that yet again I had been snubbed for a reason I was still struggling to understand.

What was wrong with me? Why didn't these producers want me for even an audition?

As I sat in my living room with the laptop open before me and a blank application before me, I was still trying to work out that puzzle.

I was a middle-aged white man who worked in the IT industry, loved watching my local football team, playing snooker, and spending time with my family. What was there not to like?

And as I described myself in that sentence, I suddenly worked out why I was being snubbed. I was just too boring for TV and my honesty about myself was probably not helping matters. TV did not want people like me, they wanted wacky and exciting contestants, not the ordinary bloke I was.

Yes, that was my problem. Honesty was not always the best policy, especially when it came to this. Yes, he was sure many contestants on these shows were indeed ordinary citizens, but they were obviously telling some white lies, so their applications shone through.

So, for the next couples of hours I did just that. I made myself sound like the most interesting person alive. Whilst the job and hobbies stayed in, they were now joined by endeavours and anecdotes that made me sound like the perfect quiz show contestant.

Looking at the completed application in front of me I did feel slightly guilty about what I had done, telling myself it was needed if I was finally to get past this application stage.

Suddenly my phone pinged with an incoming text message.

Looking down I could see it was from Sadie.

'How it's going babe' it said.

Putting the laptop down I quickly texted a reply.

'Not too bad. Nearly finished. How are you and the kids?'

Seconds later a reply burst back.

'We are good. Glad it is going ok. See you in a bit. Love you. xx'

I sent her a 'love you back' and picked the laptop back up again.

I attached the mandatory picture they needed and signed the completed form. I always used the same picture of myself at a wedding a couple of years ago, a picture I thought showed me up in the best light. I also attached the 30 second video I had done with my best Christmas jumper on and a BIG smile! It was nothing too fancy, just a video to hopefully show I had got the personality to appear.

'Well Ashley, that's the best you've got' I said, clicking the *send application* button.

There was nothing else I could do now, only wait.

Chapter 25

Stephen Howard sat in his spacious office at SMH Data Solutions with a big grin on his face. Stephen always loved Monday mornings and was loving this particular Monday even more than usual.

Staring at his computer screen he could not have wished for a better outcome than the one he was now looking at. The share price of his company had gone up by 30% since the announcement of his financial involvement in *The Duel* last week. He could never have dreamed of this happening so quickly, clearly the markets were impressed with the exposure the company was now getting and its long-term prospects due of this.

His commitment to matching the prize money with a charity donation also seemed to be having the desired effect. The predicted storm over the morality of the large prize on offer had been outweighed by his decision, with the public support being crazily positive, especially on social media.

Stephen also had his own motives for his, and it was not just to be charitable or help make one of the great British public a double millionaire.

This company was his baby and one he had nurtured into one of the fastest growing IT companies in the whole of Europe. It was the company he had founded over twenty years and to see it grow the way it had was a dream come true. It was just a shame that his circumstances had changed over the last few months.

A messy divorce from his wife was looming and he had to make important decisions about the future if he were to meet his substantial financial obligations to his wife and their two children.

That unfortunately meant selling his beloved company, and he had already received two indicative offers over the last week, offers he was currently mulling over with his leadership team. The offers were good, and he was sure he was going to accept the slightly higher one until he looked at that share price moving upwards this morning.

With that share price still rising, he now saw a different wealth of opportunities in front of him. The offers on the table were now worthless, due to the burgeoning share price It was obvious the bids would have to increase considerably if they were to be successful.

Yes, Stephen Howard liked Monday mornings, especially this particular Monday.

Chapter 26

'Great work Sarah' Mike Phelps said, as he read the list of bios that she had handed him.

Sarah Mills seated in the chair opposite him, had been working all weekend to get the bios she had gathered from her visit to the UK Quizzing Grand Prix in Brighton ready. She stifled a yawn, her lack of sleep now beginning to tell.

Mike looked happy with her efforts as he closed the file. 'This all looks really promising Sarah. Some great quizzing talent here and really pleased you have managed to find us some female contestants, a task that was not easy I bet.

'You can say that again, I've got to admit things are slightly changing in that direction though. Big credit to Miles on that score, though I still think there is a long way to go with it. And whilst the situation with women is changing, there is still not enough ethnic minorities at these quiz events in my opinion.'

'Well, we will just have to find them in the general auditions' Mike said, 'How are we getting on with that by the way?'

'Still a slog to be honest with the number of applications we are getting. The guys are working their butts off to get through it all and we seem to be sifting a lot out through the vetting process.

Mike nodded in approval.

'I'll be glad when the two weeks are over, and we finally get to meet some of these people. Always my favourite part of the job' Sarah said, taking a bite out of her vegan sausage roll.

'Yes, I know what you mean. Used to be my favourite as well until I became part of the management and got stuck behind this desk most days. You should be grateful we are letting you off the leash for them. Not often a producer gets to see some of the action of the auditions.'

'Thank you, kind sir, I'm so incredibly grateful for this great opportunity you are giving me' Sarah said in a very sarcastic tone.

'Well, we've got to keep our favourite producer happy haven't we.' He laughed back.

'Well, I better get back out there and help the troops' Sarah said, as she put the last of the sausage roll in her mouth and got up from her seat.

'Before you go Sarah there is one last thing.'

'Yes Mike?'

'Pick those bloody crumbs up from my desk please. I'm trying to run a clean and tidy ship here.'

Mike was still laughing as Sarah stuck two fingers up at him and slammed the door behind her.

Chapter 27

It had been raining consistently nearly all day and the drive here had been horrendous as the car crawled through the monsoon that was raging outside.

Now sitting in the car park outside the Harp Inn, I was glad to be away from the spray covered motorway and the crazy drivers who still thought you could do 80mph in this sort of weather. *'They certainly have a death wish'* I thought as I turned the engine and lights off on my ten-year-old Ford Focus. If I didn't have enough to worry about, the MOT on it was about to hit me, and judging from the rattling it was making recently I didn't hold out much hope of it passing without some major investment.

'Come on girl, just get me through another year' I said to myself, the thought of having to buy another car already causing me a major worry.

Reclining my seat back, I closed my eyes and tried to think of something more pleasant as I waited.

Like what would I spend two million pounds on?

Clear debts, new house, flash car and lots of holidays were just a few of the things on my wish list.

Just thinking about it all gave me a warm feeling inside. Of course, I had not even gotten onto the show yet, let alone win it. It was nice to dream though.

This could be my lifeline out of the mess I was in, and if the dream came true, I could even sort out the mess before Sadie even knew we were in one. I just needed to keep the bank off my back for a couple more months for that to happen, which was easier said than done.

I felt happy with the application I had sent off on Saturday, and really hoped it was enough to finally get that elusive call back at last.

I hoped I had finally cracked the secret to getting my application noticed. I felt I had answered all the key questions in a way that was slightly 'out of the box', hoping that was what the producers were looking for.

Suddenly I was sprung back into reality by a loud tap on the window.

Opening my eyes, I could see the face of Jenny staring back at me through the rain splattered glass.

Reclining my seat forward I hastily wound down the window as cold rain blew onto my face.

'Get a move on Ashley. It's pissing down out here if you hadn't noticed, and I have a gin and tonic with my name on inside.'

Chapter 28

Five minutes later we were seated in a quiet corner of the pub, Jenny with her gin and tonic and me with a pint of real ale.

She was dressed smartly in a white blouse, a black skirt which came seductively just above the knee and a pair of black stiletto heels.

Looking at her seated in front of me dressed like this I could remember why I was so attracted to her. Why that mutual attraction between us had finally been torn open with a drunken kiss during a party a few months ago, which no one had seen and where it should have ended. Unfortunately, it had ignited feelings in them that they could not supress, and weeks later they had booked a hotel room for the evening, telling both Sadie and Paul that they were away on business trips.

They had both agreed that it had been a stupid mistake and that passion had got the better of them. Nothing more had been said about it until now.

'So how was work today?' I said, trying desperately to make small talk instead of bringing up the real reason for this meeting.

'Same as always, I haven't come here to talk about my day at the office though.'

Looking around with paranoia at the others in the pub, I said in a hushed voice, 'So what have you come to say then Jenny, as if I didn't already know?'

Looking very anxious suddenly Jenny took a sip of her drink before composing herself.

'Well, I'm not sure how to pussyfoot around with this, so I will just jump straight to it.'

I really was not liking this. Not one bit.

'I'm pregnant' Jenny blurted out.

It was one of those moments where I imagined the whole pub had fallen silent and all eyes were on us, the secret Jenny has just shouted out being heard by the entire pub.

'And what does that have to do with me?' I whispered back.

Jenny could not contain her chuckle as she looked at me incredulously.

'Please do not insult my intelligence Ashley, you know perfectly well what it has to do with you.'

'Do I?'

'Stop playing games with me. We need to discuss this like proper adults.'

Finishing my pint, I said, 'I'm not playing any games with you and I really don't know why you are telling me this.'

'It's yours Ashley, and you know it is.'

Moving closer to her and keeping my voice as low as possible I said, 'So a one stand with me now makes me the father of your unborn child, whereas it could not possibly be man who you have been married to for the last twenty years.'

'Not unless it was an immaculate conception.'

'And what's that meant to mean?'

'Well, let us just say, me and Paul haven't been what you would say intimate for quite some time.'

Leaning back in my seat I looked closely at her for any tell-tell signs of dishonestly, in truth I could only see sincerity in her eyes.

'I thought you and Paul were incredibly happy. The perfect middle-class couple with 2.4 children.'

'Well, things aren't always what they seem. Yes, outwardly we may seem like the perfect couple, but things have been difficult ever since Evan was born.'

'But he's nearly ten!' I said in genuine disbelief.

'I know' she sighed. 'Let us just say I didn't really fancy sex for a period afterwards, and Paul found his desires elsewhere.'

'You mean affairs?'

'Yes, there were a few of those. It was more the visits to the prostitutes that disgusted me more though.'

I was genuinely taken aback by all this. Paul and Jenny had seemed the perfect couple and these revelations had shaken me to the core. For a moment I had even forgotten she had told me she was pregnant.

'I don't know what to say. Why didn't you leave him if you knew all this?'

'The kids, stability, financial security. All the usual reasons wives stay when their husbands stray.'

'You can't keep it; you do know that don't you?'

'That is surely up to me is it not. My body and my decision, surely you do agree?'

I remained silent.

Suddenly there was an almighty crash in the sky outside as the thunder that had been threatening for the past few hours roared its ferocious voice.

'Don't worry you will be the first to know my decision. I just thought we needed this little chat first, so you knew all the facts.'

She was talking to me like one of her clients, and not like the probable father of her unborn child.

'I know it's a shock, but I decide what to do next, remember that. And if I want to keep it, I will do just that.'

'This is not a bloody new dress you are deciding to keep Jenny' I said a little too loudly as the couple next to us briefly turned their heads towards us. 'This is real life and people we both care about will get hurt if what we did gets out. Do you really want your friendship with Sadie to be destroyed over this?'

Without answering the question, she got up and put her coat back on.

'We need to talk about this?' I pleaded with her.

'I think I've done enough talking for one-night Ashley. We can chat again when I've decided what to do.'

The car park outside was suddenly bathed in brilliant light as the thunder's more dazzling partner made its much-anticipated appearance. The rain was coming down even heavier now and the car park was slowly being deluged with its unrelenting power.

'You can't drive back in this weather. Let me drive you home and we can collect it in the morning after Paul has left for work. You can tell him you got the train home.'

'I'll be fine. See you soon' she said, giving me a peck on the cheek.

Seconds later, I watched out of the window as she drove out of the car park, with her taillights barely visible in the continuing thunderstorm.

Chapter 29

'So, Ashley it's come down to this. Answer this question right and you will be walking away with the biggest amount of money ever seen on television. A mouth-watering two million pounds will be all yours. Are you ready for the question?', said the cheesy host with his set of purely white teeth.

'Yes, I am' I said, sweat beginning to seep through my silk shirt.

'So, for two million pounds, here is the question' the host said as the studio lights suddenly went down, and the spotlight was upon me.

'In 1960, the song *Three Steps to Heaven* was released posthumously by which artist?'

The tension I had been feeling up to this point was suddenly lifted from me. I knew this, I bloody well knew the answer!

'I think I know this' I said, trying not to sound too cocky.

The audience let out a sigh as I took a sip of water towards my parched lips.

'Remember if you get this wrong Ashley then your opponent will win by the one point that now separates you. If you are correct, then you will win by securing the two points that have been allocated to you for this question.'

Yes, I knew all this. Just ask the question again so I can give you the correct answer, will you.

The host repeated the question and after a few seconds composing myself I said confidently, 'It's Eddie Cochran.'

There was a hushed silence in the audience as the host stroked his chin.

'So, your answer is Eddie Cochran. I can tell you the correct answer is'

The tension in the studio was unbearable as the host took the required pause before announcing the right answer.'

'Eddie Cochran' he concluded as ticker tape descended from the ceiling, and the audience clapped and cheered in unison.

I collapsed to the floor as the host came forward...

Suddenly I heard ringing in my head as the images in my mind faded into nothing.

The bedside lamp suddenly came on as I gingerly opened my eyes to the dazzling light.

Sadie next to me picked up the phone as I sat up and looked worriedly across at her. I picked up my phone and saw that the time was 3.16am. It was never good news having a phone call at this hour, and at this moment all I could think of was my mother in the care home.

'Hello' Sadie said with a sleepy weariness.

'Paul, what's wrong? Please calm down' was all I could hear as Sadie continued the conversation.

'Please god no!' Sadie screamed down the phone as tears cascaded down her face.

I looked even more worryingly across to her, as Sadie told Paul she would be there as soon as possible before replacing the receiver.

'What's wrong? I said, a deep seat of dread slowing building in my stomach as I waited for her reply.

'That was Paul' Sadie said, tears still streaming down her face. 'Jenny has been in a car accident.'

'Is she ok?' I said, not feeling good about this at all.

'She's dead' Sadie screamed!

Chapter 30

Patrick had not been in a green room since his TV career had been abruptly paused, and it now felt so odd sitting here in one after all this time.

As always Lance was by his side, and for that Patrick was grateful as he could still not shake off these bloody nerves.

Why was he feeling like this? He had been in showbusiness for over thirty years and had never felt like this. The press launch had gone way better than he had expected so why was he still feeling so panic stricken.

'Will you please stop shaking that bloody leg of yours Patrick.'

'I'm sorry. I know it sounds daft; I just feel so bloody nervous.

'Yes, it does sound bloody daft. Look, you breezed through that press launch and I know it's been a while since you have done a full-on interview like this, but you will be fine, trust me on that.'

He knew Lance was talking some much-needed sense, it still did not help at this moment in time though. He would just have to put on his showbiz face until he got back into the swing of doing this type of thing.

His nerves were not being helped by what faced him in a few minutes time.

A ten-minute slot on Britain's biggest breakfast show to talk about the show, and Patrick was not expecting an easy ride from the opiniated and sometimes downright rude male host.

Stewart Flowers was known for his fiery temper, and this was often in evidence as he grilled politicians and the showbiz fraternity with the same aggression and intensity as he tried to get true and honest answers out of them.

Patrick watched his show most mornings and the thought of now facing him was sending shivers running throughout his body.

'How long before I'm on?'

'Another thirty minutes or so the producer said. Apparently, they need to spend some time talking about the antics in the jungle before getting to you.'

'I just hope Stewart is in a charitable mood this morning' Patrick said, picking up a Danish pastry from the small selection that had been laid out in the green room.

'I'm sure he will be. I personally think it's all an act anyway, and he's a real pussycat really.'

'I'm not sure this is such a good idea if I'm being honest Lance. What if he asks questions about the court case and all the stuff that went with it?'

'I'll be pretty bloody surprised if he doesn't. Stewart Flowers is the rottweiler of morning television and will take great delight in bringing all that up again. Remember what I said though Patrick.'

'Yes, I remember. Answer the questions and don't let the bugger wind me up.'

'Indeed. Do that and you will be fine.'

'Thanks Lance.'

'For what?'

'Always being here for me.'

'That's what friends are for, and besides, you pay me well to watch your back.'

We were both distracted by a knock on the door and a young woman entered the room.

'All ready?' she said with the same breezy smile that had greeted us when we had first arrived in the studio a couple of hours earlier.

'As ready as I'll ever be' Patrick said.

'You'll be fine. We don't bite here, well not that badly anyway' she laughed.

Patrick did not laugh back at her little joke.

'We are just about to head into a commercial break, so we'll get you onto set during that' she said, briefly speaking into her headset to let the guys on the studio floor know that they were coming.

Turning towards Lance she said, 'You can watch it all on the TV in here if that's ok?'

'Fine by me' Lance said, picking up another croissant and making himself more comfortable in his seat. 'Good luck and just try to enjoy it' he said, turning to Lance.

'Thanks Lance' Patrick said with a nervous smile.

The woman led him from the room and down a narrow corridor, before stopping at some double doors that had a sign above saying, *'Studio 1 – On Air.'*

'Won't be a minute' she said, waiting for the go-ahead from her headset.

A minute or so later the *'On-Air'* sign went off and the woman opened the door, leading him inside.

It was dark in this part of the studio with the floor covered in cables, and seeing this world again made Patrick feel alive.

He belonged here. This was his domain and he deserved to be back here.

A man approached them from across the studio floor.

Extending a hand towards Patrick he said, 'Hi Patrick, I'm Rob Steele, floor manager here at Morning UK. I hope Lucy has been looking after you well.'

'Very well thanks' Patrick said, smiling towards the woman standing next to him.

She gave him a warm smile and wished him good luck before disappearing again through the double doors, no doubt to take care of another guest who was appearing on the show.

'I'm sure Lucy told you we are currently in a commercial break, which will be followed by a quick local news update. This will give us about five minutes to settle you in.

Yes, Patrick certainly had missed all this. The buzz of a studio with all the cameras and lights upon him, this world excited him in a way nothing else could. The old Patrick had returned, and it was certainly good to be back.

Rob escorted him carefully through the labyrinth of cables towards the main studio floor and the set of Morning UK.

Ahead of him, he could see the bright and cheery set that greeted millions of viewers as they switched on their TVs each morning. Viewers expecting an update on overnight news, along with the light and fluffy entertainment strands that this type of programme was famous for.

Patrick was still unsure which way his interview would go. Would he get the light and fluffy, or the serious treatment? He expected a bit of both if he was being honest.

Patrick was led towards the main news desk area where a man and woman were animatedly chatting to each other.

He recognised the man as Stewart Flowers. The main anchor of the show was dressed immaculately as always in a blue pin-striped suit and a pink tie.

The woman next to him Patrick knew as Claire Bruce. The co-host was even more stunning in real-life than she was on-screen, and it was hard not to be captivated by the sheer beauty of the woman.

Reaching the desk Rob introduced him to the two presenters, both rising to shake his hand.

'Morning Patrick, it's great to meet you. I'm not sure our paths have crossed before, have they?' Stewart said, as he offered Patrick the seat to the side of them.

'No, I don't believe they have. I am a great fan of the show though.'

'Good to know we have celebrity fans out there, is it not Claire?'

'Indeed, it is. I do hope you're a fan of mine too though Patrick?' she said, looking up from the notes she was reading.

It was not often that Patrick got embarrassed, the way she looked at him when she said that made him blush ever so slightly though.

'Of course,' he said.

'I was only joking' she said with a twinkle in her eye.

Stewart had already become bored of the conversation and was chatting to the makeup lady who was hovering around him, busily reapplying the foundation that made anyone look good on TV.

She moved quickly onto Patrick, who also received a quick application of the magic dust before she dashed from the set.

One of the runners brought Patrick some water and before he knew it the floor manager was doing a ten second countdown for the live show to restart.

10, 9, 8, 7, 6.

Patrick could feel his heart beating ever so faster.

5, 4, 3, 2, 1.

Taking deep breaths as he heard the floor manager say, 'And we are live. Good luck guys.'

The camera zoomed in front of Stewart as the theme music faded out.

Looking straight down the in front of it, Stewart said, 'And welcome back to Morning UK. Now I am sure unless you have been living on the moon this past week, you will have all heard about the new quiz show *The Duel* which is offering the biggest quiz prize ever seen. Joining us now to talk about the show and the whopping two million pounds on offer is the host Patrick Reed.'

Another camera trained in on Patrick, as Stewart continued.

'It's great to have you here this morning Patrick, and it must be great to be back on TV in a show that is generating so much interest around the country, with this insane prize money that is on offer.'

The next five minutes were spent talking about the show, with a relaxed and confident Patrick responding skilfully to the questions posed. That was until…

'We've only got a few minutes left Patrick, so I would like to just ask a few questions about what has been happening in your life this past year, if that's ok?'

Patrick knew this was coming. It was now time to put into practice the advice Lance had given him.

'Yes, that's fine.'

'Clearly it's been a tough year for you' Stewart Flowers continued. 'We all know you were cleared of the allegations against you in a criminal trial last year, but can you still understand the unease amongst some people that you are back on TV in such a high-profile role?'

God Patrick really did detest this man. Looking down on him with his sneering superiority and veiled insinuation that maybe he was not as innocent as the court felt he was.

Composing himself Patrick replied in a calm tone, 'I completely understand why some people may feel like that, the truth is I have been cleared of all these malicious allegations though and believe I deserve to return to a job I love doing.'

'And I completely understand that, though there are clearly still women who feel you acted inappropriately towards them. What do you say to those women who feel you have literally gotten away with it?'

Back in the green room Lance was perched on the edge of the couch watching the TV screen in front of him intently. *'Keep your cool Patrick, don't fuck it all up now just to please this arrogant bastard'* he mouthed silently to himself.

'I haven't got away with anything, and I'm not sure why you are implying I have?'

Raising both his hands Stewart said, 'I'm not implying anything. I was just quoting what some of your accusers have said. That you were guilty of these crimes and that you got away with it due to a legal technicality.'

'I hardly think finding out these women were telling blatant lies a legal technicality?'

Looking down at his notes again, notes which were obviously prepared extremely well, Stewart continued with his line of questioning. 'Two of the women were found to have been lying I grant you; do you feel that should have halted the entire trial though, and therefore denied the others the chance to put their cases to the court'?

Finding all his inner strength not to shout the answer directly into the face of him, Patrick said, 'I was completely innocent of all these charges and the judge agreed the trial should not continue. I have nothing to be ashamed of.'

'Do you respect women Mr Reed?'

The question from Claire Bruce took him completely by surprise. She had not said a word in the interview before this and now this question completely poleaxed him.

'I'm sorry' was all Patrick could say.

'Do you respect women?' she repeated.

'Of course, I do.'

'Well, we will have to leave it there I'm afraid, we are incredibly grateful to you for coming in this morning to chat to us. That was Patrick Reed, who is the host of *The Duel*.

And that was that. Patrick sat dumbfounded on the rather uncomfortable stool he was on shaking his head in disbelief. All the questions and they end on that one. He was not sure whether to laugh or cry.

Chapter 31

'You sure we have made the right decision there?' Sarah Miles said, muting the television that was mounted on the office wall.

Herself and Mike Phelps had watched the breakfast show interview with Patrick, a deep sense of dread building up in them as the final few minutes of it rolled by.

'Well, there's not much we can do about it now even if we think we have. Too much effort has been put into this with Patrick as the face of the show, much too late to drop him now.'

'You might be right, the guy still gives me the creeps though, and that interview just now didn't change that.'

'What's that meant to mean Sarah?' Mike said, taking a sip of his now tepid coffee.

'He just gives me the heebie jeebies, that's all.'

'You sure you're not thinking about his past and that's making you imagine things?

'Maybe, I certainly wouldn't like to be left alone with him though.'

'That is understandable I suppose, he comes across as a nice bloke though and we have to remember he was cleared of all that business. Everyone deserves a second chance Sarah.'

'Your right. Me being too sensitive I suppose, still think we should keep a close eye on him though, especially around the contestants' she said, taking a mouthful of her muesli. 'Let us just hope that the rest of his interviews today aren't as tough as that one.'

'I'm sure they won't be' said Mike. 'There's not many more Stewart Flowers out there thank god, and at least he's got him out of the way first.'

'Let us hope your right then, or this show could be getting publicity we definitely could do without.'

Chapter 32

Complete gobbledygook just stared back at me as I looked blankly at the screen in front of me.

A screen I had been staring at for the last hour. No attempt to type anything or take in what was on there. Lines of codes that usually I could decipher in the blink of an eye were now just scrambled nonsense.

All he could think about was Jenny and the awful news they had received three days earlier.

I closed the page of code in front of me and opened the website of the local paper, clicking on the short article I had read numerous times.

FEMALE DIES IN CRASH ON COUNTRY ROAD

A crash on a flooded country road in which a woman died when her car overturned, has led to a police appeal for information.

Crash investigators said the accident happened on the A12 between Bridgend and Swansea.

South Wales Police said the accident happened at 21:30 on Friday. A spokesman for the force said the woman has not yet been named.

An investigation is under way and any witnesses have been asked to contact the police.

I still could not believe she had gone.

So many things were swirling in my mind now.

Why didn't I take her home that night?

Was she even pregnant?

Was it really mine if she was?

I closed the page and rubbed my weary eyes as the rain outside bounced furiously against the window next to me.

The same weather as that dreadful night.

My phone pinged on the desk to indicate an incoming text message.

Picking it up I could see it was from Sadie.

'How's work babe? XX'

I quickly replied with the following.

'It's ok. How are you feeling?'

I put the phone back on the desk and tried once again to concentrate on my work.

After a few minutes I gave up and walked the short distance to the coffee machine.

Grateful that no one else was there I pressed the button for a cappuccino and walked over to the large set of windows that looked out onto the busy roundabout three storeys below me.

It had only just gone four, but already the traffic was building as the rush hour began. This atrocious wind and rain were not helping matters either as the long trail of traffic meandered through the surface water that had quickly gathered on the drenched tarmac.

The same road conditions as a few days ago when Jenny had ....

I shook my head and tried to erase that last image I had of Jenny as she drove away into that storm and towards her ....

DEATH!

Her death that was all my fault and no one else's. Her fragile state, coupled with that atrocious weather was a disaster waiting to happen, a disaster that did happen.

'This your drink mate?' said a voice behind me.

I turned to see a face that I knew, with no name to go with it. That was the trouble working for such a large company, with over four hundred people scattered over its six floors

'Sorry' I said, removing my drink from the machine.

'No worries' said the nameless figure. 'Are you sure you're ok though mate? You don't look too great.'

'I'm fine thanks' I said, quickly moving back to my desk to avoid any further discussion.

Slumping back into my seat I could see my phone flashing with another text message.

'I'm ok. I still cannot believe she has gone though. XX'

Sadie had taken the week off work to try her best to comfort Paul and the kids, whilst grieving herself for the best friend she had lost.

Was what Jenny said about their relationship true?

To the outside world they looked like the perfect couple. Looks could be very deceiving though.

I took a sip of my cappuccino and began to look at the screen again. Trying really hard to process the information facing me, a task that was still completely failing me.

After a few minutes I turned to face the window, once again thinking of Jenny. Dark thoughts fighting for space in my brain along with the grief. Thoughts that said I was glad Jenny was dead, as with her dead there was now no chance of Sadie finding out about us.

My secret was safe with Jenny gone. My marriage was safe.

I tried to banish these thoughts from my mind, thinking like this surely made me a monster, didn't it?'

If what Jenny had said was true, then my unborn child had also perished that night. A child that I now would never meet or hold, if indeed it was my child. If she was so willing to jump into bed with me, what was not to say she was willing to jump into bed with other men too.

All these thoughts swirling around in my head, with no clear answers forming through the fog.

Time to call it a day, I think. Not that I had been much use today anyway.

I undocked my laptop and shoved it into my rucksack. It was as I began to put my coat on that my mobile started to ring.

I looked at the number on the screen.

It started with 020, which I recognised as a London area code.

Probably another bloody call centre or worse, I thought. And to be caught in another scam was the last thing I needed.

Usually, I would just ignore calls like this, for some reason today I accepted it though. A sixth sense telling me that this call may be important for some reason.

'Hello' I said rather curtly.

'Hi. Is that Ashley White?' said a young female voice at the other end.

'Yes speaking' I said, ready to put the phone down as this had a call centre or scam written all over it.

'Hi Ashley, my name is Nadia. I was just ringing to have a quick chat about the application you put in for *The Duel*. Is now a good time for you?'

I slumped back down into my seat, shaking like a leaf.

Chapter 33

I held the phone in front of me like it was some foreign object I had just picked up on my travels. I could not quite believe what I was hearing from it, as the voice once again spoke back at me.

'Hello Ashley, are you still there?'

Shaking myself back into reality I put the phone back against my ear.

'Yes, now is fine. Could you just give me a few minutes whilst I find somewhere more private though? Bit difficult to chat with colleagues around.

'That's fine with me' she said in a cheery manner, 'I can call you back in five minutes if that's ok? Save you ringing me back.'

'Sounds good to me. Thanks Nadia.'

'No problem. Speak to you soon Ashley' she said, ending the call.

I quickly walked down the office to the meeting room. Checking through the window on the door to make sure it was vacant, dashing in quickly and closing the door behind me when I could see it was empty.

Lying my mobile on the desk in front of me I tried desperately to control my breathing which had become increasingly faster ever since I had received the phone call.

In the aftermath of Jenny's accident, I had forgotten all about the show. The call just now completely catching me by surprise.

Was the call even real?

Was I in a dream that I would suddenly wake-up from?

Six applications without even a phone call back, and now I finally get one for the biggest show of all.

Was my luck finally changing?

I felt sweat dripping slowly down my back and realised I still had my coat on. Taking it off I stared at the phone and wondered if I had time to nip to the loo before Nadia called back.

Any notion of doing that dissipated though as the phone on the desk started to ring again with the same number as earlier.

Doing a quick prayer to god for divine inspiration, I answered the call in the most confident voice I could find.

'Hi Ashley, Nadia here again. Is now a good time?'

'Yes, all good now Nadia. Sorry about earlier, you know what offices are like though, with colleagues trying to pry into every little conversation they can hear.'

'I completely understand. We want you to feel as comfortable as possible for this, we try to be very informal though.'

The next few minutes were then spent going through all the mundane stuff before the white lies, I had said on my application form came back to bite me on the arse.

'So, it's says here you are a keen marathon runner Ashley?'

God, what had I done?

'Yes, that's right' I said, desperately trying to remember what I had said on that form.

'Ultra-marathons it says here.'

Oh god ...

Racking my brain to try and remember. 'Yes, I have done about a dozen of them now, both here and aboard.

'Very impressive I must say. I feel tried just talking about it' Nadia said, laughing.

'Well, I do try and keep as fit as I can' I said, suddenly feeling a pang of terror now washing over me, the significance of this lie beginning to hit home.

How was anyone going to believe an overweight man in his early forties did Ultra-marathons on a regular basis? I had not thought over the implications of what I had said. In all the excitement I had lied in a desperate attempt to get on the show, lies that I would find exceedingly difficult to explain, especially if the researchers did some digging around.

'And all these bungee jumps you have done. You certainly do like the extreme.'

Bloody hell, I had completely forgotten I put in that as well. What the hell had I done!

'Yes, I'm a bit of an extreme junkie I'm afraid. A holiday to New Zealand is to blame for that particular obsession' I said, trying desperately to sound confident in my lies.

Nadia seemed really interested in all this and we chatted for a few minutes about the few fictitious jumps I had done. We also chatted about the fictious meal I had next to a famous Hollywood star in a local restaurant. This star did indeed have a meal in a local restaurant according to media reports, so any digging she did on that would find my account of things completely plausible.

In fact, the more the conversation was going on even I was beginning to believe some of these lies I had written on that application form.

'And you say you would emigrate to Canada if you won the two million pounds on the show?'

Now this was true. Sadie had been born there and it was her dream to live there one day, a dream that could certainly turn into a reality with all that money.

'Yes, that's correct' I said as I rattled off the reasons for this answer, with Nadia seeming genuinely interested as I spoke.

'Well, I hope that dream can be realised' she said, as I looked at the clock on the office wall.

It was just after five and I had already been on the phone to her for over fifteen minutes.

'So, to finish I would like to go through a quick ten question quiz. All the questions are general knowledge, and you will have five seconds to answer each one. Unfortunately, I will not be able to repeat a question so please listen carefully, and I am also afraid I will not be able to give your score at the end. Are you happy with all that Ashley?'

'Yes, that all seems fine' I said, slightly apprehensive at having to do a quiz right now though.

'Excellent. So, question 1 is ...' she said, quickly bursting through the following ten questions:

Q1. 'Who was the opponent of Muhammad Ali in the 1974 boxing match known as the Rumble in the Jungle?'

Q2. 'K is the chemical symbol for what?'

Q3. 'Who was the last wife of Henry VIII?'

Q4. 'What is the name of the café on Coronation Street?'

Q5. 'Who wrote the Twilight series of Novels?'

How easy were these questions I thought as Nadia continued; I could only hope the rest of them were just as easy.

Q6. 'In the Wild West, how was Henry McCarty better known?'

Q7. 'In the board game Risk, what is the colour of Europe?'

Q8. 'What is the largest freshwater lake in North America?'

Q9. 'What country was formerly known as Persia?'

Q10. 'What is the name of the currency used in Poland?'

Ah, no such luck I cursed as I finished answering the last question. Those 6th and 7th questions were real toughies and I really hoped my blind guesses on them would prove successful. I was not even sure what was considered a good score on here. Would Nadia be looking for perfection or would a couple of wrong answers be acceptable?

'Thanks Ashley. All the hard stuff is over now so you can take a deep breath and relax.'

I did indeed take a deep breath.

There then seemed to be the longest pause I had even encountered as we both allowed the silence to drift between us.

Please come on. Is it a Yes or No?

The suspense was killing me.

And then I heard the words that made all this worthwhile.

'Well, I'm pleased to say we would like to offer you an audition Ashley. Many congratulations.'

Those words meant so much to me, much more than Nadia could ever know.

Chapter 34

'How much dear?' the old lady said for the third time.

'Sorry' the woman said, staring into space.

'How much for my shopping'?

'I'm sorry' the woman said, focussing back on the till display in front her.

'That's £42.50' she said to the clearly exasperated lady in front of her.

Handing her the cash, the old woman looked at her with concern.

'Are you sure you're ok love? You don't look too good if you don't mind me saying.'

'I'm fine thanks' the woman said, although she could understand why she was worried.

She had not slept all night, and then to cap it all off she had to watch him on the TV again this morning.

The only comfort this time was that the grin had been taken off his smug face. Watching him squirm as the interviewer took him to task made her smile and she just wished it had not ended so abruptly. Another few minutes and she thought his mask may slip under the tough questioning, alas it was not to be though.

The time would come when that smirk was wiped off his face permanently and she was determined to see that day.

Handing her change back, she thanked the old lady for her concern and watched as she wheeled her trolley out of the store.

She was grateful it was time for her fifteen-minute break as she closed her till off and rose from the uncomfortable seat she has resided in for the last couple of hours.

'Sorry I'm closed' she said to a young woman with a screaming child in tow who was just about to put her shopping onto the conveyer belt.

She watched as the irate woman moved to another till, muttering some obscenity under her breath.

In fact, there was nothing she liked about this job. It was a means to pay the bills, nothing else. She particularly hated the tills where the interaction with the customer was at its most intense and where chitchat and a cheery demeanour was the order of the day. She had pleaded with her line manger to stay on the stock filling team, but he had insisted she needed to broaden her customer skills with a prolonged stint on the tills.

'Are all men bastards?' she wondered, walking towards the staff area at the back of the store.

Keying in the pin code she opened the door, instead of heading towards the staff room though she moved towards the door that backed out to the rear of the building.

Slamming the door shut behind her, she breathed in the fresh air that was so welcome after the stifling oppression of the store interior.

Leaning against the back wall she took out a cigarette from a packet in her trouser pocket. Another habit she had picked up since that night.

She had tried to forget it all, tried to forget him and that night after the failed trial. Seeing him again had reignited the hatred that had been lying dormant inside her, and which she was now finding difficult to control.

The door opened and one of her colleagues came out into the cold December day, where the light was already beginning to fade even though it had just gone past four.

'How's your day been?' the young man asked.

Before he could converse again the woman put out her cigarette and went back inside without uttering a word back.

'Miserable cow' the man shouted after her.

Chapter 35

Even the crawl through the rush hour traffic could not damper my spirits that evening.

As I looked at the brake lights of the car in front of me, I slowly brought the car to a standstill once again.

All I could think about was the audition that now lay ahead of me. An audition I never thought I would ever have.

Yes, I knew it was only the first step and there was a long way to go but I had finally broken through that barrier and got an audition!

Clearly the white lies had worked in my favour, they were lies I was now having serious doubts about though.

What was going to happen when I got to that audition in a few weeks' time and those researchers saw what was in front of them? When they saw a clearly overweight and unfit man standing there, they would surely all be thinking the same thing. How could he be doing ultra-marathons and bungee jumps looking like that?

As I crawled another few yards forward before hitting the brakes, a thought suddenly popped into my head.

Eddie Izzard!

I remembered he had done something like thirty marathons in as many days a few years ago for charity, and not trying to be mean but Eddie Izzard looked far from your typical marathon runner. If he could pull it off, then surely, I could. It was just like work, be on top of your brief and you could pull the wool over anyone's eyes. If I were prepared, I could bamboozle anyone, so I was sure a couple of TV researchers would be no problem.

I hoped ...

The rain was literally bouncing off the windscreen now as thunder shook the night sky followed by the accompanying flash of lightning. The inside of the car lit up briefly with the white flash as I quickly turned the wipers to their fastest speed.

'Will this bloody rain ever stop?' I thought, as the Robbie Williams CD I had been playing briefly stopped for a traffic report from the local radio station.

'And the M4 between Bridgend and Swansea is currently at a crawl due to a three-vehicle accident. The vehicles have now been moved to the hard shoulder although traffic build-up means it will add another hour to journey times in the area' the reporter said, as another rumble of thunder rolled by.

'Why do people drive so recklessly in weather like this?' I mouthed to myself, as my thoughts returned to that night, I last saw Jenny.

'Was she driving fast and recklessly?'

'Why did she go down that country lane that night when it would have been obvious to most people, as it was to me, how dangerous it would be in that weather?'

I slammed my fists on the steering wheel with anger and frustration about that night. I should have done more to stop her going off like that, but her revelations had *'knocked me for six'* and I was not thinking straight. If I had been, then I would have definitely stopped her going off in that state.

Paul had said the police had informed him that Jenny had been found quickly by another passing motorist who had seen her car aquaplane and leave the road. Paramedics had arrived swiftly, but tragically Jenny had died at the scene from horrific internal injuries.

Such a needless death for a woman that had so much more life to look forward to, a life cut short in the blink of an eye. It was still hard to believe what she had told me that night, her death meaning I was unlikely to really know the whole truth though. I chastised myself for feeling so damned happy whilst we were mourning the loss of Jenny. After the news I had just had It was hard not to be though.

It was ninety minutes later when I finally opened the front door of my house and walked inside its warm abode.

'That smells nice' I said, greeting Sadie inside our rather compact kitchen.

Sadie was standing over the hob, stirring a big pan of minced beef next to a boiling pot of spaghetti.

'Sorry it's nothing more exciting' she said, as I kissed her lightly on the lips.

'Don't be daft. It's looks and smells lovely, just what I fancied for tonight.'

Turning the gas down she said 'I know you've only just got in, but would you mind picking up Ellie from dance? I'm just whacked and I'm not sure I feel like bumping into anyone there tonight.'

'Sure' I replied, although to be honest I was whacked myself and could do without another drive there.

'Oh, and could you pay her fees tonight as well please? We've had a polite reminder that we are late for this term.'

'Do they really need them tonight?

'I think so, and you know what Ellie will be like if she knew we were paying late.'

Yet more money I did not have, I thought.

'I'll write them a cheque later' I said, hoping that they would delay banking it until I got paid, or it would be bouncing straight back at them.

'Where's Rhys?' I said, hanging my coat over the bannister.

'In his room' Sadie said, 'And no doubt playing on that bloody Xbox as usual.'

'He's a ten-year-old kid. Isn't that what they all do' I laughed.

Sadie was in no mood for laughing back though, which I could fully understand.

'How was Paul today?'

'Same as yesterday really. I just don't think it's hit him yet.'

'Yes, the poor fella' I said, 'I just can't imagine what he's going through.'

'Jenny's mum and sister are there now so I thought I better give them some space. Paul knows we are both here for him when he needs us.'

I nodded in agreement.

'I know it's early, but do they know when the funeral will be yet?'

'Not yet. Paul said the post-mortem will be done tomorrow and then hopefully they will release the body to him.'

'Post-mortem?' I said with surprise.

'Yes, it's standard procedure in road traffic accidents apparently.

I would soon know if Jenny was telling the truth then.

Chapter 36

'Surely the day wasn't that bad darling?' Maria said, as Patrick got into bed beside him.

Patrick had just got in from what seemed like a day that would never end. After his breakfast encounter, he had been required to do a vast array of interviews with TV, radio, and newspapers that were thankfully much less demanding than that first encounter.

'The rest weren't too bad if I'm being honest love, better than the debacle earlier anyway' Patrick said.

Whilst he thought it had been a disaster, Lance had totally the opposite opinion. He remembered their discussion earlier.

'It went as well as I expected' Lance said, as they discussed the days' events over a large bottle cognac in his private member's club. 'You stuck to the script we went through and that's all you could have done. They landed no fatal blows on you and you never incriminated yourself, so job well done I say.'

'Even the breakfast interview?' Patrick responded.

'Look we knew that would be a tough one. Stewart Flowers is hardly well known for his sensitive interviews, but you did good, believe me.'

'I just wish I had more time to answer that question about respecting women. Still can't believe that stupid cow pulled that one out of the hat at the end.'

'You got to say you did, and that's the main thing. The viewers got to hear that and that's good enough for me.'

Patrick still was not sure about that, but he trusted his agent's judgment and if he said it went ok, then so be it.

'Lance said they went well, so I'm guessing they could not have been that bad' Patrick said, as he picked up the book he had been reading for the last few weeks. A great autobiography on Pat Wall, who was one of his comedy heroes.

'Well, that's good enough for me as well' Maria said, as she stifled a yawn.

'And it's all out of the way now darling. We can now look forward to Christmas and New Year in the sunshine.'

Yes, despite his initial misgivings Patrick was really looking forward to the break Lance had organised. Three weeks in the sunshine is just what the doctor ordered, and it would be good to spend some quality time with Maria.

'Yes, your right' he said, as he put the book down.

At least he did not have to pick up the cost of that taxi ride home from Central London. There were at least some perks in marketing the show to the media.

'Tired?' Maria said, turning off the bedside lamp next to her.

'Knackered' he said, as he did likewise and suddenly their bedroom was filled with darkness, only illuminated with the full moon that shone through the curtains.

'Sure, I can't wake you up' Maria said, expertly moving from her side of the bed and straddling onto the top of Patrick.

She moved down towards him and took his head in her hands as their mouths entwined. She kissed him with passion and vigour as her tongue found his.

He responded with the same intensity, before she took off the top of her silk pyjamas to expose her beautiful firm breasts. Moving slowly down towards her breasts he cupped both with his hands before expertly taking her right nipple into his mouth. Flicking his tongue over its erect tip, she moaned with deep pleasure as he continued before moving onto the other breast.

She tugged at his top as she mouthed quietly for him to remove it. He complied and she gently kissed his chest before taking off her bottoms. He quickly did likewise as she slid slowly down to his erect penis.

She playfully licked the shaft before taking the tip of the penis into her mouth as she began slowly to suck it. He moaned with pleasure as she began to increase the tempo before she suddenly stopped.

'Don't want you to finish too early' she said as she straddled him again and took his still erect penis in her hands before slipping it gently inside her.

He moved his penis up and down her moist vulva, slowly at first before he began to increase the pace as he felt himself near climax. Both were now breathing more heavily as Maria bounced even more aggressively on him as she sensed them both nearing orgasms.

'Please cum inside me' she begged, as sweat dripped from her forehead onto her toned body.

This seemed to urge Patrick on ever faster, an urgency that finally led to his sticky fluid erupting inside her.

She screamed in pleasure as she felt him in her, and both remained where they were for a couple more minutes as they savoured the ecstasy, they both had experienced.

She slowly rolled off him and they both lay there in silence for a few moments as their breathing returned to a normal rhythm.

'And has that destressed you Mr Reed' she said, turning to face him.

'Very much so Mrs Reed' he said with a glint in his eyes.

Chapter 37

'Thanks for coming both' Paul said, leading us into the longue of the large, detached house he shared with Jenny and their two boys. *Had shared with Jenny and their two boys.*

The five-bedroom house was set in an effluent estate which had been built a few years earlier, and it certainly dwarfed our own three-bedroom semi.

'Can I get you anything to drink?' Paul said, as we both took seats on the couch.

'You sit down Paul, I'll make it' Sadie said, 'Coffee all round?'

Both me and Paul nodded in the affirmative as Sadie went off to the kitchen.

Paul sat down opposite me and there was an awkward silence between us before I said, 'I'm so sorry mate. I just can't imagine what you and the boys are going through.'

It was the first time I had seen him, albeit for a brief moment the day after Jenny had died. Now sitting there before him I was finding it hard to look at him in the face, knowing I was the last person to see his wife alive.

'I still can't believe she's gone. I'm still expecting her to walk through the door at any minute to tell me this has all been a bad dream' Paul said, tears beginning to well in his already puffy eyes.

What was I supposed to say to that?

Yes, she probably would be walking through that door again if I had not let her drive into a flooded road on the night she died.

But of course, I could never say that, could I.

'I'm still mystified in what she was doing on that road in the first place. It wasn't on the route back from work, in fact it was over twenty miles out of her way.'

'Drink with colleagues?' I offered as an explanation.

'Maybe, but surely they would have said that was the case by now. And even if that was true why meet in a pub that is so far away from work?'

I shook my head, hoping that Sadie would be back soon to save me from all this.

'How are the boys?' I said in a bid to move the conversation on.

'Hard to know how they are coping really. I am more worried about William if I am honest, you know how quiet and reserved he is.'

Yes, I knew where Paul was coming from there. On all the occasions I had met the boys William had always seemed more reserved than his more confident brother Archie. William reminded me a lot of Rhys in many ways, both quiet and sensitive boys who would both rather stay in playing video games than socialising with their friends.

At last Sadie came back into the room carrying a tray with three coffees and a plate of biscuits.

Setting it down on the table she resumed her seat next to me.

'Are the boy upstairs?' she said.

'Their spending a couple of days at their Grandmother's so I arrange the funeral, amongst other stuff. I am regretting that now though.'

'I'm sure they will be fine' Sadie said, picking up her coffee.

'I know they will be fine and Jenny's Mum loves having them, but they should be here with me, shouldn't they?'

I am not quite sure what Paul expected me and Sadie to say to that. We both remained silent.

'I'm glad you have both come anyway' he said, looking at us both with a hint of tears still in his eyes.

'You know we are always here for you Paul' Sadie said, as I nodded in agreement.

'The police called this morning with the results of the Post-Mortem' Paul continued.

My heart was beginning to thud ever so slightly faster.

'They confirmed she died of massive internal bleeding due to blunt trauma caused by the impact of her car hitting the barrier alongside the road.'

Nothing unexpected there then, I thought. Unfortunately, Paul had yet to finish.

'They also wanted to offer their condolences again for the tragic loss of my wife and unborn baby.'

'Baby?' said a shocked Sadie.

'Yes. Apparently, my wife was ten weeks pregnant when she died.'

'I'm so sorry Paul. I had no idea she was expecting.'

'You and me too' Paul replied with a hint of venom in his voice.

'She never told you?'

'Not a word.'

'Maybe she didn't know herself' I said.

'Maybe, I have a feeling she did though. She just didn't want me to know.'

'And why would you say that Paul?' a puzzled Sadie said.

'Because it wasn't mine' he said as if it was the most natural thing to say.

'I don't understand. Why would you say it wasn't yours?' an even more perplexed Sadie replied.

I was beginning to feel more and more uncomfortable as this conversation continued.

Paul laughed mockingly as he continued 'Well, let us just say, me and Jenny have not led a normal marriage for a quite a while.'

'I thought you were so happy' a visibly shaken Sadie said.

'And that's what we wanted the outside world to see. A happy couple who had everything. The only thing missing was the intimacy a husband and wife should have.'

So, Jenny had not been lying that night. The baby and her marriage woes had all been true. The baby Paul was talking about was mine and I had to muster all my inner strength not to burst into tears right there.

'I'm so sorry' was all I could say to him.

'Not your fault. I blame her and the bastard she was shagging.'

'Please Paul, don't say things like that' Sadie implored.

'Why not Sadie' Paul hissed back 'It's all true.'

None of us spoke for a few moments as we all processed the revelations that Paul had just revealed.

'At least I know what she was doing that night now.'

We both looked at him puzzled.

'Meeting her fancy man, isn't it obvious?'

'We don't know that Paul' Sadie said.

'So please explain to me Sadie what she was doing driving along a quiet country road so far out from her commute home?'

Sadie did not have an answer for him.

'I do know one thing though' Paul said, 'Once I find out who she was meeting that night I'm going to bloody kill him.'

Chapter 38

'I just can't believe what Paul just told us, I really can't. Jenny pregnant and their marriage a sham. It just does not make sense. Do you believe him?'

It was only a five-minute drive home and ordinarily we would have walked there and back if it had not been for the persistent rain falling.

'I don't know. He certainly seemed convincing, and why would he lie.'

'As he ever discussed any problems they were having in their marriage with you?'

'Why would he?' I said, as if it was the stupidest thing she had ever said.

'I thought you were friends?'

'Hardly' I said, 'We only see each other down the pub quiz, surely you had more chance of Jenny confiding in you.'

'Well, she never did. In fact, I'm beginning to wonder how close we were now.'

I slowed the car as the traffic light turned red and turned to face her.

'She never said anything about another man then?'

'Never' she said, 'I thought they were the happiest couple we knew, how wrong could I have been.'

The light turned green and I turned left into our road.

Of course, I had a selfish reason for not wanting Jenny to confide in Sadie. It did seem that the secret of me and her had died with her, along with her unborn child.

There was of course Paul. Naturally, he seemed angry tonight and who could blame him. His wife had been pregnant by someone else and he was determined to find out who by. I just hoped that his detective skills were not up to scratch, if they were then I was a *'Dead Man Walking.'*

Reaching the house, I drove into the small parking area in front of our house.

'Shit' I suddenly said as I turned the engine off.

'What?' Sadie said.

'I've just remembered the MOT is overdue.'

'How overdue?'

'Only a couple of days but I could well do without that now, especially being so close to Christmas.'

'I'm sure it will pass, and even if it does need work, we are doing ok now, aren't we? she said. 'Especially after the windfall from your Aunt.'

'Yes, we do not want it all going on car maintenance though, do we?' I laughed.

'Very funny' she said, getting out of the car.

I watched her open the front door as I sat in the car for a few moments.

How long could I keep lying to her about all this?

Christmas had been paid for with credit cards and the bank was now constantly leaving me messages for *'a chat about my financial wellbeing.'* I was desperately trying to keep it all together but knew that in only a few months' time this huge financial mess I was in was likely to collapse all around me.

Should I just be straight with her and say what a fool I had been?

That the house may be taken off us?

And that exposing this secret was a whole lot better than the other secret I was keeping from her.

.

Chapter 39

The familiar sound of Roy Wood came out of the speakers as the staff of Gem Productions sat down to their annual Christmas lunch.

Mike Phelps and the management team had really splashed the boat out this year to celebrate what had been another bumper year for the company.

The venue was one of these fancy clubs that had sprung up all over London, a club where membership was exclusive to the media and creative industries. The leadership team at Gem Productions were all members and had manged to hire the premises for the afternoon.

'Cheers' said Tony Vine to Mike, the man who co-founded Gem Productions with him all those years ago, and who was now seated by him.

Tony had been highly active in the business during those early years, his expertise in factual programming being invaluable as they concentrated on that genre of programming, winning many industry awards for their documentaries. Unfortunately, when that type of work dried up in the ever-changing TV landscape, so did the active involvement of Tony. Now semi-retired and in affect a silent partner, he did still enjoy the social gatherings the company had, as well as the substantial share of the profits that came his way.

'So, things are still very much on a high I can see from the latest annual report' Tony said, finishing off the last of his red wine, before topping it swiftly up again.

'Yes, it has been an exceptionally good year as you can see, and next year looks even better with our brand-new show hitting the airwaves in the Spring' Mike proudly replied.

'Ah yes the new show. I am banking on that topping up my retirement fund nicely' Tony said, as Wizzard and Roy Wood had now been replaced by the nauseous tones of Michael Buble who was belting out one of his many cheesy Christmas tunes.

'We are expecting big things from it so I'm sure it will help top it up. Already we have many countries interested in the format, including America. I'm expecting a tidy little earner from it all' Mike said, tucking into his Christmas pudding with the vigour of a man who had not eaten for days.

'I'm surprised we hired Patrick Reed as host though' Tony said.

'You mean because of all that business last year?'

'Yes, there was that, and the rumours that continue to fly around about him.'

'And that's all they are Tony; remember he was found not guilty.'

'Well, that's not strictly true is it. The trial collapsed if I remember rightly, so he never actually got the chance to be found *guilty* or *not guilty*.'

'You know what I mean.'

Looking thoughtful for a few moments Tony continued, 'I remember working with Patrick at the start of his TV career.'

'You've never mentioned that before' Mike said, polishing off the last of his pudding.

'Well, I've never had a need to until now. Us hiring him has brought back memories of that time though.'

'I'm all ears, let me have another drink first though' Mike said as he tried to get the attention of the waitress.

Finally managing to grab her he ordered two cognacs for himself and Tony.

'If this is going to get heavy then I think I need a comfier seat than this. Shall we move over there' Mike said, nodding towards two leather bound chairs that were situated in the far corner of the room.

Tony nodded in agreement and both men made their excuses from the table.

Sarah Mills who was seated further down the table mouthed a silent 'Everything OK' to Mike.

'All good' he mouthed back.

'So, what's the gory gossip you have to tell on our Mr Reed then?' Mike said, as both men settled into the leather chairs.

'Please don't say it like that Mike. What I have to say is not really a laughing matter' Tony said as he quietened his voice slightly, despite the music and the exuberant chatter of the other occupants of the room.

'Sorry, wrong term of phrase I know. Please go on.'

'Well, like I said it was one of his early TV shows, though he was already a big star on the radio at the time, and I was learning the trade as a lowly junior researcher.'

'Life at the bottom of the ladder, I remember it well' Mike said.

'Yes, the money was poor, and I was treated like a dogsbody if I was honest, but it was a great learning experience and gave me a great footing for the rest of my career.'

Tony paused for a few moments as the waitress arrived with their drinks, setting them both down on the table between them.

'So, what was Patrick like to work with in those days?'

'Well, it was his first foray into TV like I said, despite that he quickly built up quite a reputation for being a smooth operator in front of the camera and a ...'

Mike paused a few seconds as he tried to find the right word.

'And a sexual predator behind it' he finally said.

'And you saw this in action?' Mike said.

'I saw Patrick Reed behave in what would now be perceived as inappropriately, what at the time I thought as him being friendly. How times change eh?'

'What inappropriate things did you see?'

Tony took a large intake of breath and continued even more quietly as to avoid any eavesdropping from any of the other partygoers. 'Well, it was things like slapping female staff on the bottom, giving them playful massages, pecks on the cheeks, sometimes the mouth. Like I said, at the time I thought these things seemed creepy, but just passed them off as being over familiar. That was until the business with Lesley.'

'Lesley'? Mike said, moving slightly forward in his seat, his interest piqued even more now.

'Lesley Horner, a name I will never forget' Tony said, draining what was left of his cognac.

'Another?' Mike said.

'Yes please. I think I will need another to get through what I'm going to tell you next.'

'I'll get them at the bar' Mike said, 'Save waiting for the waitress.'

A few minutes later he returned with the drinks.

'Thanks pal' Tony said, gratefully taking the drink.

'All on the company anyway, so in theory you're paying' Mike laughed back. 'So, who was Lesley Horner and how does she fit into all of this?' he said with a deepening sensation of dread at what he was about to hear.

'Lesley Horner was a junior researcher like me and one of the female staff that Patrick took a particular shine too.'

'More than the others?'

'Looking back, I would say so. It was the same sort of overfamiliarity like the others, but you always sensed he wanted more from Lesley, and it didn't help she led him on.'

'Led him on?'

'Yes, the others would laugh it off, and try to keep their distance from then on. Lesley liked the attention from him though, and it all seemed harmless fun until...'

Until what?'

'Until she accused him of sexual assault and all hell broke loose.'

'I never heard anything of this. Yes, the more recent accusations, nothing that far back though' Mike said in shock.

'You wouldn't have. It was all hushed up by the bosses at the time. Rumours were that they offered her a promotion elsewhere for her silence. Unfortunately, that was the last I ever saw of her.'

'You never kept in touch to see how she was?'

'Never got the chance' Tony said with tears in his eyes. 'She tragically took her own life a few months later.

Mike stared at him open mouthed, unable to utter a response at this tragic revelation.

An hour later Mike was paying the bill at the bar when Sarah slid up beside him.

'So, what did Tony have to say then? I could see you both engrossed in the corner about something.'

'Nothing exciting' Mike lied. 'Wanted an update on how we were doing and bragging about how life in semi-retirement is so wonderful.'

'Yes, life must be so tough on him' Sarah laughed, 'He was telling us earlier about his hectic social life!'

'So, where are you guys off to next then?' Mike said as the bartender returned his credit card.

'Thought we would go to the Oak next, apparently it's quiz night there tonight. Aren't you coming then?'

'I might give it a miss if you don't mind Sarah. Think those cognacs with Tony have tipped me over the edge and I told Melissa I wouldn't be home that late.'

'Party pooper!' Sarah said, making her way back to her table.

Mike hated lying to her, but what choice did he have? If he told her what Tony had just relayed to him, there would be no chance she would ever agree to work with Patrick.

Mike had to keep this secret, otherwise the show he and the company had worked so hard on would be blown to pieces.

Chapter 40

'The garden could do with a makeover' Sylvia said, manoeuvring the last piece of Turkey from the plate into her large gaping mouth.

God, I hated this day more and more each year, and it seemed to me that this Christmas Day was even worse than previous years that had gone before it.'

Sylvia Morris really was the mother-in-law from hell and her never-ending criticism of me was winding me up more than usual.

Mother-in-law from hell was probably a bit extreme, and to be fair she was a lot more laid back since the death of her beloved husband over five years earlier. Stan Morris was a great bloke, and his death had hit us all hard after a two-year battle with dementia. The illness turning this once sociable person into a withdrawn and frightened old man. A disease that was now ravishing my Mum too.

I could usually turn to my mum for most things, her illness now made that impossible though. Admittedly the situation with Jenny would have been difficult due to the close relationship she had with Sadie, though the financial peril I now found myself in would have been nice to talk to her about. And of course, there was the real possibility she could have got me out of it. There was no way that could happen now, and I was not going to go cap and hand to my brother for help.

'And the state inside isn't much better' Sylvia continued as she finished her third glass of wine. 'When was the last time this room had a lick of paint for instance, and don't get me started on the state of the bathroom.'

'Another glass Sylvia' I said in the hope of shutting her up about my lack of DIY skills.

'I thought you would never ask' she said, moving her now empty glass towards me.

I topped up her glass and handed it to her.

'At least you have a couple of weeks off now to get these jobs done Ashley' she said, taking the glass without even a word of thanks.

The kids laughed as their gran said that and I gave them both a steely stare across the table.

'I do work Sylvia, you know. I'm not literally sitting on my arse all day whilst the house falls down around me, which it isn't in my opinion anyway.'

'I'm sure mum didn't mean it like that love, did you mum?' Sadie said, giving me an evil look.

Sylvia just grunted a non-comital response.

'So, who fancies Christmas pudding?' Sadie said in an attempt to bring an end to the spat between me and Sylvia.

'You know I can't stand Christmas Pudding mum' Ellie groaned.

'Don't worry I have cheesecake for you love. Is pudding ok for everyone else though?'

We all nodded in confirmation as Sadie went off into the kitchen.

'You should really put that phone away at the table Rhys' his gran told him with anger in her voice.

'Sorry gran' he said, putting his new and awfully expensive iPhone down.

More bloody expense I could have done without I thought. I had tried to dissuade Sadie on the need for him to have such an expensive model, but she said he would have been ridiculed if he had a different model to his friends. I relented as usual, though it still sounded bloody ridiculous to me.

I tried to put all these negative thoughts out of my mind though. It was Christmas and I had a whole two weeks off to forget about all this and hopefully look forward to better things to come. I had my audition a few days into the new year which I dearly hoped would be a positive sign of things to come, unfortunately the sad event of Jenny's funeral was due the day before.

Two events that could not be more different.

Understandably Sadie was still devasted by the death of her best friend, and the revelation that she had been pregnant. I just counted myself lucky that she did not know the true identity of the father, a secret I hoped she would never know.

The thought of it all still chilled me to the bone.

'I'm just going to give her a hand' I said, leaving the table.

Entering the kitchen, I watched as Sadie plated up the desserts in a room which now resembled a bomb site after the usual hectic morning of Christmas day.

'Need a hand' I said.

'I think I'm nearly there thanks, you can help to take them through though.'

I moved behind her and wrapped my hands around her.

'God I'm knackered' she said, turning to face me.

She really did look tired and I was beginning to worry about her if I was being honest.

'I really wish you would see the doctor' I said.

'And what's that going to achieve?'

'He can sign you off work for a couple of weeks at least. You need a rest with all that's happened recently.'

'And risk another disciplinary? I took a few days off after Jenny and you know that was frowned upon.'

'At least see what the doctor suggests.'

'I'll think about it' she said, handing me two bowls of Christmas pudding.

'I love you' I said.

'I love you too. 'Now get that bowl of pudding to my mum pronto, before she criticises you for that.'

We both laughed. The first time in weeks we both had.

Chapter 41

The woman watched as the inane blonde presenter she could not stand introduced another z-list celebrity onto the dancefloor.

She had returned to her flat a few hours earlier after another fraught Christmas day at her parents. She knew they meant well and only wanted the best for her, she genuinely believed neither of them knew what she was going through though and probably never would.

'Why don't you try to go back to a law firm?' her father had said during lunch.

'I'm happy where I am' the woman replied.

'How can you be love? Working in a bloody supermarket.'

'And what's wrong with working in a supermarket?'

'Well, nothing for some people, but you are so much better than that. You had such a brilliant career ahead of you and now your stacking shelves for a living.'

'You are so patronising Dad, and hasn't it ever crossed your mind that my reluctance to continue in law has something to do with what happened?'

'Surely that's all behind you now love. You can't wreck your career prospects for something that happened so long ago.'

And that is when she really flipped. She could take most crap from her dad, but his total lack of empathy for what happened that night still astounded her.

'Behind me' she shrieked.

'I'm sure your father didn't mean it like that' her mum interjected.

'Oh, I'm sure he did. Just like he did not want me to go to the police when all those other women came forward. He just wanted me to forget the whole thing and carry on like the good girl he thinks I should be.'

'I thought no such thing' he insisted, 'But you have to admit it got you nowhere in the end.'

And that was the point she stormed out of the house in tears, leaving her half-eaten dinner on the plate.

She ran all the way down the deserted residential street that her parents lived in before stopping at the end of the road.

Suddenly her phone started to ring, and she could see her mum's number on the display. She quickly rejected it and instead dialled the number of a local taxi firm.

Minutes later she was in the back of a taxi, where soon she was leaving the Surrey countryside behind for the harsh reality of the capital.

Now sitting here in her bleak and tiny flat she looked at her phone, could see there were ten missed calls from her mum.

She picked up the phone and thought about ringing her back to say she was ok. In the end she decided against it, unable to face speaking to her at the moment.

Instead, she texted her the following:

'I'm ok mum. Back home safe and sound now. Just need a bit of time on my own. Happy Christmas by the way. xxx'

She put the phone down and picked up her glass of wine. She was already on her second bottle since she got home and could now see that it also looked alarmingly empty.

Her heavy drinking was one of the consequences of that night and has much as she tried, she just could not stop. Drinking was her way of coping, and more importantly forgetting.

Her phone pinged on the table. Picking it up she read the reply from her mum.

'I'm glad you you're ok love. I wish you had not left like that though. Your father does care, he just does not know how to say it at times. Will ring you tomorrow. Love you. xx'

'Did her father really care?' the woman thought.

Yes, she knew both her parents loved her, but she did wonder if they genuinely cared about what happened to her that night.

She felt her father only cared about his reputation with friends and neighbours, and how that reputation would be affected if it ever got out his only child was one of the many women accusing Patrick Reed.

Did her father think she was a tart who led him on?

The worst thing was her mother nearly always took his side.

A mother she should have turned to for comfort as soon as it happened, a mother that should have been there for her, a mother that had sadly done none of those things.

She had to keep the secret bottled up for so long, until she finally summoned up all her inner strength to go to the police once the reports of the other women had surfaced.

Still, she felt her parents support had been lukewarm though and could feel their relief when the trial collapsed. No need for their daughter to testify and no chance of her name getting out, even though anonymity of the victims should have guarded against that.

'No harm done love' she could imagine them saying. 'Now time to get back to work and that brilliant career in front of you.'

She could never return to that normality though. NEVER!!

She picked up the remote and moved aimlessly through the channels before finally returning to the inane blonde and those stupid dancers.

After a few minutes she turned the TV off and sat there in silence.

At least this nightmare would be over soon she thought.

Chapter 42

Looking out towards the endless and glistering blue sea, Patrick felt the most relaxed he had for many years.

Taking a mouthful of the lobster that had been fished out of the restaurant aquarium less than thirty minutes earlier, he marvelled at the stunning view in front of him. Situated right on the golden beach that seemed to stretch out forever, the restaurant looked out over the stunning panorama of Los Cristianos harbour.

He had always loved Tenerife and was glad Lance had chosen this destination for the much-needed holiday for all of them.

'Merry Christmas everyone' Lance said, raising his glass.

'Merry Christmas' everyone around the table said, also with raised glasses.

Yes, Patrick could get used to this, Christmas in the sun was a world away from the dreary ones they usually spent in the UK.

'Thanks for arranging all this Lance' Maria said, as she washed down the last of her paella with a large glass of sangria. 'It certainly beats the wind and rain back home.'

'No worries. We all needed a break, and I cannot think of a better place than this to spend a few weeks. Also, it is great to be back here if I am honest. I must admit I do miss spending time here ever since I sold the villa.'

Lance had a villa here for over twenty years before selling up a few years ago, and Patrick knew how much he missed his visits to the island.

'Yes, it's much appreciated' Patrick said.

'Like I said it's no bother, and it's not like I've paid for the whole thing is it.'

'Yes, your generosity doesn't quite extend that far unfortunately' Patrick said with a grin.

'Usually I would, but I am not the one making millions from this new show, am I.'

'Millions? You never said it was that much love' Maria ribbed.

Putting his finger to his lip Patrick said, 'I thought I told you too keep quiet about all that Lance.'

They all laughed as the waiter came to take away their empty plates.

'You sure I can't persuade you for a round of golf tomorrow?' Lance said as the waiter moved away.

'You know how awful at golf I am. It's takes me about ten swings to actually hit the damn ball and then it only trickles tamely along the ground.'

'Surely you can't be that bad?' Cindy said.

'Oh, believe me he is darling' Lance quipped.

'So why do you want me to come then?'

'Well, we all need a good laugh at times, and you being there will make us all look good.'

'Well, I'm definitely not coming now after that insult' Patrick said, watching as a jet ski skimmed gracefully across the clear blue sea in front of him. 'And I could do with topping up my tan by the pool anyway.'

'I fancy a cocktail' Cindy said, getting up from her seat. 'Shall we move onto that nice bar we went to last night after I've freshened up?'

'Sounds good to me my love. You both ok with that?' Lance said, turning to Patrick and Maria.

Both voiced their agreement.

'I think I could do with freshening up too' Maria said, getting up to join Cindy.

'Thanks again for all this Lance' Patrick said, with the ladies now out of earshot.

'It's fine mate. You don't need to keep thanking me.'

Silence remained between them for a few moments until Patrick spoke again.

'Do you think all the fuss would have died down by the time we get back?'

'Of course, it will have, and I think you're overreacting anyway. One tough interview does not constitute a fuss in my book. You also must remember that this show will be much bigger than you once we get back. The contestants will be the focus, just remember that.'

'Well, I just hope your right.'

'Trust me I am. Now let us enjoy the rest of our Christmas in the sun and forget all about that until we get home.'

Chapter 43

I never did quite understand the need for a reception after a funeral, and that unease was even more acute as I sat in one to celebrate the life of Jenny.

A life cut short at the age of forty-two was hardly something to celebrate, was it?

No funeral service could be called a pleasant experience, but the sudden and horrific death of Jenny had made this one even more unbearable for the congregation that gathered in the local Catholic church.

Watching that coffin enter the church as Paul and the boys walked behind it was one of the saddest sights I had ever witnessed. The boys looked robotic, like as if they could not quite believe they were walking behind the coffin of their mother. Paul stood in the middle of them gripping their hands tightly, as he looked tearfully at the wooden box containing his wife.

Crocodile tears I thought as he passed us, or was this genuine grief, and maybe remorse for all Jenny had alleged he had done to her.

Both Paul and Jenny's older sister had given readings, and whilst the raw emotion had been plain to see in her, Paul had given a calm and measured reading. Only minutes earlier he has been emotional walking behind that coffin, and now he could give that performance. It certainly seemed strange to me, but I guess we are all made different, and knowing what Jenny had told me should I really have been surprised by his erratic behaviour.

'Such a sad day' the woman next to me suddenly said.

'Yes, it certainly is' I said, turning to look at her.

The woman seated by him was in her early thirties he guessed and was dressed in a simple black dress, with her blonde hair tied back into a bun.

'Are you a relative?' I asked.

'No, I was a colleague of Jenny's. You?'

'Close friend' I replied.

'I still can't believe she's gone. We were planning a night out for that Friday and now I am sitting here in her funeral. It's all so surreal.'

'Indeed' I said, picking up the tuna and cucumber sandwich from my plate and taking a small bite from it. 'You really don't know what's around the corner. That's why my motto is to always live this day like it's your last.'

'Good advice and something I wholeheartedly agree with.'

I looked across the room at Sadie, who was talking with two other women by the bar.

Sharon Rose and Tamara Lee were part of the group of school mums that had all met on that first day of school and had remained friends ever since. A group that was tragically minus one of its members now though. Sadie even remarked last night, through a flood of tears that the WhatsApp group they used would now have to change its name from All Saints. That name signifying the four members in their favourite pop group.

Both Sharon and Tamara were now divorced, and according to Sadie enjoying their new-found freedom as single women. I often worried that Sadie one day might also be persuaded to take that leap, especially given how much influence both women seemed to have over her.

Did that influence also have a bearing on the one-night stand Jenny had with me?

Would Sadie on one of her night's out also decide she needed more excitement in her life?

Just like me and Jenny did?

'I thought it was a lovely service, didn't you?' the woman said, interrupting my thoughts.

'Yes, it was lovely' I said.

'I never thought she was that religious though, in fact in work she seemed more anti-religion than anything.'

'I think she was brought up catholic and I know her mother is still active in the church' I responded.

'Still, it does not seem Jenny to me, not that it really matters now. Once you are gone and all that.

The woman seemed nice enough and ordinally I may have wanted to chat more with her, today I was not in the mood for small talk though.

'I'm sorry, would you excuse me for a minute? Need to get some air.'

'Of course,' the woman said, disappointment in her voice that her sole source of conversation was now leaving.

Leaving my seat, I made my way towards the exit of the local rugby club where the funeral reception was taking place.

It was bloody freezing as I stepped outside and walked towards the smoking shelter. Snow was on the way later this week according to the weather reports, and I zipped my coat right to my chin to try and minimise the effects of the icy chill.

I thought back to the scene at the graveyard a few hours earlier as the coffin was lowered slowly into the ground. The anguished tears of some, whilst Paul and the boys stood forlornly as *wife and mother* slowly disappeared from their lives forever. I had never attended a graveside burial before and that was a scene that will probably never leave me for the rest of my life. The woman entering the ground was most probably carrying my child when she died, as I stood next to the woman I loved most in the world. A woman who was streaming with tears as she mourned her best friend, a friend who had betrayed her with the man she loved most.

What a sorrow mess it all was. The most important thing now being the need to keep it all a secret, at all costs.

I lit a cigarette and slowly blew smoke out into the cold air.

'Need company?' a voice behind me suddenly said.

Turning around I saw the figure of Paul behind me. Dressed immaculately in a black suit, tie, and a crisp white shirt, he gave out a tired smile.

'Of course, mate' I said, 'And I'm sorry I haven't been over to chat since the church, I could see you were busy and didn't want to intrude.'

'No worries pal. Been a day I want to see the back of, for the boys' sake more than anything.'

I remained silent, only nodding my head in agreement.

'Do you mind if I have one?' he said, pointing to the cigarette I was holding.

'Sure' I said, holding out the pack for him to take one.

After lighting it for him he took a deep drag before gratefully blowing out the smoke.

'God, I really needed that' he said. 'Apart from an occasional cigar at Christmas that is my first cigarette since university.'

'It was a lovely service. You all did Jenny proud' I said.

'All her mother and sister really. You know I am not religious Ashley; they are completely hooked on the nonsense though and it's how Jenny was brought up.'

'It was a lovely send-off anyway' I said, immediately regretting my choice of language.

Paul did not seem offended though or was just trying to ignore my poor choice of words.

'I'm going to find that bastard that got her pregnant though, believe me' Paul suddenly said.

I was taken by surprise that he was even mentioning this now, and at the funeral of his wife of all places.

'Sadie and I were so sorry about the baby.'

'Why? It wasn't even mine, so why should you both feel sorry?'

'It's still a baby Paul. Another human life that went that night.'

Paul just laughed.

'I suppose you are right in some ways, and perhaps I should be mourning that child more than the lying bitch we just buried.'

'Please do not talk like that, especially here.'

'Yes, your right. She was the boys' mother and they do not deserve me talking like this about her. I'm sorry.'

I was not sure he was that sorry but said nothing more.

'Anyway, I'm hoping I will know who it was very soon.'

'Really?' I said in astonishment.

'Yes, I am hoping I can unlock her phone, I was hoping for your help on that though?'

'My help?'

'Yes, according to Apple there is no way they can physically unlock the phone, but if Jenny were syncing it to a computer then it could be unlocked that way. Far too technical for me, not for someone of your ability though I hoped.'

'Of course, I can take a look. I would need her password to access her laptop though.'

'I'm one step ahead of you with that one.'

'You are?'

'Fortunately for us, Jenny always wrote her passwords down in her diary.'

You stupid idiot Jenny, I thought. Who bloody writes their passwords down!

'Great' I said, 'I can pop down later this week if that suits?'

'Perfect. Now I better get back inside before they wonder where I am' Paul said, stubbing his cigarette out and making his way back inside.

I stood there in shock, hoping that Jenny had not been so stupid as to keep the messages between us. If she had indeed synced her phone to her laptop.

If she had then my whole life was about to come crashing down.

Chapter 44

Patrick leant back on the sun lounger as the rays from the midday sun hit his already tanned body.

In the week they had been here it had been a balmy 70 degrees on average and Patrick had been taking full advantage of this weather to reinvigorate his mind and body.

He had always loved the sun and felt so much more relaxed in this type of weather, so he was determined to enjoy it as much as possible before returning to the drabness of back home.

'Bloody hell, how could I be so stupid' Maria said on the lounger next to him.

'What's wrong love?'

'I've only gone and forgot the suntan lotion, haven't I'?

She rose to get up, Patrick stopping her.

'I'll go and get it. Could do with stretching my legs and I can get us all a drink on the way back.'

'Gin and tonic for me please.'

'What can I get you Cindy? Patrick said.

'Just an orange juice for me please Patrick' Cindy said, lowering her sunglasses slightly to look at him. 'Far too early for me to be hitting the hard stuff.'

'Well, it's after twelve and I'm on holiday, so make no excuses for letting my hair down a bit' Maria said, as if Cindy's decision to have something non-alcoholic was a slight on her.

'Of course, Maria. I hope you did not think I was having a go at you in some way. It's just I prefer to pace myself, especially in this weather.'

Maria decided not to bite back and returned her attention back towards Patrick.

'You do remember where I keep it don't you?'

'Yes love.'

She looked back at him and frowned.

'Second drawer down on my side of the bed' he groaned.

'I'm teaching you well' she said, laying back down on the lounger.

Patrick put on his flip flops and made his way back to their apartment, which was about 200 yards away from the pool area.

It pained him to say, but Lance really had chosen well here. As well as a great location this accommodation was also superb, with the 4-star complex being only 200m from the beach and within easy reach of the bars and restaurants of the town centre. Its other big attraction was its *'adults only'* rule which suited the four of them perfectly. Yes, it was a big regret that he and Maria had not managed to have children, unfortunately it was not to be after three miscarriages. Yes, there was the option of adopting but both had always dreamed of being natural parents so that option had been a non-starter really. Patrick had always been glad in some ways that the problem had been on both their parts, which meant there was no resentment that had lingered between them due to their childless marriage.

They were happy with their life now as it was. Yes, there had been ups and downs, with the biggest down of them all being the accusations and the trial that followed. They had got through it all though and were now stronger than ever.

As he walked through the lush greenery that separated the pool and bar area of the complex, his mind wandered back to what awaited him when he returned home in a couple of weeks. More media attention due to the show and then the hard slog as run-throughs and rehearsals took place to get everything near perfect before the actual contestants entered the studio.

He would not have it any other way though. He was back doing what he loved, and he was in his element being back in the studio. He could not wait to get stuck in again to be honest, and just hoped those bloody media appearances were kept to a minimum from now on.

As he walked down the pathway that led to their apartment, he could feel the heat picking up and removed his hat to wipe the sweat that was steadily dripping from his forehead.

Certainly, a different way to spend Christmas he thought, as he approached the front of their white walled apartment block.

He could see the familiar cleaning trolley outside the bottom apartment as he climbed the short flight of stairs towards the upper level. The door of the apartment was open, and he could see a mop and bucket outside with various cleaning products by its side.

Entering the room, he saw the maid coming out of the bathroom with a couple of dirty towels in her hands.

'Hola' Patrick said.

'Hola Senor' the startled maid said. 'Shall I go?' she continued in broken English.

'No, its fine. I just need to get something, and I will be out of your way' Patrick said.

The maid smiled and dumped the towels into the laundry basket before moving it outside.

Patrick watched her go before moving towards the bedroom door to retrieve the suntan lotion he had returned for.

He was just about to leave when he felt a sudden need to pee. He had already been three times today without consuming much liquid and was beginning to worry about it if he was being honest. He resolved to make an appointment with the doctor if the problem persisted.

As he stood in front of the toilet, he watched the never-ending flow of his urine hit the white china bowl with the relief of a man who had just been told his test results were clear.

Finally finished, he zipped up his trousers and quickly washed his hands. The bathroom was overly spacious with a shower in the right-hand corner and a large jacuzzi type bath covering the left. Yes, Lance had chosen very well indeed.

As Patrick opened the door out into the living room area, he could see their bedroom door was ajar.

Looking in, he could see the maid was now busily making up the bed.

She looked in her late teens or early twenties and was dressed in the smart black and white dress that all the housekeeping staff at the complex wore. Unlike their usual maid who was in her early sixties, this girl wore a much shorter version of the uniform.

Patrick watched transfixed as the maid bent over the bed to tuck the fresh blanket under the mattress, exposing her shapely stockinged legs as he did so.

As he continued watching he could feel the growing hardness down below, and quickly moved this hand there as if that simple action might supress his growing excitement.

He quickly averted his eyes and moved towards the front door to exit the apartment, when suddenly a flick of a switch in his brain made him walk back towards the open bedroom door.

Entering the room, he looked as she made the finishing touches to the bed before she turned towards the door.

She seemed startled to see him standing there, guessing he had already left the apartment. She smiled politely at him before trying to leave the bedroom.

Using his muscular frame Patrick stopped her attempt to leave.

'Senor?' she said, a look of bewilderment on her face. 'I must go.'

It was then that the red mist that had descended on him so many times in the past suddenly enveloped over him.

He grabbed the maid by her left wrist and before she had the chance to even scream, let alone fight back, he had dragged her across the room towards the bed.

Throwing her down on the bed he looked straight into her terrified eyes as he pinned her down with his large frame.

Her slight frame was no match for him, and he easily maintained his grip of her as she struggled in vain to get away.

She stifled a scream before he used his right hand to cover her mouth before her protestations could be heard from outside.

His erection was now beyond his control as his excitement grew and the helpless woman lay before him.

His free hand yanked her skirt down as he tried to pull down her tights to free her knickers, her now frenzied kicking making this task extremely difficult.

As Patrick desperately tried to stop her kicking legs, the woman suddenly managed to free one of her pinned hands and grab the right hand he had covered over her mouth.

With his hand now in her grasp she bit into the top of it as hard as she could.

'Bitch' he yelled.

With his hand now in searing and agonising pain Patrick momentarily loosened his entire grip on the maid.

Amid this brief respite she managed to push his frame off her as he rolled onto his back next to her.

Taking this chance before he managed to regain his composure, the maid leapt from the bed and ran towards the door screaming. She stopped for a brief second to pull her skirt back up, this was not long enough for Patrick to get off the bed and begin a pursuit of her though.

By the time Patrick had managed to fight off the pain and leap off the bed, the woman had shot out of the bedroom and slammed the front door of the apartment as she made her escape.

Patrick ran outside and down towards the lower level of the apartment block but could see no sign of the maid.

'Shit' he said, as he took in the magnitude of what had just happened.

Reaching inside his pocket he pulled out his mobile phone.

Holding it in his right hand he grimaced as he saw the teeth indent that now glared fiercely back at him.

The pain was excruciating as Patrick struggled to dial and hold the phone with his uninjured hand.

Waiting for the call to be answered Patrick looked around him for any sign of the maid.

Where had she gone?

To the police? The hotel manager? One of her colleagues?

He was still thinking of all the possibilities as the phone was answered by a familiar voice.

'Hello Patrick, what can I do for you?' Lance said at the other end. 'Getting bored of sunbathing with the girls already?'

Patrick was struggling to breathe as he tried to respond.

'Are you ok?' said the now concerned voice of Lance.

'Have you finished?' Patrick finally managed to get out.

'Just finished the last hole. What's up?'

'Are you heading back now?' Patrick said through gritted teeth, as the pain in his hand worsened.

'Well, I was going to have a few drinks in the clubhouse and then head back. Why don't you join us?'

'Please can you get back now Lance?'

'Please tell me what's wrong? Are the girls ok? You?'

'Please just get back here now Lance' Patrick literally shouted at the phone.

'You're frightening me now. Can't you tell me on the phone?'

'No, I can't. I'll meet you in thirty minutes down at that beach bar we go to.'

'Why there? What's wrong with meeting at the hotel?'

'Bloody hell Lance. Stop asking stupid questions and just get back here. I need your help and a bloody need it now!'

Chapter 45

Patrick had been sitting alone at the beach bar for well over an hour now and was starting to worry that not all had gone to plan.

His meeting here with Lance had been a strange affair and he was still debating his agent's reaction as he watched the world go by before him.

Lance was obviously angry, though he did not seem overly surprised when he told him about the incident with the maid. He listened with pent up anger and then left Patrick here alone as he told him he would sort it, like he always did.

What did Lance mean by that?

Just when things were getting back on track his demons had returned, and maybe this time it would be his downfall.

He drank the last of his beer and was just about to summon the waiter for another when his mobile on the table pinged with an incoming text message.

'Meet me at my apartment now!' it said.

Had Lance sorted it? It was near impossible to tell from that message and whilst he was tempted to text back, he knew the wise option was just to talk to Lance at the apartment.

He paid the bill and began the five-minute walk back to the hotel.

As he walked his thoughts returned to the events of the past couple of hours, and the ramifications it would cause if it got out. If Lance had not sorted this and that maid had gone to the authorities, then his career was definitely over. A career that had been resurrected, now only to be shot down in flames by his utter stupidity.

He could feel the burning heat from the sun on his feet as he walked on the frazzled promenade next to the packed beach, as people enjoyed the afternoon sunshine.

Not a care in the world he thought. He was just like them until ...

He blanked it all from his mind for a few moments as he turned right and made his way up the short tree lined hill that took him towards the hotel.

A few apartments graced the lower half of the street whilst their hotel and another opposite took up resident at the top end of the short road.

Close enough to the hustle and bustle of the main town but also far enough away for the peace and quiet he craved. Peace and quiet he had until what happened that morning.

'YOU BLOODY FOOL PATRICK' he could hear a voice inside his head say.

His heart began beating faster and faster as he approached the entrance of the hotel and the dreaded encounter with his agent. He smiled at the hotel receptionist as he walked towards the short flight of stairs that would take him to the apartment block where Lance and Cindy were staying.

As he got to the bottom he hesitated, and instead of turning right towards the apartments he made a left turn towards the pool and bar area. Keeping a safe distance as not to be seen, Patrick watched the sleeping figures of both Maria and Cindy, both of them still settled on the sun loungers.

Maria was the *'love of his life'* and the person he had hurt the most with all this business. Was he about to hurt her yet again? When he had returned to the pool after what he could only still call *'the incident'*, his nerves were understandably all over the place and the concern from Maria was evident from the outset.

'What's up love? You look as white as a sheet' she said, as he arrived back carrying the suntan lotion in his good hand.

'I'm fine. Think this heat is just getting to me a bit' he lied.

'You should get in the shade' Cindy said, looking up from the book she was reading.

'Good idea. In fact, Lance just texted to see if I fancy a beer up at the golf club.' he said, handing the lotion to Maria.

He winced with the motion, and a concerned Maria said 'Patrick?'

'I'm fine love. Just knocked my hand against the bed when I was getting the lotion.'

'Let me look' she said, as she looked to remove the towel that was covering my injured hand.

'No, it's fine' he said before she could take a look. 'Just a sprain, I think. I'll pick up a bandage from somewhere in town for it on my way to the golf club.'

He gave her a quick kiss and was heading back towards the hotel lobby before she could even reply.

'Hey, Patrick' Cindy shouted, 'You've bloody forgotten our drinks.'

Patrick heard but kept walking.

Snapping back to the present, he watched them both for a few more seconds, before reluctantly making his way towards Lance's apartment.

He wished he had stopped at the hotel bar now for some *'Dutch Courage'*, in truth he had already drunk enough today though.

Now standing at the apartment door, he knocked lightly in the hope Lance would not hear and he could turn back. There was no such luck for that though, and the door was opened almost immediately.

'You took your time' Lance said, closing the door behind him.

'Sorry' Patrick said, as he grew accustomed to the gloom of the room. All the blinds were closed he noticed.

What happened next stunned Patrick, as he had never, in all his years' knowing him, witnessed a violent bone in his friend's body.

Lance grabbed him by the throat and pinned him up against the wall with a rage in his eyes that Patrick had never seen before. A rage that been building since he had first told him.

'You fucking idiot!' Lance yelled right into his face, whilst still keeping a firm grip on his neck. 'Are you determined to wreck everything? And for what, a quick 5 minutes of pleasure?' Lance continued to rage.

Patrick was struggling for breath as the vice like grip continued.

'Please Lance. I can't breathe' he managed to gurgle.

Lance released his grip and Patrick slumped to the tiled floor, trying desperately to catch his breath.

Lance sat down on the chair opposite and watched as Patrick slowly got to his feet.

'I'm not saying I didn't deserve that, but I'm not sure nearly choking me to death is the answer.'

'Don't exaggerate, and yes you did bloody deserve it.'

Patrick made his way slowly to the other chair in the room and sat gingerly down, whilst still clutching his neck.

'Well?' he said.

'Well, what?' Lance said, desperately trying not to make eye contact with him.

'Did you find her?'

'Ah yes, the woman you tried to rape.'

'Please don't say it like that.'

'And how else should I say it then? Shall we say the woman you came onto and things got out of hand ever so slightly. Does that sound better for Patrick Reed?'

Patrick said nothing to that.

'Well, to answer your question, yes I did find the poor woman after a friendly chat with the housekeeping manger here. She finally let me speak to her after I made it worth her while.'

'Glad to hear extortion is still alive and well' Patrick said with a grin.

'Not even close to being funny' Lance retorted.

'Had she told anybody about what happened?'

'I don't think.'

'Did you explain how sorry I was? I truly never intended for it to happen, it was like a red mist descended over me, and once it had started, I just couldn't stop.'

Lance leant forward and put his head into his hands before looking straight at him, 'Why though Patrick? Why risk all this again, just as things are on the up.'

It took Patrick a while to answer before he eventually said, 'I really don't know. She was there and I just could not help myself. I knew it was wrong, but once the thought came into my head it just would not go away. I knew I should not have acted upon it; I have been so damn stupid.

It was at that point that Patrick began to sob.

'I'm so sorry Lance, you have to believe me.'

Lance watched this performance from his so-called friend and began to feel real pity for the sorry man in front of him.

'You knew, didn't you?' Patrick said through the tears.

'Of course, I did' Lance said with contempt. 'I've been your agent for nearly all your career. You really think I wouldn't know what you did.'

'Why did you keep quiet then?'

'Probably for the same reason all those producers, directors and others that knew kept quiet. The power you held over everyone at that time was extraordinary, and I think most of us turned a blind eye in a misplaced sense of loyalty towards you.'

'I never realised' Patrick spluttered.

'Why would you?' Lance said. 'Any women that complained were quietly moved on or told to keep quiet if they valued their careers. The others I presumed never said anything due to the power you held over them or through the shame of it all.'

'What did you say to the maid?' Patrick said, trying to bring the conversation back to the matter in hand.

'That you had severe dementia which affected your decision making. That your moral compass for right and wrong had gone haywire due to the illness. Her grandfather is also suffering with it which helped, she understood how an illness like that can change the personality of a person.'

'Thank you, Lance,' Patrick said contritely, 'So she won't go to the police?'

'I can guarantee that for sure, I don't believe she will though. The thousand euros I gave her also helped in that regard. Which you will be returning to me, of course.'

'Of course, do you think that buying her silence is a good idea though?'

'I prefer to call it a goodwill gesture and what choice did I have after your stupidity.'

Patrick said nothing as he began to rise from his chair.

'Just one other thing before you go.'

Patrick resumed sitting.

Lance cleared his throat before continuing, 'Once the show is over, I want to end my role as your agent. I won't put either of us in an awkward position by ending it before then, but when it does finish, I want to terminate your contract as my client.'

'If that's what you want' Patrick said with a note of resignation.

'It is. Now I think it is about time we got back to the girls' Lance said, standing up.

'And act normal?' Patrick enquired.

'What else can we do? Am I supposed to ignore you and make Maria suspicious? No, we act normal and hope that this maid has bought the story and keeps quiet.'

As both men moved towards the front door of the apartment Lance turned to Patrick before opening it.

'And Patrick, if you ever do anything like this again, then I will personally break every bone in your body.'

Chapter 46

I cut the engine and looked at the illuminated clock on the car dashboard.

9:05 it read.

The audition was at 10:30 so I had over an hour to kill before then.

Much better to be early though, and I could do with a strong coffee before it all started anyway.

I opened the car door and climbed out into the darkly lit multi-storey that was crammed full of cars, driven here by office workers and early morning shoppers. Not fancying the stairs, I took the lift down to the ground level and exited out into the cold January morning.

A small dusting of snow had fallen the night before, although it had already virtually disappeared now as I made my way across the busy street towards the coffee shop. To my left were the foreboding outer walls of Cardiff Castle, whilst to my right was the magnificent sight of the Millennium Stadium, rising above the buildings that surrounded it. The sight of it always gave me goose bumps, and I hoped that I could draw inspiration for my audition from the great performances that had graced that hallowed turf.

After ordering a latte in the coffee shop, I found a quiet seat near the window, so I could compose my thoughts for the ordeal to come.

I still had not told Sadie about all this, and so right now she believed I was sitting at my desk in work rather than in a coffee shop in the centre of Cardiff. Maybe I should have been honest with her, but after the funeral yesterday it was probably for the best she did not know quite yet. Indeed, if she would ever know. It was likely this was where the short journey would end and the need to tell her would no longer be required.

There I was again. Being pessimistic even before the audition had started. It was a big issue for me and one that had plagued my whole life, with the consequences often manifesting themselves in my dark periods. A *'Glass-Half-Empty'* person summed me up, and it was a habit I needed to get out of, especially if today was to be a success.

I looked at the confirmation email on my phone yet again.

It stated that arrival for the audition was required fifteen minutes before the requested start time, so I determined to leave here just after ten for the two-minute walk to the hotel, which was viewable from my current location.

Proof of ID and address were also required, so for what felt like the hundredth time today I checked that my passport and a utility bill were safely tucked into my coat pocket.

I scrolled down to the end of the email where the following words shot starkly back at me.

'Remember just be yourself.'
'Prepare to be chatty.'
'Think about any funny stories you may have.'
'Relax and enjoy the experience.'

Just reading these words made my heartbeat faster and cause those awful butterflies in my stomach, which I always seemed to get when I was nervous. I was tempted to run out of that coffee shop and just drive home but what would that prove? That I was a gutless coward who was running away from something I wanted so badly and had waited so long for.

I inhaled deep breaths and told myself to calm down or this whole thing was going to end in disaster. Putting my phone down I tried to put the audition out of mind for a few minutes in the hope that my frazzled nerves would begin to calm down.

This did not really help though as my thoughts returned to Jenny and the aftermath of her tragic death.

I was due to see Paul at the end of the week to help him unlock her phone and the secrets it contained. I was still hoping that Jenny had not synced her phone to that laptop, but given she had the habit of writing down her passwords it did seem likely. Surely, she would not have been so stupid to have kept the messages between us though.

I had thought about lying to Paul and tell him the phone had not been synced if I found out it had been. I quickly realised this would be a bad idea though. He could always get a second opinion, and for all I knew he already knew the phone could be unlocked and this was part of some elaborate test to trick me.

Why would he want to trick me though?

Did he already know about me and Jenny, and was just waiting for the right moment to unleash his revenge?

I quickly put these thoughts out of my mind. I had known Paul for several years, and I doubted he could have kept that knowledge inside him.

Still, I had a nagging doubt in the back of my mind about it all though.

Looking at my watch I could see it was just past ten. Time to leave.

Quickly drinking what was left of my latte I made sure I had all the required documents with me before putting on my coat and vacating the table.

Upon exiting the café, I was struck even more than earlier of the biting chill in the air and wished I had brought my scarf and gloves with me now. The street was full of shoppers trying to bag a bargain in the January sales, and this cold weather with the threat of more snow to come was not going to deter them. I took my time to weave between the throng as I made the short journey to the hotel.

Less than five minutes later I was standing outside the Victorian hotel, with its large and impressive portico entrance. They certainly did not build things like this anymore I thought, as I tried desperately to compose myself before entering.

'Calm down Ashley. You have waited so long for this chance. Don't blow it now!' the voice in my head said. And that voice inside me was definitely right. I had waited years for this opportunity and to blow

it now due to my erratic nerves would indeed be crazy. Attempting to clear all negative thoughts out of my head, I walked up the short flight of stairs under the portico and entered the hotel.

All I could think was 'wow' when I walked through those doors, to see what I could only describe as a reception area from a begone era. Straight ahead of me was a majestic central staircase that led to the upper floors and was topped with two gilded columns. Above me was a chandelier that hung from a fresco ceiling that looked like something you would see at the Sistine Chapel.

Walking towards the reception area to my left I wondered if all TV show auditions were held in venues like this.

'Good morning Sir, how can I help you?' the smiling woman behind the desk said.

'Morning. I'm here for an audition' I said rather nervously.

'Just down the corridor and it's the first door on the left Sir.'

'Thank you' I said, following the directions she had given me.

As I walked down the corridor the urge to turn back once again yet me like a hammer coming down on a nail.

Yes, I had waited so long for this opportunity, but was now beginning to think if it had come at exactly the wrong time in my life. With my mental health so low, coupled with Jenny's death, was I capable of making the best impression here.

As I contemplated this, the door to my left suddenly opened, where a blonde woman in her early twenties and dressed in jeans and white trainers appeared before me.

'Are you here for the audition?' she said rather exuberantly.

'Yes' I said, before my brain had even registered another response to say.

'Just take a seat in there please' she said, pointing to the open door. 'One of my colleagues will take your details and a quick photo for our files. Just waiting on a few others to arrive but we should be starting soon I hope.'

'Thanks' I said, watching her walk back towards the reception area with phone pressed to her ear.

I walked confidently towards the open door, in the hope of masking the bag of nerves I was feeling at this exact moment.

As I entered the large conference room a young man, who also looked in his early twenties greeted me.

'Hello, I'm Sam' he said with a cheery smile that instantly made me feel at ease. 'Can I take your name please?'

'Ashley White' I said.

Sam looked at the file he was holding as I took in the surroundings around me. The twenty or so seats in the room had been arranged in a semi-circle which were fully occupied apart from a few empty spaces, one of which I guessed was reserved for me.

'Ah yes, Ashley' Sam said, crossing my name off his checklist. 'Is it ok if I take a quick picture for our records?'

'Yes. That is fine' I said, not really sure what he would have done if I had declined.

Sam then proceeded to stick a name badge on my shirt and take a quick picture before asking me to take a seat with the others in the semi-circle whilst we waited for the latecomers to arrive.

Taking a seat next to a slightly overweight man dressed in a white shirt and blue tie, I studied the varied group of individuals around me.

It was clear to see that many people in the room were white, middle aged and even more predictably male. The five women I counted clearly had the advantage of their gender, due to the large number of men here. The same could be said for the Chinese man here too, as the producers would want a balanced ethic makeup of contestants on the show. This meant I was largely competing against the white men in this room for that coveted place.

'First time?' the man next to me said.

'Sorry?'

'First time at one of these?' he said, emphasising his point by theatrically gesturing to the room.

'Yes, is it that obvious?'

'You do look a bit like a *rabbit in headlights*, but we all experience that a bit when we first do one of these. I certainly was no different when it was my first time' he laughed.

'You've done one of these before then?'

'A few you could say Ashley.'

I looked at him in puzzlement.

'Don't worry Ashley I'm no magician, but I am a good reader.'

I still looked at him blankly.

He pointed at the sticker on my shirt and we both laughed.

'I'm Ross by the way' he said pointing to his own name badge.

'Pleased to meet you Ross' I said as I shook his hand.

Looking over my shoulder I noticed that the two latecomers had arrived whilst I had been talking to Ross.

An older black woman and a younger man of Indian descent.

My task here had just got considerably more difficult.

I watched as they went through the same process, before taking the last seats in the semi-circle. The woman I had met in the corridor then arrived back in the room and made her way towards us all.

'Good Morning everyone' she said with the same beaming smile on her face that I had seen earlier.

'Just in the way of a couple of introductions before we get started. I'm Mel and I'm the casting producer for the show and this is Sam' she said, acknowledging the man next to her.

I reasoned that to do a job like hers, you needed that type of personality and I must admit it was having the desired effect of settling my nerves.

'First of all, I would like to thank you all for making the effort to come here today, especially considering the inclement weather we are having now.'

As if anybody was going to miss the opportunity to win two million pounds due to a light dusting of snow I thought.

'So, your audition here today will consist of a 30-minute written quiz, a fun icebreaker game to hopefully relax you all and finally a chat to camera where we will get to know you all a bit better.'

That last bit really filled me with dread.

'What we really want, and I cannot emphasise this enough, is for you all to enjoy this experience. Remember you have all done incredibly well to get this far and we really want you to get the most out of this opportunity. So be chatty, let us see your personality, and above all give us your biggest smile.'

Chatty and smiling were not natural habitats of mine, and that would have to change if I were going to have any chance of getting on the show.

Mel then instructed us to look under our seats, where a single piece of paper with a 50-question quiz was attached to a clipboard.

'So, you have 30 minutes to complete this written quiz. If you finish earlier than that then please raise your hand and either me or Sam will collect it.'

She look closely at her phone, which I guessed she was using as a stopwatch, before announcing 'You have thirty minutes, starting from now.'

And suddenly the sea of faces around me dropped, their focus now concentrated on the sheet of paper in front of them.

I quickly wrote my name on top and scanned the questions in front of me.

The twenty-five questions on that first page looked straightforward enough, although as always there were the splattering of science and arts questions, my real nemesis when it came to quizzing. Turning over the sheet I could see the questions got a lot tougher and reckoned I would need at least ten educated guesses to complete it.

With a chance to win all that money I could hardly expect your bog-standard pub quiz so would have to make the most of the cards I had been dealt.

I looked discreetly at the man to my right who was busily writing in answers like it was the easiest quiz he had ever done.

Ross on the other hand, like himself, was still looking over the questions.

Rubbing my eyes to concentrate, I picked up the pen in front of me and began writing.

I always tended to work the same way in these sorts of written quizzes, and that was leave all the questions I did not know, whilst racing through all the ones I did. The logic being that with the obvious ones out of the way, it gave me the maximum time to try and formulate an answer to the difficult ones.

Before I knew it, Mel announced that there were only five minutes left.

Five bloody minutes! Where had all the time gone, I thought?

I had been staring at the same question for what seemed like an eternity now, but still no credible answer came out of the top of my pen. The others I had not known had been dealt with by that all-important educated guess, but even that was proving impossible on this one.

I looked perplexed at the question in front of me.

St Lucian poet who received the 1992 Nobel Prize for Literature?
I know this quiz needed some hard questions, but who on earth would know something like that.

OK, most of the room probably, but I certainly did not.

'One minute' Mel said.

I was wracking my brain for any inspiration. None was forthcoming though and that minute was quickly counting down.

The only thing that came to mind was a holiday to the country when I was nine to attend my cousin's wedding, fabulous holiday from what I could remember even though the marriage had ended acrimoniously less than a year later.

'Thirty seconds.'

What was the name of that drive-thru volcano we visited with its two peaks, rising into the sky like church spires?

Come on brain, THINK!

'Ten seconds.'

P. It began with a P, didn't it?

Then suddenly that drawer in my brain that was stubbornly staying shut, flew open with astonishing speed.

PITONS, it shouted out.

'Five seconds left.'

I quickly wrote down Pitons and then let out a huge sigh as I dropped the pen onto the clipboard. Clearly it was not the right answer, but I was hoping that a knowledge of St Lucia would be appreciated anyway.

'Time's up, please stop writing' Mel said, as I watched the few others still writing also drop their pens with a mixture of relief and exasperation on their faces.

'Nice and easy, wasn't it? Ross said next to me with a big grin on his face.

'You think so? I said.

'Nah, I'm kidding with you mate. Some of that was pretty bloody hard if I'm being honest, but it's what you expect for this calibre of show.'

He was right of course, although I am sure those who finished much earlier would certainly disagree. Such a shame we would not be given our scores, but then again, maybe that was for the best.

The ice breaker game of Pictionary we played for the next thirty minutes was certainly a lot of fun and lightened the tension in the room that had been hovering during the written quiz. I was not sure my mother-in-law would have been too impressed with my artistic skills and could picture her now chastising me for my technique.

'Well, I hoped you all enjoyed that' Mel said as the last person finished their round. 'We certainly believe it's a great way to relax everyone and see which of you amongst us are budding Picasso's.'

The room tamely laughed at that poor expression of humour.

'As I said earlier, we will now finish off with a five-minute chat to the camera. This will be very informal, and we want you to feel relaxed as possible, so forget about the camera and just try and talk naturally about yourself. We want to hear all about you so make sure you include family, work, hobbies, and any interesting stories you may have. I am here to move the chat along if you get stuck, but hopefully that will not be necessary. Your chats should not last longer than five minutes and I will prompt you to wrap-up if you are you in danger of going over that time. If it is ok, we will start with you Jenny and then make our way across.'

The sense of relief washed over me when she said that. Now at least I could watch most of the other auditionees have their ordeal before having to endure my own.

Jenny strode up confidently towards Mel and stood in front of the camera that had been erected upon a tripod.

I then witnessed at what could only be described as a masterclass in auditioning. It transpired that Jenny was a 45-year-old midwife from Cardiff who had us all in stitches with her tales from the world of childbirth which included delivering a set of quads. She exuded confidence and hardly stopped for breath before Mel had to prematurely bring her to a halt as she hit the five-minute mark.

That was certainly the standard for everybody to follow, and boy did they.

After Jenny came *'Paul the Policeman'* whose stories of nicking villains also had us all in stitches.

And so, it continued...

A teacher, nurse and even an undertaker followed, the line quickly getting closer to me. I was getting more and more nervous as it did, my nerves frazzled as my confidence waned watching the competition in front of me.

And then it was time for those dreaded words as Mel said, 'Your turn, Ashley.'

'Good luck mate' Ross said as he sat down following his supremely confident chat to the camera.

It was clear from watching it, that he had indeed done it many times, and was indeed exceptionally good at it.

As I walked those few metres towards the camera, many thoughts swirled in my mind.

It was one thing doing this in front of my phone, but here in front of all these people was another matter.

'You can do this Ashley!' said the positive voice floating inside my head. *'This is you dream, don't blow it now and accuse stupid nerves on your abject failure.'*

Unfortunately, it was fighting against my all too frequent negative voice.

'How delusional are you Ashley? Do you really think you can stand in front of all these people for five minutes and talk about your mundane life?

'Of course, you can. Remember all the hard work you have done and stop being such a fool' that positive voice shouted back.

'But you are a fool, and a timid one at that. Forget all this nonsense and walk straight back out of this room before you make an even bigger idiot of yourself.'

My nerves were in shreds as I stood before the camera, with my prepared script now scattered into tiny fragments all over my mind.

'Hi Ashley' Mel said with the now ever-present beaming smile projecting back at me. 'Like the others I will count you down from three, is that ok?'

'Yes' I replied in a shaky voice.

'Three, two, one' Mel said, before pointing a finger at me to begin.

I cleared my throat rather theatrically as the first beginnings of sweat dripped from my forehead.

My mind was just blank, and at this point I could barely remember my name; let alone the highly polished speech I had planned to give. The sweat was now slowing seeping through my shirt, as I stood there like a statue with an expectant Mel waiting for me to start.

I looked nervously around at the rows of faces and wondered what they thought as I stood there like a complete lemon. Maybe some were willing me on, some hoping for me to fail so their own chances of success increased.

Before my ordeal turned into a complete and utter disaster a piece of good fortune came before me.

'Can we stop for a minute please' Sam said as he looked up from the video camera. 'Just a technical issue with the camera I need to sort out, shouldn't take too long hopefully.'

Mel gave me an apologetic smile and turned to speak to Sam.

Breathing space at last, and boy did I need it. Now I had to use this time to sort myself out.

Images of people that doubted me floated before me whilst I stood there. Dad and my old English teacher Mrs Hicks standing firmly in front of the queue, as they sternly put me down as they always did.

'Accept your limitations and work with the little talent that god has given you' they said, 'Forget these ridiculous pipe dreams dear boy!'

Others took their place from the queue to give the same negative news to me.

But something happened to me at that moment, something that had never happened before.

I fought back at last.

'I'm better than you all think, I'm determined to prove you all wrong and make my dreams a reality. You can mock me, you can put me down, but one thing you will never do is defeat me.'

As those words stayed with me, the images of those before me disappearing into the ether.

'Right, I think Sam has got everything sorted, so if you ready we can start again?' Mel said.

'Yes, I'm ready, and raring to go.'

'Great' Mel said with a rather perplexed look, given my stumbling start at the first attempt.

My second attempt though, was a vastly different matter.

Timid and awkward Ashley was replaced by a confident and relaxed person, that even I had trouble recognising. It was just like I had rehearsed it that last time, with no slip ups or awkward silences. Mel seemed engaged with it, as did the others in the room, with my anecdotes generating laughs in the right places. Who cared if it was only marginally true, I certainly did not and I wasn't sure even Mel did to be honest? She wanted contestants that were good TV, and a few white lies did not matter if that objective was met.

As I resumed my seat after the five minutes, it was with the satisfaction of a job well done.

'Great job' Ross said beside me.

'Thanks.'

'Never would have guessed you did extreme marathons' he laughed.

I laughed back, saying nothing in response.

Clearly, I was not fooling him, not that it mattered. I only needed to impress Mel and her superiors; I could worry about my white lies later.

The black woman and Indian man who had arrived late were the last to make their pitches before Sam addressed us all again.

'Thanks everybody for coming here today, we hope you enjoyed the experience, even the dreaded chat to camera. I'm sure Sam will agree with me that the standard here today has blown us away and has certainly made life difficult for the producers.'

Sam nodded his head in agreement.

'I'm afraid the next stage of the process is a bit of a waiting game, those that are shortlisted will receive an email no later than a week today. If you have not heard from us by then, you have unfortunately been unsuccessful on this occasion.'

And then it was all over.

Mel wished us a safe journey home and I was heading out of the room in a much more positive frame of mind than when I arrived.

Now all I needed to do was be patient and wait.

Chapter 47

The woman reached across to pick up the glass of water from her bedside table.

She took a large swallow of the now tepid liquid before replacing the glass and returning her head to the warmness of the pillow. Her mouth was parched, like it was most nights, probably the result of her nightly bottle of wine. She knew it was bad for her but just could not stop. It was the only way she could deal with what happened, the only way to forget, even for the briefest moment whilst the alcohol took hold.

She stared at the illuminated digits of her alarm clock.

05:00.

In one hour, the alarm would shatter the silence of her small flat to signal the start of another day. A day like all the rest in her mundane life, a day that would ultimately end like all the others, with a bottle of red in front of the TV.

She was tempted to ring in sick when her alarm eventually went off, but knew if she did, then the chances of her retaining her current employment would be slim. Already on a final written warning for her absence record, she knew another indiscretion would result in instant dismissal. She hated the place but could not face the prospect of starting somewhere else, not now anyway.

Sleeping was proving impossible despite her desperate need for rest after another late night. She was barely getting a few hours of sleep now and felt the effects constantly throughout the day.

She switched the alarm clock off and reluctantly manoeuvred herself out of the bed.

She had to steady herself as she headed towards the bedroom door. God her head hurt liked hell and judging by her unsteadiness, the alcohol was still very much present in her bloodstream.

She walked gingerly along the dark landing as she reached her tiny bathroom. Pulling the cord beside the door she was momentarily dazzled as the room was lit up by the brilliant light. Reaching the sink, she stared at her reflection in the mirror, and as often was the case these days, she was horrified at what stared back at her. The heavy bags under her eyes, the red blotches on her face was not the sight of a healthy thirty-year-old woman. She ran the cold tap and splashed the freezing water onto her face in a forlorn hope that it might magically improve her appearance. Looking back to face the mirror with the water still dripping from her face she could see that indeed miracles did not happen.

Quickly drying herself she moved into the living room and switched on the TV, before making herself some breakfast. Whilst waiting for the kettle to boil she looked at her pet goldfish who was looking expectantly at her with his mouth bobbing up and down.

'Hungry are you Stewie?'

As if to answer yes, he swam frantically around his tiny bowl before finishing back in the same place he started. She dropped the small flakes of food into his bowl and watched as he greedily devoured them. She had always loved animals and as a child had a dog and rabbit, keeping animals like that was near impossible in a flat like this and unfair with her out most of the day working. Therefore Stewie, who was named after a character from her favourite TV show was a happy medium.

Settling into the sofa with her coffee and toast she watched the morning news. Like most days it seemed just as depressing as her own life, and she wondered at times why she even bothered to watch. The opinionated and rude host was currently lambasting a helpless politician about the state of the health service, with his cornered victim trying desperately to end this line of questioning. Usually, she could not stand this wretched specimen of a man, but her estimation of him had gone up slightly after his encounter with Patrick Reed.

Yes, she liked watching him squirm that morning as the host probed him with questions he did not want to answer. Of course, he should have never been on the show that morning. If justice had taken its rightful course, he would have been rotting in jail instead.

Justice would be dealt soon though, and when it did Patrick Reed would wish he were languishing in a prison cell instead.

Chapter 48

As I stood on the steps of the hotel entrance, I still felt a sense of euphoria at what I had just achieved.

Had I imagined it all? Had little old me really stood in front of all those people and just done that?

If I were not standing here and feeling the icy wind hit my face, I would indeed think it was all a dream and I would suddenly wake up.

'Excuse me' I heard a voice behind me say.

I turned to see a rather irate woman trying to move past me as she attempted to leave the hotel, only to find her exit blocked by my rather large frame.

'Sorry' I said, moving aside.

The woman walked quickly down the steps without acknowledging my apology.

'Rude cow' I silently mouthed after her, watching her cross the busy main road in front of the hotel.

I could see she looked visibly upset and it was then that I remembered her from the audition earlier. Whilst most of the room had given great performances, I remembered this poor lady giving a stumbling and nervous account of herself, as she desperately tried to impress.

She disappeared and I felt immense aguish for her, knowing that would surely have been me if lady luck had not shone down on me with the camera malfunction.

What will be, will be, I thought, as I climbed down the steps and turned right onto the pavement.

As I turned the corner, I could see a recognisable face coming towards me. Really not wanting to speak to them at that moment I made a quick about turn, unfortunately it was too late though.

'Ashley' I heard behind me.

Now I could have kept walking on and pretend I had not seen them but being just a few yards in front of them I could hardly say I could not hear them.

I turned to look behind me and was confronted by the figure of Simon Tucker, with his piercing blue eyes and clear-cut features, dressed smartly in a pair of jeans, black polo shirt and what looked like one of those quilted designer coats which he had unzipped.

'Simon' I said in mock surprise.

He came towards me with an outstretched hand, that usual big grin of his plastered on his face.

'Well, what a surprise to see you here' he said, releasing his grip. 'Now, as I know you're a happily married man and wouldn't be coming out of a place like this for that reason, I'm guessing you were there for the same reason I'm going in.'

Shit, I completely forgot there was another audition here after mine.

'Yeah, same reason' I said.

'You finally got it then?'

'Sorry?'

'An audition' he said in that sarcastic tone he often had.

'Yes, finally got here.'

'Well, congratulations mate. How did you find it?'

'Not bad' I said in a non-committal tone.

'Any tips before I go in?'

I hesitated before saying 'I probably shouldn't' discuss anything ....'

'Only joking mate' he said, giving me a playful punch on the arm. 'You know I've done this type of thing many times before.'

And indeed, he had. With his good looks and easy-going charm Simon had been on many shows in the time I had known him. The manager at the local snooker club I frequented had many successes to his name, in contrast all I had were failures. A fact that offered grated on me.

'I should really be on my way' I said, looking at my watch to exaggerate the point.

'Me too mate, I really don't want to be late either.'

'Good luck' I said, beginning to move off.

'Cheers Ashley, you know me though, tend to make my own luck.'

And with that he disappeared into the hotel.

'Well let us hope it finally runs out today' I muttered under my breath.

Chapter 49

Patrick looked out at this snow-covered garden and marvelled at the sight before him. With the winter sun glistening on the powdery soft snow that had just hit the grass a few hours earlier and once naked trees now looking like ice sculptures, his pride and joy now really did look like a winter wonderland.

A robin suddenly flew onto the windowsill in front of him for a few seconds before once again flying off into the winter sunshine. No other bird could capture this scene like the robin could, and this fleeting appearance of this beautiful bird rounded off this picturesque postcard scene perfectly. He suddenly remembered that his dear old Mum had always felt that a robin appearing close by indicated a long-lost family member or friend wanting to show themselves to you in the form of this beautiful small bird. He had always shaken this off as a stupid *old wives' tale*, but today he was not so sure. Had its appearance been a warning to him, maybe from his long-departed mum. A warning that his actions in life were wrong and he needed to change course quickly or face the consequences yet again.

He moved away from the window and sat back down at his desk to once again mull over his actions over the last week.

They had returned from holiday two days ago, and in that time, Patrick had not stopped thinking about what had happened there. Thought how stupid he had been to put into jeopardy all the hard work he had done to get back to the top.

Talk of what happened had been scant for the rest of the holiday, with Lance being true to his word and acting normally around Maria and Cindy. When they did get the chance to be alone together, he had sought more assurances from Lance that everything would be ok.

'I bloody well hope so, as I'm up to my neck in all this now as well.'

'I'm sorry Lance, I really am.'

'Are you really though? If this was a one-off, I may believe that, but it's not is it?'

He was right of course. This had been a terrible affliction that had consumed him from early in his career and showed no sign of abating even after the brutality of the court case.

'I know it's wrong, I really do. It's like another person doing those things and I'm looking down on him with a sense of despair at what they are doing. I'm willing them to stop but can't physically end it.'

Lance had laughed at that statement before replying.

'Of course, you can stop it, you just don't want to. You have the power on these women and do not want to let it go. I warn you though Patrick, this has to stop, or next time you will be thrown in a jail cell and there will be nothing else I can do to save you.'

We had not spoken another word about it since and the holiday had continued in an air of surreal normality.

It had consumed Patrick's thoughts ever since though as questions without any reasonable answers floated inside his mind.

What if that maid found out who he really was?

How long had Lance really known?

Had he been protecting him?

He had no answers to any of them.

Yes, some people had protected him as he used his power and influence for their help, but Lance hadn't been one of them, or so he thought?

He had always thought he was the good actor by keeping all this from his agent, had he read it completely wrong though and the real actor in all this was indeed Lance.

Switching his laptop on he tried to banish all this from his head for a few moments.

Scrolling through his emails he could see a flurry from Gem Productions. Studio rehearsals were due to start in the next couple of weeks and both Mike and Sarah were anxious for him to go into the office to discuss things before then.

Lance was also copied in and would ordinarily have replied on his behalf, but for once Patrick did the job himself.

Hi Both
Yes, that date would be great for me.
Look forward to seeing you both then.
Patrick

There were also more media appearances required, which he would leave for Lance to deal with.

After spending the next few minutes deleting junk mails, which seemed to grow larger by the day, he logged off.

He debated whether to go for a walk in the garden but could from the window that it had begun to snow once again, with large flakes now relentlessly sticking to the pane.

The clock on the wall of the study showed that it was just after 2 o' clock.

He reached for the bottle of whiskey and poured himself a large glass.

Chapter 50

Mike Phelps was a worried man. A very worried man.

Sitting in his office, all Mike could think of was the conversation he had with his partner just before Christmas.

Was Tony exaggerating the situation or had Patrick indirectly caused the suicide of a young woman.

It was playing on his mind so much that he really did wish that Tony had said nothing now.

He had even contemplated ringing James Pullman at the network with his concerns, but in the end had decided against it. Even if he shared the same concerns, it was far too late to do something about it now without serious questions being asked on why they thought hiring Patrick in the first place was a good idea.

No, they just had to get on with it now and hope that the decision to hire Patrick Reed would not backfire on them.

His computer pinged with an incoming email.

He checked the screen and could see it was from the man in question to confirm their meeting next week.

He quickly replied.

That is great Patrick. Will be great to catch up.
Hope you had a relaxing holiday.
Cheers
Mike

He was worried about the meeting with the knowledge he now had, but it was essential that Patrick was well briefed before they went into studio rehearsals.

Should he bring it up at the meeting and maybe get his side of the story?

He quickly rubbished the idea as one of the stupidest he had ever had. Did he think the answer he would receive would be *'of course, I raped a woman all those years ago who then tragically took her own life, but all that's behind me now so can we please move on.'*

No, he just had to make sure the right safety measures we there to protect everyone involved in the production. He had to protect his staff and the contestants as much as he could from Patrick Reed, or this show could be the last he would ever make.

Chapter 51

'Any joy?' Paul said.

I was tempted to lie and say no, but that could prove disastrous, especially if Paul got a second opinion or had indeed already got someone to check.

'Yes, it looks like Jenny did indeed sync her phone to the laptop' I said, turning to look at him.

'Excellent' he said as he peered over my shoulder, 'Can you tell when the last backup was?'

I told him the last backup of the phone.

'That's three days before she died' Paul said.

'You sure you really want me to restore the data?' I said in the forlorn hope he would change his mind.

'Why would I want to do that?'

'I'm just thinking of you, do you really want to put yourself through all this?'

'You mean putting myself through all the anguish of finding out who my wife was having an affair with and whose child she was carrying. If you did indeed mean that then I will have to politely reject that advice and insist you continue restoring the phone.'

'No problem' I said, starting the restore process, 'Should take about twenty minutes to finish.'

'Fancy a beer whilst we wait?'

'Sounds good' I said, watching the progress bar of the restore slowly inch along.

'Be right back' he said, moving off to the kitchen to get the beers.

Immediately I regretted saying yes and wished I had just made my excuses. The techie stuff already done; I was sure Paul could have coped with the rest of the process. Thinking about it, Paul was not a stupid guy, far from it, and could easily have googled this sort of thing.

Was there a reason he wanted me to be here when the phone was finally unlocked, and he could check its secrets.

Did he know, or was I just being paranoid yet again?

As I pondered this a beer bottle was plonked down in front of me.

'Cheers pal' I said as Paul took up a seat beside me.

Looking at him now, I could see how awful he looked. With heavy bags under his eyes and considerable beard growth, he looked so much older than his actual forty-eight years.

'So, how are Sadie and the kids?'

'Good thanks, Sadie is back doing her degree and Ellie is spending my money like it grows on trees.'

'Aren't I glad me and Jenny only had two boys' he replied with a laugh.

Sadie always told me that Jenny had craved a girl and that John was adamant their family would end at two children. Had his success in that been another source of tension in their marriage and one that ultimately led to both committing adultery.

'And how are you and the boys?' I said, taking another look at the laptop.

Please bloody hurry so I can get out of here, and this awkward small talk with Paul can then finish.

'They are fine, coping much better than me to be honest, and them being back in school gives them more normality.'

'And you?'

'I'm getting there' he said, polishing off the last of his beer, 'Another?'

'I'm good thanks' I said, picking up my nearly full bottle.

He headed back into the kitchen to fetch another one.

Clearly knocking back the alcohol was another factor in his dreadful appearance.

He arrived back just as the restore was ending.

'Success' I said, handing him the phone.

'Fantastic mate' he replied with excitement that reminded me of a child receiving their Christmas presents.

'No problem, I'm only glad I could help.'

I watched nervously as he scrolled through its contents.

'I should go' I said, getting up from the hard-wooden chair I had been sitting on for the last hour.

'You sure?' he said whilst still looking down at the phone.

'Yes, give you time to look it over alone.'

He finally lifted his head to look at me, 'I'm really grateful for this Ashley, you'll never know how much.'

He came towards me and gave me a big hug.

'No need for all this mate' I said, pulling away, embarrassed at his sudden act of emotion.

'I just need to know who this bastard is and destroy his life like he's destroyed mine' he said, venom clear to hear in his voice.

Please god you do not I thought, for everyone's sake.

Chapter 52

'That was delicious love' I said, polishing off the last of the lasagne.

'Glad you enjoyed' Sadie replied, taking my empty plate into the kitchen.

'I could hear her stacking up the dishwasher as she shouted, 'Is Crème Brulee ok for dessert?'

'Fine thanks, but I should really be clearing up as you cooked.'

'It's ok. You can do both tomorrow night' she laughed.

I switched aimlessly through the TV channels where I was greeted by the usual stream of soaps and reality shows.

'Anything worth watching?' Sadie said, returning with two glasses of wine.

'The usual rubbish' I said as she settled down next to me.

'So, do you think Paul will find anything?' she said.

'Well, that all depends on whether Jenny left any traces for him to find I guess.'

'I still can't believe all this, I really can't.'

'And she definitely didn't say anything to you about an affair or the baby?'

'Don't you think I would have said by now if she had' she replied as if I had insulted her integrity by even asking.

We sat in silence for a few minutes as the TV showed a woman from Manchester trying to impress four others with her lavish, or so she thought, dinner party.

'I'm sorry' I said.

'How do you think I feel though? My best friend has just died carrying a child of another man, a man I knew nothing about. And now I find my husband is excusing me of covering the whole thing up.'

'I never meant that, and you know it.'

'I'm not sure which is worst, her not confiding in me or you and Paul not believing me that she hadn't.'

Jenny clearly had not told her about who the man really was, otherwise, I would not be sitting here with all my limbs still intact. I had wondered if she had spoken about an affair with a generic man, but those doubts had been extinguished after tonight.

'I believe you and I'm sure Paul does too' I said, gently gripping her hand.

She released my grip and held my head in both her hands as she tenderly kissed me on the lips.

'I love you' she said as her lips slowly left mine.

'And I love you too Mrs White.'

'Good' she said, taking control of the remote and changing the channel to one of her favourite cookery shows.

'I'm just worried he's becoming a bit obsessed' I said as I scrolled through Twitter on my phone.

'How do you mean?'

Looking up from the phone I said, 'Well I think if he doesn't find the answers he wants on that phone, then he will keep going until he finds them elsewhere. He's like a man possessed which isn't healthy for himself or the people around him, his priority should be the boys now.'

'Wouldn't you be the same though? He has just lost his wife and now must deal with the awful truth she was pregnant by another man; it is natural he would want answers.'

'I guess so, but I just don't see where those answers will come from if the phone draws a blank. I don't want him to spend the rest of his life chasing answers that will always prove elusive.'

'Well let us hope he already knows from that phone and he can move forward' she said, getting up and returning to the kitchen.

I watched her go with only one thought in my head.

Please god he does not, or you will hate me and your best friend forever.

Chapter 53

'And that concludes the first grand prix of the year' Miles Harrison announced to the sea of concentrated faces that had packed into the room. 'Now does anyone need any questions repeating?'

A flurry of hands shot up and Miles spent the next ten minutes going over this usual end of quiz ritual.

This was high end quizzing and the questions found here you were very unlikely to find at your bog-standard pub quiz. Yes, him and his fellow question setters did put in the odd popular culture question, but this was for the serious quizzer and therefore had to be tailored for this audience.

'Right, if you are all finished will you please hand in your papers to Archie as usual' he said, turning to the man seated next to him.

Archie Lane was his right-hand man and who he had co-founded the UK quiz association with nearly twenty years ago. Both men had been proud to see their baby steadily grow in that time as quizzing became an ever-popular pastime, with the explosion of shows such as The Chase, Eggheads and Millionaire making this once niche hobby accessible to millions of new fans.

When Millionaire had started on the TV the association had seen a mini boom in its membership, but that was nothing compared to what they were currently seeing. Membership had now gone past two thousand and they had currently suspended any new applications as they struggled to process the ones they already had.

Of course, it was great to see this renewed interest, though Miles suspected this would be short lived once *'The Duel'* was over. Important to make the most of it while it lasted then, and of course all this extra money in fees helped in that respect.

'Another busy one' Archie said, looking at the pile of papers in front of him.

'Think of all the extra income all this is generating though Archie, more beer money for both of us and a nice little top up for the retirement fund!'

Both men were keen members of CAMRA, or the Campaign for Real Ale to give its proper name, and they often travelled far and wide to taste the best beers around. With only one other person employed on a part-time basis this unexpected flood of income would also give them the chance to employ more help in running the association.

'No producers joining us today then?' Archie said as he began the process of marking the papers.

'Not today' Miles said, taking a pile of the papers himself to mark. 'We have gone past being useful unfortunately.'

'So how many they have got for the show?'

'Ten I've heard.'

'Only ten?' Archie said, shocked by his answer.

'Well, they only need thirty-two contestants, so taking more from us would make a mockery of the audition process I guess.'

'True' Archie said, returning to the laborious task before him.

'Anyway, I'm fairly sure we are looking at the winner already' Miles said as he looked at the crowd before him as they waited excitingly for the results to be revealed. 'Pretty sure indeed.'

Chapter 54

I re-read the email again just to make sure I was not dreaming.

Hi Ashley,

Thank you so much for taking the time to audition with us. We are delighted to let you know that you have been **SHORTLISTED** *for 'The Duel' – well done on getting through to the next stage.*

I stopped and read this first paragraph yet again.

No, I was not dreaming. That word **SHORTLISTED** confirmed that.

Had I finally cracked it. Had I finally realised my dream and got on a show.

I continued reading the rest of the email.

Unfortunately, even though you have been shortlisted for 'The Duel' we cannot guarantee you a place on the show. If you have not heard back from us by the 20th January, then unfortunately you have not been successful on getting on the show this time.

We hope to speak to you very soon.

Once again thank you and good luck!

'The Duel' team.

I double checked the date on my phone. Exactly three weeks today.

I struggled to contain my excitement as my breathing became more erratic and those all too familiar butterflies in the stomach returned.

Gripping the steering wheel tightly I shouted 'YES!! YES!! YES!!' at the top of my voice, just as a woman I recognised from accounts passed the car.

I smiled apologetically at her as she hurried quickly pass, and towards the exit of the staff overflow car park. There she turned left, but not before looking over her shoulder to look once again at the demented man she has just encountered. And then she was gone, and once again I had the car park to myself.

I realised this was just another step in this tortuous journey, but just could not stop shaking with the excitement of what I had just read.

Suddenly my phone started ringing on the passenger seat next to me. I looked at the display as I picked it up and my heart sank.

It was Paul.

It was just after 9.30 and I was already running late for work, but I knew I had to answer despite the consequences that may follow.

Composing myself I hit the answer button and said, 'Morning Paul.'

'Morning Ashley, I hope you don't mind me ringing so early?'

'No, it's fine mate, just in the work car park so got a few minutes. What can I do for you?'

'Well, I just thought I would let you know how I got on with Jenny's phone.'

My hand started to visibly shake as I gripped the phone more tightly to my ear.

'Of course, any joy?'

There was a couple of seconds of silence until the response came back which made me even more anxious.

'Afraid not' he replied, deflation in his voice.

Relief washed over me as I heard those words, though I knew I had to act with as much disappointment as him to avoid suspicion.

'I'm really sorry to hear that Paul, I know you really wanted to find the answers on that phone. Are you sure there was nothing?'

'Zilch mate, no suspicious texts, phone numbers or anything in her internet history.'

Good girl Jenny, I thought. At least you had the sense to cover your tracks.

'I don't know what to say, I really hoped you would find something' I lied.

'Well, it seemed that as well as being a deceitful and lying bitch, my wife was also exceptionally good at concealing those lies.'

I hated Paul talking like this about Jenny. If it were Sadie though, I would surely feel the same way so felt my protestations slightly hypocritical.

'I also wanted to ring to say thanks again. Really appreciated what you did.'

'Like I said, it was no problem.'

I looked at the dashboard clock and could see it was now approaching 09:45.

'I'm sorry but I really need to get into work now mate.'

'Of course, I'm sorry for keeping you so long.'

'Not a problem and I'm glad you let me know. Just sorry it wasn't the result you wanted.'

Promising to go down and see him later in the week, I ended the call and looked out of the windscreen at the ominous black clouds that were passing overhead.

The weather might have not looked promising, but my mood had certainly brightened up after these two bits of good news this morning.

Chapter 55

Patrick thanked the driver and stepped out onto the wet and greasy pavement.

Watching as the car disappeared back into the busy London traffic he stood for some moments before ringing the buzzer that was situated at the entrance of the building.

'Gem Productions, how can I help you?' a pleasant female voice said from the intercom.

'Patrick Reed, I have a meeting with Mike Phelps at 11.'

'Yes, please come up' she said, clicking the door open so he could enter.

As he sat in the now familiar reception area, his mind once again drifted back to the incident on holiday. His presence here alone today was one of the consequences of that day and probably the one he regretted the most. The lame excuse of having another appointment could not hide the truth that Lance did not want to be here today to support him.

His thoughts were broken by the inescapable voice of Mike as he came out of his office.

'Morning Patrick' he said, extending his hand out. 'Hope the journey in was ok?'

'Very pleasant, and thanks again for sending over a driver to pick me up.'

'All part of the service we offer here' he laughed in reply, 'Shall we take a seat in my office.'

Patrick followed him into the office and took up the seat opposite him.

After ringing through to reception for some refreshments, Mike enquired 'No Lance today then?'

'Prior appointment with another client I'm afraid.'

Watching the look of surprise on the face of Mike he added 'We aren't joined at the hip you know; Lance does have other clients to deal with.'

'Of course, I never implied he didn't.'

'We don't need him today, do we?'

'Not at all. Today is just a quick chat to discuss what will happen in the studio rehearsals next week, and to make sure you are comfortable with it all.'

They spent the next hour going through all the details of what would happen in the studio next week, this included another run through of the format, which Patrick still considered as dull and uninspiring.

'Comfortable with all that?' Mike finally said.

'I have done all this before, you know?' Patrick sarcastically replied.

'I really didn't mean to offend; I know you have done this plenty of times before.'

Patrick just sighed in reply, no apology or anything resembling one for his aggressive manner.

To lighten the mood Mike said, 'So how was the holiday, good relaxing break I hope?'

'It was fine thanks, weather lovely, food and drink great, and thankfully no one mentioned this bloody quiz show all the time I was there. Now is that it with the small talk, as I would really like to get going?'

'Yeah, I'll get the driver to pick you up' replied a startled Mike.

'Thanks, I'll wait outside for them if that's ok.'

'Sure, I'll see you next week at Elstree then.'

And following a quick handshake he was gone.

Patrick sat there in bewilderment at what had just occurred. Still in shock, he rung for their driver to pick up Patrick and then returned to his thoughts.

What on earth had just happened here, had Patrick in affect just stormed out of their meeting?

Mike had never seen Patrick in that light. Usually the personification of charm, the person he had just witnessed was angry and uptight. Had something occurred whilst on holiday for him to be suddenly like this?

His concern about hiring him suddenly hit a new level which made him very scared.

Very scared indeed.

Chapter 56

'Ashley'?'

'Sorry' I replied, shaking myself back into reality.

'Where are we with defect 1976' his boss asked again impatiently.

Yes, defect 1976' I said as I looked frantically at my laptop to find the status of the defect he had inquired about.

My manager Charlie Roe did not look pleased as I continued searching for the answer.

'Shall we come back to that whilst you keep looking?' he said.

'No, it's fine Charlie, I've just got the info now.'

I rattled off what he needed and then relaxed again as he returned his focus to other members of the team.

All I could think about was that email as I waited patiently for any news. Yes, it said to wait three weeks, but surely, they knew who they wanted on the show by now. Was the lack of news a sign that I had fallen at the final hurdle?

The drone of Charlie and the others in the room continued as the clock in the room ticked slowly towards one o' clock, and the sanctuary of lunchtime.

'So, anything else?' Charlie said, looking around the room.

The sea of faces shook their heads.

'Ok, we will leave it there then guys' he said, watching as everyone took this as the cue to leave, gratefully leaving their seats after two hours of this meeting.

As I picked up my laptop and began to follow them out of the exit Charlie called me back, 'Do you have a minute Ashley'?

'Sure' I said, resuming my seat.

'Is everything ok, you seem a bit distracted today?'

'I'm fine thanks Charlie.'

'Well, if you're sure there's nothing wrong, remember I'm here for a chat if you need it though.'

Of all the managers I had over the years Charlie was one of the best, yes, he wanted to get the job done and could be hard when required, but there was also a softer side to him which made him popular with his team.

That did not mean I could pour my heart out to him about my money worries or my ill-fated liaison with Jenny though.

Suddenly I felt my phone ringing in my trouser pocket.

'Thanks Charlie, is that all?' I said, desperately wanting to leave the room to take the call.

'Yes, that's all. Thanks Ashley.'

I quickly stood up and left the room, just as the vibration of the phone stopped.

'Bugger' I mouthed.

Returning to my desk I took the phone out of my pocket and saw that an answerphone message had been left.

Dialling my answerphone, I listened excitedly to the message:

Hi Ashley,

Its Nadia from 'The Duel', I hope you are well.

If possible, please could you give me a ring back on 020 467875 when you get this message.

Thanks

Could this really be happening, could I be on the show? Why else would she be ringing me if that was not the case.

I was tempted to ring back right away but knew it was awkward from my desk, and didn't fancy searching for a vacant meeting room, so decided to go for a walk back to my car and make the call from there.

As I walked back towards the car park all manner of thoughts were flying through my head.

What subjects should I revise? Should I buy new clothes for my appearance?

How excited would Sadie and the kids be when I told them ...

Minutes later, I sat in the car and gave myself a moment to gather my thoughts and control my breathing before making that all-important call.

With trembling fingers, I dialled the number Nadia had given me and waited anxiously as it rung.

'Hello, Nadia Smith speaking, how can I help you?' the welcoming voice echoed back at me.

'Hi Nadia, it's Ashley White, I was just returning your call' I said back in a rather rushed tone.

'Ah yes Ashley, many thanks for ringing back so promptly.'

'No worries.'

'First of all, we would like to say many thanks for auditioning. We were overwhelmed by the response for the show and you should be immensely proud of getting to the audition stage and subsequently being shortlisted.'

Come on Nadia, just get on with it please!

'Thanks' I replied.

'We were extremely impressed with your audition and it's been an extremely difficult decision for us to get down to the final contestant line-up ... '

Get on with it!

'And I'm sorry to say you haven't been selected on this occasion ...'

Those dreaded words that once again said - I was a FAILURE!

'But ...'

Wait, there was a 'But?'

'We are delighted to be able to offer you a place on top of our reserve list.'

'Reserve list?' I said rather perplexed.

'Yes, if one of the contestants drops out for any reason, we would offer a place to someone on the reserve list. We hope you will accept our offer to be part of that list.'

I was so tempted to decline, as who in their right mind would drop out of the chance to win two million pounds, but something in my head told me not to be that hasty.

The words 'Yes, I guess that will have to be ok' stumbled out of my mouth before I knew it.

'That's great. Now as I have said you are on the reserve list, which unfortunately means no guarantee you will be appearing on the show. Are you ok with that?'

What choice did I have, this was my only slim chance of still appearing on the show so had to take it.

'What are the chances of anyone pulling out though?' I said in a rather downbeat voice.

'I can't guarantee anything I'm afraid, saying that all the other shows I have worked on there are always contestants unable to appear for various reasons so don't lose hope at this stage.'

'I'm guessing those shows didn't have so much money at stake though?'

'Yes, that will make a difference I'm sure, but circumstances of life still happen, however big the prize money.'

I was not too convinced by her argument, but it was all I had at this precise moment.

'And I'm top of the list?'

Suddenly aware of what she had said earlier, Nadia tried to slightly backtrack on that claim. 'Yes, you are top of that list with others, please bear in mind we have to consider many things when selecting a player from the reserve list.'

'Which are?' I asked.

'Well, matching that person as well as we can with the contestant that has dropped out, so we consider age, where they live, etc.'

'So, you will be in touch if someone drops out?'

'Hopefully, like I said no guarantees, but I would say the chances are good.'

I could not tell if she was just trying to keep me interested, or whether she really did think I still stood a chance.

After once again expressing hope we would speak again she ended the call, and I was left to digest what had just happened.

All that hard work at the audition and I was still just a bloody backup, hoping that someone would miraculously drop out of the biggest quiz show of all time. I rated my chances as non-existent to be honest, despite what Nadia had said on the phone. Clearly, they needed a big pool of reserves just to make sure they had the right mix of people to step in, which made my task even harder. Another failure to go with my many others I thought.

I slammed my fists onto the steering wheel just as the same HR woman from a few days ago passed. The look of horror as she once again encountered the crazy man in the car made me chuckle. I tried to offer a hand in apology, but the poor woman had already hurried passed to the safe sanctuary of her own car.

Chapter 57

The red ball rattled the jaws of the pocket for what seemed like an eternity before stopping tantalising at the edge.

'Hard luck mate' Dan Hedges said, returning to the table and easily potting the overhanging ball.

I watched rather disinterestedly as he potted a further three reds and blacks, before missing a rather difficult yellow. Already needing numerous snookers, I conceded the frame and shook the hand of my opponent.

'Really not your day mate, don't suppose you fancy another?' Dan said.

'I think 3-0 is quite enough punishment for one night, thanks for the offer though' I said as I began to help him clear the balls away.

I had known Dan since the first day of Comprehensive school and we had remained firm friends ever since. A shared love of all sports, especially snooker, had seen us meet weekly at the Q Club for over 25 years. Dan had led a much more colourful life than me though and was already going through a messy third divorce which had forced him to reluctantly move back in with his parents.

As we returned to the bar, I noticed that Simon Tucker had started his shift.

'Good evening gents' the snooker manager greeted us in his usually cheery manner, 'So who was the victor tonight then?'

'It was close, but Dan just edged it 3-0' I said with more than a hint of sarcasm in my voice.

'Well, the offer of my free coaching still stands Ashley. I'm sure we can iron out all these weaknesses in your game soon enough' Simon said with such delight in his voice.

'Very funny' I said, 'Just get us two pints of lager please.'

Whilst he was pouring the drinks and Dan had nipped off to the toilet, I broached the subject that had been playing on my mind since I had arrived here.

'So, have you heard anything back from that quiz show?' I asked casually.

For once in this life Simon looked slightly embarrassed as he placed both glasses on the counter, 'Yes, I heard back yesterday actually, you?'

'Yes, I had call today, good news for you I take it?'

There was still a reluctance on his face to tell me, but I was determined he would say before my lips expelled my own news.

'Yes, you could say that.'

Just spit it out you bastard!

'And?' I said with a growing sense of knowing what was coming.

'I got on, going up to film it in a few weeks' he replied rather sheepishly, an uncharacteristic trait for him.

'That's great news mate, congratulations.'

'Cheers Ashley, what about you?'

Should I lie and tell him I had got on too? That would be a foolish thing to do though, especially as Simon would already have expected me to have blurted out my wonderful news.

'Mixed' I said, taking a sip of my drink.

'Mixed?' Simon said as he waited for me to elaborate.

'They liked me, they really did, but you know how these things work. They need the right mix of people for all sorts of different reasons.'

'Indeed' Simon replied as he waited for me to continue.

'Well, to cut a long story short, they're asked me to be a reserve.'

'I see, well I wish you all the best for that. I'm sure you will have good news soon' he said in a rather condescending manner.

Of course, you know as well as I do, that I have a cat and hell's chance of getting on.

'You too, hopefully the drinks will be on you when you get back?'

'I'm not sure about that' he laughed. 'I will definitely give it my best shot though.'

I had no doubt he would. Simon might be an arrogant bastard at times, but there was no doubting his ambition to succeed at whatever he did. Taking over the management of the club five years earlier, he had completely turned around its fortunes from near bankruptcy to the premier snooker venue it was today.

And then of course, there was his many TV appearances. I could not quite remember how many times he had been on the box, but it must surely have entered double digits by now. He had the looks and personality that TV obviously loved, he did not in my opinion have the brains though. Of course, he was not stupid, but for a show like this I expected intelligence to outweigh personality and looks, and I beat Simon hands down in that department surely.

So why was he on the show, and not me? It was a statement I could just not get my head around.

I took the drinks back to the table where Dan was seated and watched as Simon laughed and joked with some other customers. Watched as he charmed his audience, it was like he had them on an invisible rope that drew them in to his every word.

And it was at that moment that I knew what I needed to do.

Chapter 58

'Thirty-two players. The biggest cash prize ever seen on television anywhere in the world. The show where knowing your opponent's strengths and weaknesses is as important as your own. Watch TV history happen this Spring with me, Patrick Reed.'

Patrick kept looking at the camera until the floor manager gave him the thumbs up.

'Great stuff Patrick' he said as the lights went up in the studio, 'That's a wrap.'

And Patrick was certainly glad of that. For the past three days he had been stuck in this windowless space rehearsing for the show, with the culmination now being this talk to camera, which would form part of the trailer that would go out in the weeks prior to the show being aired.

After a sound technician had taken off his microphone, he moved off the stage where he was greeted by both Mike and Sarah.

'Great job Patrick' Mike said, giving him a pat on the back.

'Yes, I second that' Sarah said with that infectious smile of hers. 'A phenomenally successful, if tiring few days. Thanks for all your efforts Patrick.'

Patrick certainly had to agree with her on that. Yes, it had been exhausting, with lots of the hanging about that was synonymous with a show like this. Despite all that he had really loved being back in this environment though. Yes, he was glad these rehearsals had ended due to his sheer exhaustion of it all, though he had loved the sheer buzz of being back here in a studio. He really could not wait until he was back here in a few weeks with real contestants and an audience to spark off.

'Thanks guys, I have to admit I really enjoyed it, despite the long hours you forced me to put in.'

'Well, I have to say it has really paid off. The set looks great and I'm really pleased with how the gameplay has worked' Sarah said.

Patrick still was not sure the format was that interesting, but did it really matter. The viewers would flock to see who would win the phenomenal prize on offer, with the actual format of the show being of secondary importance in his opinion. He did like the tension the show conveyed though and was sure it would be even better once real contestants were sitting in those seats and not members of the production team.

Mike looked at his watch and said 'The driver should be here in about an hour to take you home Patrick. In the meantime, take the time to relax in your dressing room. Would you like some sandwiches brought in?'

'Yes, that would be great.'

'Lizzie, could you escort Patrick back to his dressing room please' Sarah shouted to the young runner who was close by.

Mike shot Sarah an anxious glance before saying 'It's ok Lizzie, I think Matt is free to take Patrick back.'

'No worries' Lizzie said, stepping away from the group as Matt was called to take Patrick back to his dressing room.

When they had left, Sarah turned to Mike, 'Well, what was all that about?'

'I just thought it best Matt took him back, I thought we both agreed that was for the best, don't you remember?'

'Sorry Mike, I completely forgot. I've felt less uncomfortable around him these past few days anyway.'

'That's fine, but I still think we should stick to what we agreed.'

'Of course, is there anything else I need to know?'

Mike had contemplated telling her what else he had found out about Patrick at the Christmas party, but in hindsight had decided not to. He could control the situation like this for the time being, and in truth he did not want to cause panic by spreading what he knew.

'Nothing' he lied, 'Just want to make sure everyone feels comfortable.'

Safely back in his dressing room Patrick took a bite of the tuna salad baguette that Matt had brought for him minutes earlier.

Thinking about it though, it was always a male member of the crew that had looked after him these past few days. Was that just a coincidence or was there more to it? The incident just now where Mike had stopped that female runner escorting him back here suggested it was not.

But why would that be?

Suddenly the realisation that Lance may have told them more than he should have hit him. Surely, he would not have though, as doing so would have risked his whole participation in the show. It would also have been a stupid thing to do giving what he had done to cover up the incident on holiday.

Something had changed with Mike though, so if Lance had not told him, had someone else?

Chapter 59

I had driven through this gateway many times before over the years without any trouble, tonight though my hands were trembling so much I made slow progress as I made sure I got through the narrow opening without incident.

Finally, the car was safely through and I slowly drove up the winding driveway as the headlights lit up the white façade of the house I knew so well.

I stopped the car at the double garages at the rear of the property and cut the engine. It was a pitch-black night with no visible moon, so I was glad of the glow permeating from the light that was situated on the side of the garage.

Stepping out of the car into the chilly night air I closed the door behind me. Still finding it a struggle to control my trembling hands I reached into my coat pocket to retrieve the cigarette packet there. Still shaking I managed to light one before leaning back on the garage wall to take in my surroundings.

The house that stared back at me had been my childhood home for over twenty years, and even though I had not lived here for such a long time it still felt like home. The four-bedroom house had been built in the 1930s and was surrounded by two acres of garden, which until her illness, had been meticulously attended to by my mother. Since she had been in the nursing home a gardener had been popping around regularly to tend to the lawn and general upkeep of the garden, but not in my opinion to the standard my mother had kept it.

Stubbing out the cigarette I fished out a bunch of keys from my pocket, standing under the light I selected the one I required and headed towards the back door.

Opening it I entered the narrow corridor that connected the original house with the extension that my parents had built around fifteen years earlier. I flicked on the light and the corridor was suddenly bathed in a warm light. The house felt musty as it often did on my visits here now, the obvious effect of not being lived in. To my left was the room we always called the back room or more affectionately *'Dad's Room.'* An integral part of the extension that he had built after finishing work as a manager for a local health board due to ill health, the room had in affect secluded him from my mother in those final years as he unfortunately smoked himself to an early grave. They had loved each other deeply though and I knew it had been a deep regret to her that they had lived so separately before his death, the only solace of her illness now was that she had largely forgotten that period of their life together.

Turning right I entered the utility room where the icy cold of the house really hit me. I was tempted to turn on the heating, deciding against it in the end as I hoped my time here tonight would be short-lived.

I headed towards the small white door that was to the right of the room and slowly turned the key that hung from its lock. Opening the door, I looked down into the pitch black below me, before quickly flicking on the light switch. The room below was lit up in a dull glow as was the stone steps that led to it. Slowly I made my way down, holding carefully onto the rail as I always did when I ventured down here. It always felt eerie descending these steps and tonight was no different as my feet reached the last step and hit the cold concrete floor of the cellar.

Originally my father had wanted to make this into a wine cellar, but with that dream never realised it had just become a place to store all the unwanted junk we had. Boxes of old toys, bikes and other household rubbish littered the room, the task of clearing this and the rest of the house something me and my brother dreaded as its inevitable sale drew closer.

'Shit' I exclaimed as what looked like a mouse or rat scurried across my path and into the dark gloom of the boxes. My nerves were frazzled as it was, and the appearance of this furry monster with its long and skinny tail was the last thing I wanted to see. I tried in vain to find the little bugger, finally giving up and making a mental note to buy some poison for the next time I came down here.

Leaving the light on I returned upstairs, glad to be away from the cloying dampness of the cellar. Leaving the door wide open I checked the time on my watch, 12.15am stared back at me as the start of a new day began. I really did need to get a move on, or Sadie would really start to worry back home.

Reaching the back door, I picked up the small ceramic bowl that lay by the side of it and tears began to form in my eyes. The name 'Sam' emblazoned on its front, it symbolised how much had changed within this home over the last couple of months. The cat that my Mum adored had sadly been rehomed since she had gone into the nursing home, with this bowl being the last sad reminder of his existence here. I knew I was stalling now. I had come here tonight for a reason, and that reason was not to get sentimental about a cat bowl.

Placing the bowl back down I opened the back door and entered the chilly night once again. Digging my car keys out my coat pocket I headed towards the boot with trepidation, tempted to abandon this reckless act and just drive off back from where I came. I knew that was not an option now though.

With trembling hands, I hit the boot release button and very slowly began to lift it. Fully open, it took me a few seconds to finally look at the sight that confronted me in there.

That of the still figure that lay inside.

Chapter 60

For god's sake, what had I done I thought, as I just kept staring down at the prone figure before me?

The figure of Simon Tucker, manager of the Q club.

I lightly prodded him and could thankfully see he was still breathing, my fear of him dying whilst incarcerated in that small space not realised.

Gently I lifted his legs over the rim and planted his feet on the tarmac of the drive, then taking my hand around this waist I managed to carefully manoeuvre his whole body out of the boot so eventually I was holding up his whole frame next to me.

I managed to drag his body along to the open back door, thankful that whilst Simon was quite tall, he was also of slim build which made moving him along beside me much easier. Reaching the inside, and with the sweat now dripping from my forehead, I placed him in one of the patio chairs in the corridor to gather my thoughts.

The sedative I gave him should last a good ten hours I hoped, which would mean him regaining conscious around 8 this very morning. And what then, I thought?

Looking at the sleeping form of Simon Tucker my thoughts returned to the events of a couple of hours earlier. Events that shaped the predicament I was in now.

'Sorry mate' Dan Hedges said as the blue ball fluked its way into the top right pocket.

'No worries' I said as I held my hand up. Usually, I would be hopping mad at the amount of flukes Dan had sunk, but not tonight. This evening I had much more important things to think about.

Minutes later I was at the bar getting the drinks in whilst Dan occupied one of the few free tables in the packed club.

'Busy one tonight then?' I said as Simon pulled the pints.

'Always is when the Champions League is on mate.'

Taking the drinks, I said 'Actually Simon, I was wondering if I could have a chat later?'

'Sure, nothing serious I hope?'

'No, nothing serious. Just a bit of advice really about what I should do about the show.'

'Of course, not sure how much help I can be, but happy to offer some advice. Might have to chat whilst I clear away after closing time though, hope that's ok?'

'That's fine, thanks Simon' I said, 'Will even help you clear up as a thank you.'

'Will definitely hold you to that' Simon laughed, as he moved away to serve another customer.

Two hours later, and with the last of his customers on their way out, Simon finally locked the doors for the night.

'So how can I help?' he said as we both began clearing the tables.

'Well, like I said earlier, it's more advice I'm after really. It has been a week now since I had that call saying I was on the reserve list. I know you are going on next week so just wondered if I should give up any hope of getting on the show?'

Simon turned to face me, 'I'm no expert on this, but my advice would be to never give up hope until all the filming is done and dusted. Someone might pull out of the show at the last minute, you never know.'

'Yes, your right of course, must keep positive and hopefully the impossible might happen.'

'That's the spirit mate.'

'Thanks for the advice, I know I must sound like a spoilt kid who hasn't got what he's wanted.'

'Don't be daft, I know how important this is to you. I would feel the same if I hadn't got ...' Simon said, stopping in mid-sentence.

'It's ok, I'm pleased you have got on mate' I lied.

'Cheers, I'm not sure how far I will get but will give it my best shot' Simon said as he loaded the last of the dirty glasses into the dishwasher.

'Can I buy you a drink?' I said as Simon turned it on. 'This chat has really helped me stay positive and I would like to say thanks in some way.'

'No need for that mate, I had better get home anyway. It's been a long day.'

'Come on, one drink and we can have one quick frame so you can show me some of that snooker coaching you have been promising.'

Simon thought about if for a few seconds before saying 'Ok, it will have to be quick though. Another pint for you?'

'Better not, had a couple already and I'm driving. Coke will be fine.'

Whilst Simon was pouring the drinks, I set up the balls, pleased that at least the first part of my plan for tonight was working.

'There you go' Simon said, returning with the drinks and setting them down on the table. 'Let us see how your game is shaping up then.'

Halfway through the frame and I was 20 points down, with criticism of my posture and bridging from Simon ringing in my head.

'Just nipping off for a quick piss' Simon said after playing an excellent safety shot which kept the white ball tight to the top cushion. 'No re-arranging the balls whilst I'm gone' he laughed.

Whilst I had planned tonight meticulously, I still had to rely on many things to fall into place if it was to be successful. I could not know for certain that Simon would leave his drink unattended so I could do what I did next, fortunately for me, he did though.

I took the small clear plastic bag out of my pocket and quickly deposited its contents into the Simon's glass. I had crushed what I hoped was enough sedative to knock him out till the morning, then

I could decide what to do next. I watched as the powder interspersed with the beer in the glass just as Simon returned.

'So, let's finish this job off then' he said, taking a swig of his drink.

'Smug bastard' I thought as I returned to the table to take my shot, you won't be so cocky later though, I can assure you of that.

'I was meaning to ask if you were still having issues with your CCTV?' I said as I totally misjudged my shot and left an easy red on. 'If you are, then I have a mate with a security systems business that could take a look.'

'Yes, it's still bloody down. I'm still waiting for someone to look at it, so if your friend can get here any quicker, then that would be great.'

Another piece of the jigsaw that was falling nicely into place.

'No worries, I'll let them know you need someone asap.'

Simon returned to the table and easily potted the red, followed by a scoring streak which took the frame out of my reach.

As the final yellow disappeared into the pocket, he suddenly leant against the table to support himself.

'Are you ok?' I asked from my seat.

'Just suddenly feel very giddy' he slurred, 'So very giddy ...'

I raced over to him and just got there in time to stop him slumping to the floor.

'Let us get you sitting down' I said, leading him back to his seat.

'Sorry' he mumbled, 'I just don't know what's come over me, I've only had the one drink tonight.'

'Don't worry, you just sit there and take it easy and I'll get you a glass of water.'

Returning from the bar with it, I found that Simon had now passed into unconsciousness.

'Simon?' I said.

No response.

'Simon' I said again with more urgency.

Still no response.

I had never expected the sedative to work so fast, had I inadvertently killed him?

I poked him and thankfully the rise and fall of his chest told me he was still alive.

Everything had gone like clockwork so far, but I knew the next part was going to be the most tricky and dangerous. Fail here and all the good work that had gone before would be for nothing.

I picked up the glasses we were using and left Simon where he was as I tipped the contents of both down the sink that was behind the bar. Keeping both the glasses in my hand, I raced through into the back area of the club and its dark recesses. Reaching into my pocket I took out the gloves I had brought with me and disabled the alarm located by the back door, taking a few seconds to reflect on the enormity of what I was doing here tonight. As desperate as I was currently, was this course of action really the answer?

Pushing those thoughts out of my head I slowly opened the door and stepped out into the cloudless night.

Knowing what I was going to do tonight, I deliberately parked at the rear of the club, which I hoped would offer me the privacy I needed as I carried out the most difficult part of the night.

Only two cars now occupied the car park, my old and battered Ford Focus and Simon's flashy BMW. With the only light hitting the car park coming from the security light attached to the rear of the building, the relevant darkness and lack of CCTV was definitely a big advantage as I prepared for the next step.

I walked to my car and opened the back door, where I flung the two glasses I still held. With one laced with sedatives and the other with my fingerprints, I could not leave them in the club with the risk that would open up.

Locking the car back up I walked to the entrance of the car park and could thankfully see no sign of life on the street outside, relieved that it was a Monday evening, and the city centre was quiet. Confident that the coast was clear, I made my way back into the club, where the sleeping figure of Simon awaited me.

Time was of the essence now and I really did not want to be here any longer than I needed. I had read in one of the many true crime books I loved that the longer a criminal was at the scene of their crime, the more chance of mistakes being made, and evidence left behind. I could do neither tonight.

Carefully I lifted Simon from the seat and dragged his tall and slender frame towards the back door. Carefully sitting him by the side I opened the door for one final check to make sure the coast was clear, which again it thankfully was.

It was a chilly night and I whilst I was wrapped up well, I suddenly realised that Simon was only wearing a thin cotton shirt. Heading to the cloakroom I picked up his jacket from the peg and quickly put it on him just as I felt the first beginnings of sweat drip from my forehead. Rummaging through his pockets, I found his wallet, mobile phone, and a set of keys. Leaving the keys and wallet in his pocket I removed his mobile and switched it off, placing it again in his pocket when I was certain it had been powered down.

When the police attempted to track down the phone, which they undoubtedly would, they would find its last tracked position would be in this club.

No mistakes. There really must not be any mistakes tonight.

Before talking him out towards the car there was one final thing I needed to do before I finally left the club.

Moving back to the bar area I stuffed as many notes as I could from the till into my coat pockets. I needed to make this look like a robbery, the absence of money from the till and the disappearance of Simon's personal possessions would hopefully show this to be the case.

Satisfied I had done everything I needed, I carefully lifted him from the floor and slammed the back door behind me. I then walked him or should say dragged him towards the waiting car.

I had originally thought of sitting him next to me in the passenger seat but had now dismissed that idea, fearing an over enthusiastic copper might stop me and ask awkward questions about my unconscious passenger. No, Simon had to be out of sight as I drove him to my destination.

Opening the boot, I managed to somehow lay him into the enclosed space by pulling his legs up towards his chin before gently letting it close shut. I was only glad he was not a heavy man as I slammed the boot shut, the thought of moving an overweight Simon would have filled me with dread.

The sweat was now dripping off me despite the cold night and I mopped my brow as I sat in the car. Still not quite believing what I had done here tonight, I started the engine and left the car park with my precious cargo tucked safely away in the boot behind me.

I physically shook as I remembered those events, all the time looking at what I considered my precious cargo as he continued his medicated slumber in the chair.

It was time to stop pondering what I had done though, it had happened now, and I just had to get on with the next phase. The repercussions of it all had to be debated later, now was not the time for all that.

I once again lifted him and dragged him towards the open cellar door where the dimly lit light shone the pathway down to the bottom.

Taking the journey down these steps with an unconscious body was the part I had most dreaded about tonight. Images of me losing my balance and both of us tumbling to the bottom uppermost in my thoughts. The reality though was much different, as I, much to my surprise, managed to walk him down with relevant ease to the cavernous space.

Lying him against one of the boxes down there, I raced back upstairs to retrieve more items from the car that I needed to finish my night's work.

Returning to the cellar I laid one of the blankets I had got on the floor and moved him to lie on it, covering his body with the second blanket I had brought. I would leave the heating on low before I left but it would still be bloody chilly down here and I certainly did not want to find him dead of hypothermia in the morning.

Unsure whether to still use them, I looked at the heavy-duty handcuffs in my hands that I have bought on-line a few days ago. Even though the cellar door would be locked when I left, I was still paranoid that he would somehow manage to break his way out. Impossible as it seemed I could leave nothing to chance, so decided I would have to use them to ensure my prisoner did not escape. Pulling him closer to the water pipe that ran across the wall, I attached one part of the handcuff to his right hand and the other part to the pipe. Satisfied that both ends were secure I dropped the key into my pocket and returned to the top of the stairs.

Taking one final look at the still body below me, I switched off the light and slammed the door shut behind me.

It was just after one when I finally arrived home and dropped myself onto the living room couch. As the enormity of what I had done suddenly hit me, it felt like someone else had done all those things tonight and the real me was only a curious bystander.

How could someone as mild mannered as me sedate and then imprison a man?

'Because you are desperate, that is why' *the voice inside my head answered.*

The justification of what I had done was interrupted by footsteps coming down the stairs and the living room door being opened by a sleepy Sadie.

'Your back late' she said, 'Everything ok?'

'Sorry love I didn't mean to wake you, Dan wanted to go for a couple more drinks after snooker and then I had to drop him home' I said with as much conviction as I could muster in the circumstances.

'That is fine, how is he anyway?'

'You know what Dan's like, trying to put on a brave face but really struggling behind the façade.'

'Finding life back home tough then?' Sadie said, stifling a yawn.

'I imagine we would all find it tough to move back in with our parents, and to top it all off Kelly is being difficult about the divorce settlement.'

'I'm sure he will bounce back, helps he as a friend like you to talk to.'

Who could I talk to though?

'Anyway, I'm back off to bed. Don't be too late babe, work in the morning remember' she said, blowing me a kiss goodnight.

'I won't' be' I said as I replicated her show of affection.

As I heard her retreat upstairs, I made my way into the kitchen where I found Riley sleeping soundly in his basket. Careful not to wake him and cause the expected pandemonium that would come with it, I opened the cupboard and took out the bottle of whiskey sitting there, pouring myself a large glass from it.

Taking the amber liquid down in one go I poured myself another large measure.

Tomorrow I needed to plan the next steps, at this moment though, I needed to forget the awful things I had done tonight.

Chapter 61

The woman wiped the sweat from her forehead as the timer on the exercise bike continued its countdown to zero. Already cycling for twenty-five minutes, she still had another five to go before she could finally relax.

Whilst most of her life before the attack had now disappeared, her regular visits to the gym had not. This was the one place where she could forget about that night and just be her old self, albeit for a short period of time. Her regular gym classes had ceased though as the least interaction she had whilst here the better. The timer finally hit zero and she stopped pedalling. Literally dripping with sweat she used the towel that hung around her neck to wipe her face as the relief of finishing washed over her.

It had just gone past seven in the morning and only a handful of people were in the gym this early on a Sunday morning, and that was just the way she liked it. She did not want to make small talk with others or be hassled by a personal trainer, and this budget gym she had found close to her flat was perfect for that.

She got off the bike and made her way back to the changing room, feeling refreshed after her hour here. Usually, her thrice weekly trips here were made after work, an attempt to unwind after the tedium of shelf stacking and trying to be polite to obnoxious customers on the till. Today though, she had made the effort to get up early and come here on her weekend off.

Laying off the drink last night helped in that regard. It had been tough, but she had to admit she felt so much better for it. A clear head for the first time in months felt like some sort of liberation from the drunken pit of self-pity she had dug herself into since that awful night.

And she really did need a clear head if she were to get her revenge.

Chapter 62

He tried to turn over, his movement suddenly stopped by something attached to his right hand.

'What the fuck!' Simon Tucker shouted as he looked at the restraint that was holding him back.

He tried desperately to break the handcuff free from the pipe that it was attached to, but it was a fruitless task, the pipe looked secure and the handcuffs heavy duty in their design.

He pulled off the thin blanket that covered him and tried to take in his surroundings despite the eerie gloom of the room.

Boxes and crates dominated the space, with a flight of stone steps leading up towards a door where a thin layer of light was trying its best to penetrate the gloom. So, he was in a cellar of some kind he guessed. The question was why was he here, and more importantly who had brought and left him here?

'HELP!!' he shouted with as much strength as his tired body would allow.

'HELP!! HELP!! HELP!!'

He shouted continuously for a few minutes, his throat becoming more and more hoarse in the process. He eventually stopped as he came to the grim conclusion that no one was coming to his rescue.

His throat parched and head feeling like he had gone twelve rounds with Mike Tyson, he desperately tried to search his frazzled mind to unpiece the mystery of how he got here.

He could remember working last night, club was busy due to the football. He could remember locking up and sending Harry home early, telling him it was ok, and he would clear up with the help of
...

Help of who?

Come on brain, THINK!

What happened after he locked up.

He remembered clearing the tables, loading the dishwasher, and then playing a frame of snooker.

But with whom?

Why could he not remember, why was his brain blocking this memory.

His head began to hurt even more as he tried to remember this mystery figure, the person who helped him clear up and then played a frame of snooker with him. He tried going further back in the night, in the hope that it would trigger a reaction.

Live football always brought the crowds in, the club packed with a mixture of regulars and 'off the street' punters enjoying the atmosphere of watching the match on the big screen whilst having a few pints and playing a few frames. Yes, it had been busy, but he liked it that way, and of course it all helped with his profits.

And then the clarity of last night hit him like a bolt of lightning. The two of them clearing up and then the pep talk that calmed his guest. Being sat down as drowsiness took of hold of him and finally falling into the oblivion of unconsciousness.

The image of the last person he saw before that now firmly stuck in his memory.

The face of Ashley White!

Chapter 63

'Ashley!! Ashley!!' was all I could hear as I was shaken out of my slumber.

'What, what time is it?' I managed to garble.

'Time you should be getting ready for work' Sadie chastised.

I slowly rose from my lying position on the couch and looked at her from hazy eyes as she continued to shout at me.

'It's seven o' clock, why the hell didn't you follow me up to bed last night?'

'I fully intended to, just felt like a nightcap before I did that's all.'

'I can see that' she said as she held up the bottle of whisky on the table, now only a quarter full. 'Do you think it was sensible drinking all this, especially when you have work to go to the next day?'

'I didn't realise I had drunk that much, I only meant to have the one' I replied, shocked at how much I had drunk and now paying the price with a throbbing headache.

'Well, if that were just the one then I would say you poured the measure into a jug' she said with a smirk.

At least her foul mood at me was mellowing, I thought.

'Well, you better get a few black coffees down you before you even think of going to work' she said as she went back upstairs to get ready for work.

I gingerly got up and went into the kitchen to take her up on her advice. As I waited for the kettle to boil my mind drifted back to last night.

The disbelief of what I had done still had not sunk in. Yes, it is one thing to think of doing something bad, but another to actually carry it out. Last night I put into reality that shocking thought inside my head, with the consequences still unknown to me and my prisoner.

The kettle boiled and I poured myself that strong black coffee which I took with two paracetamols. I really hoped they would quickly work their magic as I needed a clear mind today, a day I needed to sort out the mess I had created.

'Head a bit better now?' Sadie said as she came into the kitchen to interrupt my thoughts.

'A little' I said rather sheepishly.

'Well. I would leave it a while before you drive to work, last thing we want is for you to lose your licence.'

'I won't' I promised, although it was always my intention to phone in sick today anyway.

'Good' she said, giving me a quick kiss. 'I've woken the kids, so please can you make them some breakfast and make sure they leave for school on time?'

'Of course.'

'Great, I'll see you tonight then' she said, before rushing off out through the front door.

And left me to my own devices to plan the next stage.

Now, over three hours later I was once again driving carefully through the narrow gateway towards the big white house.

Parking around the back once again, I could now in daylight take in the vast grounds that surrounded the house. With the nearest neighbour around half a mile away the property was self-contained and isolated, which was the primary reason I had chosen it. It also helped that my brother Marcus was in Australia for a month visiting his in-laws, meaning only I would have access to the house for all that time.

Picking up the carrier bag on the seat next to me, containing sandwiches and bottles of water I had bought on the way here, I headed towards the back door.

My head was still throbbing, and I now regretted the copious amount of whisky I had consumed last night. Yes, it had made me forget my actions for a few hours but now I really needed a clear head.

As I opened the door, I was struck at how quiet it was inside the house, no shouting or screaming which slightly unnerved me.

What if he had not woken up? Had I given him too much sedative and now he was lying down there dead?

I put that thought out of my mind, deciding that the lack of activity from downstairs must be down to the fact that Simon had just got tired of screaming for help. It was just past eleven, and I presumed he had now been awake for hours.

I walked into '*my Dad's*' room which was bathed in gloom despite it being mid-morning. Switching on the light made the room a bit lighter, though the apple tree that dominated the outside window made it impossible for the room to be fully light and airy. The room had been stuck in time ever since my Dad had died with the same tobacco-stained décor scattered throughout, the only thing missing being my Dad sitting in his chair smoking one cigarette after another.

Tears began to form in my eyes as I remembered those days. A man who should have enjoyed his retirement with Mum had instead smoked himself to death in this room. A sad room in so many ways, and one I always tried to avoid when I came here now.

Today I needed to come in here though, today I needed something from here that would help me deal with the problem in the cellar.

I selected the key I needed from the many on my keyring and opened the filing cabinet that was in the corner of the room. Sliding the top drawer open I took out the white box located in there. I had not opened this box for many years and my hands trembled slightly as I did so now.

Slowly lifting off the top of the box revealed the black revolver that lay underneath, an item that still gave me goose bumps as I wondered at its beauty and the history behind it.

The Enfield No 2 was the standard British/Commonwealth sidearm of the second world war, and this one had belonged to my

Grandfather. A member of the Royal Tank Regiment who had seen active service in North Africa, the gun had passed down to my Dad when he died and largely been forgotten in this box for most of that time. How my Grandfather had remained in possession of it had never really been discussed, but at this moment how grateful was I that he had.

I lifted the gun from the box and held it in my hands, something I had not done since my teens. It felt good to hold and was in remarkably good condition considering its age. Using my left hand to hold it steady I pulled the trigger, of course it had no bullets in it and I was not even sure it would still work if it had. I needed to show my prisoner I could handle it though; however useless it was now as a weapon. I needed him to believe I would use it if required, I needed him to be scared of me.

I stood there for a few minutes to compose myself and then made my way towards the cellar door, the gun now lowered against my right side.

Deep breaths Ashley, the hard work was done last night. This is easy compared to that surely.

I did not think that was strictly true though, yes getting Simon here was tough but at least he was unconscious. Now I had to deal with a fully conscious Simon to try and explain my actions of last night.

Well, I hoped he was conscious.

I had considered wearing some sort of mask before I went down the cellar again this morning, but on my way here decided against it. My guess was he would have already pieced together what had happened, and with that, guessed I was the perpetrator.

I turned the key in the lock and slowly opened the door, the darkness of the cellar once again making it impossible for me to see the bottom.

'Who's there?' I heard a voice from below shout. 'Is that you Ashley?'

As I suspected he knew it was me, I had hoped the sedative may have confused him, but alas that was not to be.

I switched on the light and the cellar illuminated the figure of my prisoner below.

'What the fuck are you playing at?' Simon shouted as I shut the cellar door and made my way carefully down the stone steps.

'Just answer me god damnit' he shouted even louder as I finally made my way down to the bottom.

His face turned deathly white as he saw the gun in my hand.

'What the fuck is that?' he said as he made a frantic attempt to free his handcuffed hand from the pipe it was attached to.

'I would not waste your energy trying that if I were you.'

Simon stopped his struggles, continuing his terrified stare on the weapon by my side.

'This is just an insurance policy to make sure you don't do anything silly' I said, indicating the gun by my side. 'If you do as I say it will never be used, if you don't though, I won't hesitate to use it.'

'Why? Why the hell have you done this?'

'Isn't it obvious' I said as I moved further into the room.

'Not to me it isn't.'

'And I thought you clever' I laughed.

'Just fucking tell me!' he screamed back.

'The quiz show' I said matter-of-factly, 'It's all about the quiz show.'

'Quiz show?' he said incredulously, 'What are you talking about?'

God he really was stupid I thought.

'You were guaranteed to be on the show, and I wasn't. I had to take action to try and rectify that.'

'You've imprisoned me here to get on a bloody quiz show, are you fucking mad or what!'

'Maybe' I replied, 'I need to get on that show though and this was my only option.'

I could see by his reaction that he was stunned by the revelation of why I brought him here, the risks I had taken for such a crazy reason.

'You think I'm deluded, don't you?' I said, breaking the silence that had suddenly formed.

'Yes, I do' he spat out with ferocious venom, 'A bloody madman who has made the biggest mistake of his life. Now get me out of these bloody handcuffs and don't make this situation even worse.'

'I can't do that; you know I can't.'

'You have to, it's the only thing that makes sense now' he pleaded.

'And you are just going to forget about this minor indiscretion on my part, are you?'

His silence told me he would not. If I let him go now, I would be facing the full force of the law and a likely prison sentence. It was something I could not allow to happen.

'Just let me go' he shouted.

I shook my head to indicate the answer was still no.

'You can't be sure they will give you my place anyway, this is a big risk to take for a reward that may never materialise.'

Whilst agonising over whether I should carry all this out, I had endlessly thought about that, deciding in the end it was a risk worth taking.

'I'll take my chances' I said.

Simon shook his head as if mocking my reasoning.

'I need a piss' he suddenly said.

'You will have to use a bucket I'm afraid. I'll pop upstairs to get one.'

'Whatever' Simon grunted back.

I walked back up the stairs to fetch the bucket from the garage, locking the door behind me and once again leaving Simon in solitude.

Simon knew he had to get out of here now, there was no chance that Ashely was going to set him free and the longer he was down here, the greater the chance he was going to die down here.

It was clear to him that he was dealing with an extremely sick man, who in the end would probably have no other choice than to kill him, however much he denied that was his intention.

Yes, when Ashley returned, he would have to overpower him somehow and make a run for it.

Returning with the bucket I set it down next to him before moving back towards the stairs.

'Hard to take a piss with one hand handcuffed' Simon said.

'Try.' I said in reply.

'Come on, I can't even stand up with this on me. What am I going to do with that thing pointing at me anyway?' he said, looking towards the gun that I still held firmly to my side.

I thought about his request for a few minutes before throwing the key for the handcuffs towards him.

'Open it and then move slowly to the back with the bucket.'

'Thanks' he said as he eagerly released the handcuff, the relief of finally being free evident on his face.

'Just go to the back and quickly do what you need too' I ordered as I pointed the gun on him.

Simon did as he was told and slowly moved towards the back wall with the bucket in his hand.

'So why are you so desperate to get on this show?' he said, sighing with near ecstasy as the warm liquid hit the bucket.

'Let us just say I have financial challenges at this time.'

'Still a big ask though, getting on the show and then winning it.'

'Well, we all need to take risks from time to time, don't we'?

'You that skint then? That desperate to do all this?'

'Enough questions' I snapped back. 'Just hurry up, will you.'

'I'm done' Simon said, zipping back up his trousers.

'Good, now leave the bucket where it is and slowly move forward towards the pipe. Handcuff yourself back up when you get there and then throw me the key.'

Now was the chance he had, with the handcuffs off him there was the opportunity to overpower Ashley and make a run for it. There was one obvious problem though, and that was the gun that was pointing at him. He had been looking at it very closely as Ashley kept it trained on him and from these observations it looked incredibly old, antique even. Of course, none of that meant it was not in perfect working order, it just looked so old that they may be a chance it was not. Whether it was working or not did not really matter though. This was his chance to overpower him and he had to take it. Ashley was clearly not the fittest guy in the world, and Simon was hoping that his extra fitness and stamina could provide the element of surprise that was needed.

I watched as he walked slowly towards me, the gun clasped firmly in my hands as my finger hovered over the trigger.

And then without warning he picked up speed and charged directly at me. Caught unawares I dropped the gun to the ground as he pinned me on the cellar steps.

'You bastard' he shouted as his face practically touched mine. 'You really thought this crazy plan of yours was going to succeed.'

The suddenness and speed of the attack had shocked me, the speed and agility of Simon clearly being advantageous as he took me down. That advantage was now clearly a weakness though as I managed to regain my senses and push his slim frame off me.

Simon staggered backwards as I lifted myself from the stairs and we both faced each other, neither quite sure what to do next.

'Not so brave now without your gun, are you?' he chided.

I tried to see if the gun were nearby but could see no trace of it. It had probably gone behind one of the many crates and boxes down here, and I certainly did not have the time to seek it out now.

He then ran at me again with that immense speed he had shown minutes earlier. The difference being I was now fully ready for the new assault, with that element of surprise of moments ago now lost.

Before he had the chance to pin me down again, I extended my right arm and punched him forcibly in the face, the sickening sound of his nose breaking fully audible in this small space.

He staggered backwards a few steps, stunned by the force of the blow that hit him as blood spurted from his ravaged nose. Fully expecting him to lunge at me again I put up both fists to defend myself, this time there was no further attack though.

Instead, I watched as he fell backwards onto the stone floor below, the crack as his head hit the floor feeling so powerful that I fully expected to see a crack in the stone also.

What I did see was a large pool of blood form around his head as his body lay perfectly still.

Chapter 64

I froze.

Froze like a statue, my body unable to move as I watched the red river of blood continue to pour out of Simon's head.

Move you idiot, he needs your help. You must help him.

Shaking myself back onto reality I raced over to the lifeless body.

'Simon' I shouted as I knelt beside him, 'Can you hear me?'

There was no response.

'Simon' I shouted again.

Still no response.

The amount of blood pouring out of the wound seemed to have decreased slightly, the amount that had already formed on the floor suggested his injury was extremely serious though.

I fetched the blanket that was nearby and moved it under his head, some of the blood being soaked up by it.

I picked up his hand, which already felt cold to me, and placed my index finger on his wrist.

I could feel nothing, no beats coming from his wrist. NOTHING!

I looked at his chest for the reassurance of its rise and fall, there were none.

My heart was beating so fast it felt like it was going to explode out of my chest like a runaway train. Sweat was dripping off me and my whole body was shaking, as panic took hold of me at the scene I was witnessing.

SHIT, SHIT, SHIT!!

This was not meant to happen.

I had taken some basic CPR training in work about ten years and was now trying to desperately remember the technique I was taught.

'Place the heel of your hand on the breastbone at the centre of the person's chest' the rather overweight St John's Ambulance volunteer said to the assembled room, 'Then place your other hand on top of the first hand and interlock your fingers.'

I did exactly that on Simon's chest.

'Position yourself with your shoulders above your hands' he continued.

I did that.

'Using your body weight, press straight down by 5 to 6cm on their chest.'

I did this very carefully, aware that my full body weight could do even more damage to Simon.

'Keeping your hands on their chest, release the compression and allow the chest to return to its original position.'

I once again followed the instruction I remembered from all those years ago.

'Repeat these compressions at a rate of 100 to 120 times a minute until an ambulance arrives or you become exhausted' he finished with.

I did exactly that, working as hard as I could for five minutes until I did indeed become exhausted. The other option of finishing when an ambulance arrived, was of course, not an option.

Gasping for breath after my exertions, I sat forlorn next to the lifeless body of Simon.

Despite my best efforts I could not save him, could not undo the damage I had done to him.

And then I cried, cried in a way I never had before. Tears streaming to show my remorse at what I had done, begging for forgiveness at what I had done. Actions that had culminated with me now sitting here next to the dead body of Simon Tucker.

Chapter 65

'And you're sure you said nothing to Mike?' Patrick said.

'No' replied an exasperated Lance.

It was just after midday and Patrick was in the Covent Garden office of the Lance Poole Talent Agency.

'Well, someone has, he was acting so strangely during the rehearsals that I'm sure he knows something.'

'What do you mean by acting strangely? He seemed perfectly fine when I was there.'

'Ah, yes. You mean the few hours you could be bothered to turn up on that first day.'

Lance laughed back.

'Something funny?' Patrick snarled back.

'Yeah, something is funny now you say it. I do find it really laughable that you criticise me for not being constantly at your side after all that business in Tenerife.'

'I apologised for that' he said sheepishly, 'What more do you want?'

'Nothing, I want nothing but for this show to be done and dusted so we can end our association together.'

Patrick made no attempt to reply, instead he just looked forlornly out of the window.

'How has been Mike acting strangely anyway?'

Patrick continued to stare out of the window.

'Patrick?'

'Sorry' he said as he turned back to face him.

'I said how has Mike been acting strangely?'

Patrick hesitated for a moment before finally saying, 'His constant insistence that I was escorted back to my dressing room by male members of staff for instance.'

'That is hardly acting strangely, have you considered only male members of staff were available to do that?'

'I think it was a deliberate act on his part myself, even when I did ask a female staff member to bring me something he would always intervene and send over some young chap.'

Lance pondered this over before saying, 'Well I certainly have not said anything. Maybe he's just being cautious in the circumstances and you're being slightly over sensitive.'

'I was found *not guilty,* remember?' he snapped back. 'There should be no reason for him to think like that.'

'You keep saying that often enough, and you may start to believe yourself.'

'Don't be a tit Lance, it doesn't suit you.'

'Look anyone could have told him something, if indeed anyone did. Over the years lots of people, including myself, have covered up for you. Anyone of them could have let the truth slip out to him.'

'And I bet that would please you so much, seeing me back on the scrapheap.'

'I'm not even rising to that; you know how much I've done over the years to protect you. And getting you this gig did not come out of thin air either, I worked bloody hard to get you that so show me some bloody respect please.'

'I'm sorry, I know you have.'

The phone suddenly rang on Lance's desk and he picked it up.

'Thanks Louise, I'll be out in a few minutes' he said before replacing the receiver.

'I'm sorry Patrick, I have another client to see. Was there anything else?'

'No, I guess there isn't' he said as he moved to get up.

'Look Patrick, I will be by your side for the filming ok' Lance said as he led him to the door.

'Thanks, I do appreciate all you've done for me Lance. I'm lost without you by my side and scared of what I will do when you are not there.'

As Lance watched him leave the office, the words he had just uttered chilled him to the bone.

Chapter 66

The car behind me continued its incessant beeping as I kept my vehicle in its stationary position, frozen like a statue as I watched vacantly at the green light ahead of me. Lights now also flashed behind me as the irate motorist got more and more frustrated at me. Eventually he came up beside me and wound down his window, shouting an array of obscenities before driving off into the distance.

I watched as the lights turned red once more and an elderly lady crossed the road in front of me, smiling in gratitude as she passed.

I looked at the clock on the dashboard. It read 13:04.

I had left the cellar and its macabre scene ten minutes earlier, shutting the door behind me and driving away. The relief at being away from that scene washed over me after what I had witnessed in there.

Finally driving away as the lights turned green once again, I knew I had to face the mess I had created. Right now, I just needed to get home and work out a plan.

It should not have ended like this.

Or was this the way it was always going to end?

Was I being delusional in thinking it could end any other way? That I could keep Simon prisoner for weeks and weeks whilst I appeared on the show, and then what, release him back out into the real world in the hope he would not say anything about his ordeal?

That was not going to happen, it may have been a nice happy ending in my head but there was no way it was going to happen.

The only way this was going to end was in the death of Simon, whether that happened this morning or later on, it did not matter. It had happened much earlier than expected though. All the plans in my head had been to keep him a prisoner and now I had a dead body to deal with instead.

With my brother away for the next month at least I had time on my side. The question was, did I really want to leave his body inside the cellar for a considerable amount of time though?

Moving the body elsewhere was not a task I relished but it was one that had to be done. Once Marcus returned, the process of selling the house would begin and the opportunity to move the body would disappear. The thought of a perspective buyer finding a dead body in the cellar made me chuckle slightly before my brain told me this was no laughing matter. I had a dead body lying in my mother's house and that was definitely not something to be laughing about.

I also knew from my love of true crime books that rigor mortis could set in within four hours of death in a human. The thought of disposing of a stiff corpse was not something I relished.

As I stopped the car outside my house, I had already resolved what I needed to do.

I needed to move the body, and I needed to do it tonight.

Chapter 67

Patrick swirled around the amber liquid in the glass as he looked out of the pub window at the frantic London life passing him by.

He had come straight here after his meeting with Lance and was already on his third whisky, the warm and fuzzy feeling of the alcohol beginning to work its magic.

When he was in London, he would usually go to his private members club in Mayfair, that unfortunately was no longer an option though. His membership was cancelled when he was charged, and even his subsequent acquittal had not seen it reinstated despite his protestations that it should be.

Those bastards, he thought. He was good enough for their stupid club when he was at the top of his game, then cut adrift as his world came crashing down. The irony now being, as he looked to be climbing to the top yet again, these spineless bastards still refused to let him grace their stuffy club.

He finished off his drink and returned to the bar to get another. Already busy with the lunchtime rush, the pub was packed with the diverse clientele that this part of London attracted.

Taking his drink back to the table, Patrick made a mental promise that this would be his last. Though he was sure no one in here had recognised him, it would not be a good look if the star presenter of the biggest quiz show on TV was found drunk and alone in a central London pub during the day.

He had regretted his outburst to Lance earlier, he should have known his agent would not have spilled the beans to Mike, as doing so would have put him at risk of implicating himself in the cover-up.

Mike was acting so weirdly during rehearsals though, the way he seemed so overprotective over his female staff members suggested to him someone had spilled the beans, and if it was not Lance, then who was it?

Many people had covered for him during the years, many people knew what he was doing, most kept quiet and those that did speak up were shot down before it could go further. The threat of losing their dream job in television being enough to make sure it did not go any further. Could one of those many people now be trying to jeopardise his return to television? Of course, he was unlikely to ever know unless he confronted Mike directly. Doing that would be admitting to the dark things he had done though, and even if Mike did have suspicions, he could not allow that. He would just have to put up with it, there was no other option for him.

His eyes were diverted to a young woman sitting alone at a table opposite him. Dressed smartly in a skirt and blouse, he guessed she worked in one of the many legal firms that were littered around this area. He had always been partial to young and intelligent women, ones he could chat to on his level and have some fun with later on …

He smiled at her, she smiled back.

He finished his drink and got up to leave. As he passed her table, she smiled at him once again. Fully expecting him to sit down, she moved her coat off the chair next to her.

Patrick made no attempt to sit down though, instead he smiled politely and made his way towards the exit. The fun and games he enjoyed had to stop, for the time being at least.

Chapter 68

It felt like Deja vu.

Once again, I stood at the same door, the same door I had stood at over twelve hours earlier.

This time was so different though. This time I was not going to feed or look after my prisoner. This time I was here to remove his body.

I unlocked the door and switched on the lights, once again the bottom of the room being swathed in light. I closed my eyes for a few moments, not wanting to confront the image that was visible at the bottom of those stone steps.

I opened them again, knowing I had to face what lay down there.

As I got closer to the bottom of the stairs, I could clearly see the prone body of Stuart, now covered with the blanket I had put over him.

The blood that had poured from his head earlier now stained the stone tiles next to his body. Blood had also seeped into the blanket that covered him.

I walked closer to the body, a chill now hitting my bones as I neared it. I had only seen a dead body once in my life, at the funeral parlour as my father lay in his coffin. That image of his ghostly white face still haunted me to this day.

I slowly lifted the blanket to reveal the ravaged face of Simon. The broken nose had caused considerable damage and his face was splattered with congealed blood. Despite this, he did look like he was just sleeping and a gentle nudge from me would awaken him from his slumber at any moment.

I had closed his eyes before leaving here earlier, so at least did not have the frightening prospect of him staring back at me now.

It was just after two in the morning and the cellar was freezing during this late hour. Now that Simon was dead the need to warm the cellar was not required although I still wished I had left the heating on.

I had left Sadie in bed an hour ago, explaining my absence at this late hour on the need to go into the office to sort out an issue with one of the servers. I was on call this week and it was prefect cover, I could be gone for a few hours without causing her any suspicion.

I had been dreading this moment all day. It was one thing to bring a drugged, yet still alive Simon here, it was another to bring out his dead body.

I fully took off the blanket that covered the rest of his body, and with a grimace on my face lifted his body from the cold stone floor. The idea was to drag him upright once again and move him to the car that way. I had considered carrying him, but my worry of falling backwards on those cellar steps had discounted that idea in my mind.

His body now felt much heavier as I lifted him to stand beside me, the muscles he had used whilst alive now redundant as I used all my strength to prop up his limp body. No sign of rigor mortis setting in yet it seemed, a fact I was incredibly grateful for.

It was such a struggle dragging him up those steps, the exertion so much I needed to rest him back down on the floor when I reached the top.

The chillness of the night was now a distant memory as perspiration dripped down my face and back.

Thank god I never carried him, I thought.

I picked him up and resumed my trek back to the car outside, dragging my human corpse alongside me. Reaching the car, I dumped his body onto the dust sheets I had laid down inside the boot, a rather clumsy way to conceal any evidence if this car was ever searched by the police.

I slammed the boot shut, breathing in the night air for a moment before returning to the house. Turning off all the lights I secured the back door, the cleaning up of the cellar could wait. Tonight, was all about disposing of Simon and nothing else.

Five minutes later I was driving through the country lanes of rural Gower. With the narrow roads devoid of street lighting, I carefully wound through them with full headlights blazing as I fully concentrated on the road in front of me.

One of the reasons I loved living in this Area of Outstanding Natural Beauty was the isolation it offered, the opportunity to live a quiet life with Sadie and the kids whilst still being close to the numerous amenities of Swansea was a perfect balance for me. And that isolation now offered me something else, it offered me a perfect place to conceal a body.

I stopped the car and cut the engine.

Getting out of the car I was struck by the silence around me, only the solidary sound of a distant owl intermittently cutting through it. I was all alone here with only a corpse to keep me company.

I ascertained that this spot was ideal to dump the body, not that close to any of the villages that were dotted around this sparsely populated area, which I hoped would mean discovery of the body less likely.

Putting on the gloves that were in my pocket, something I had done every step of the way when touching Simon, I opened the boot and lifted out his body for one final time. Ignoring my misgivings about the heaviness of his corpse, I decided this time to carry him the short distance to the grass verge by the side of the road.

'Bye my friend' I whispered as I stood at the edge of it, the weight of him already making me start to sag slightly. 'I'm so sorry it had to end like this.'

And with that I dropped his body into the dense undergrowth, watching as the body became concealed by the thick foliage of shrubs and bushes that littered the wooded area that ran alongside the road.

I switched on the torch of my phone and shone it down into the undergrowth.

Now covered with the thick undergrowth, the body of Simon was barely visible. I was confident that only someone literally standing at this spot and making a very conscious effort to look would think anything was amiss.

Satisfied I had done all I could to conceal the body I turned quickly back towards the car and shut the boot. The sound as I slammed it down reverberating in the still night.

I jumped into the car and sat just sat there for a few minutes. Yes, this place was remote and deadly quiet, especially at this hour, but I still knew that just sitting here was not the best thing to do. It only took one police car to pass and stop for a chat for potentially all my good work here tonight to unravel. I started the engine and put my still shaking hands onto the steering wheel, knowing I needed to get a grip and finally leave this place.

As I finally drove away, I looked into the rear-view mirror and the scene I was leaving behind. The scene that contained the final resting place of Simon Tucker.

Chapter 69

'Come in' Mike Phelps said.

Sarah Mills opened the door, a look of concern etched on her face.

'Everything ok?' Mike said as he gestured for her to take a seat.

'We may have a problem' she said as she took the seat opposite him.

'You know I don't like problems Sarah' he grinned, 'What's up?'

'Seems one of our contestants has gone missing.'

'What do you mean by missing?' he said, as if he did not quite understand what Sarah was saying.

'Well, it's the usual meaning of missing Mike. As you know we have been liaising with all of the contestants to make sure they are comfortable with all the arrangements to record their shows next week.'

'Yes' he nodded back in acknowledgment.

'Well, all has gone well in that respect, apart from this one contestant' she said, looking briefly at her notes as she continued. 'We have not been able to contact a Mr Simon Tucker for the last four days, that is until today when we finally managed to get hold of his wife.'

Mike nodded for her to continue.

'Well, the poor woman was frantic on the phone, literally in tears as I spoke to her. She told me her husband has been missing for the last four days and that the police had been informed. Apparently, he did not return from a night shift at the snooker club he owns.'

'Bloody hell' Mike said as he digested what he was being told. 'Have the police got any idea what happened?'

'Robbery they think. Money was taken from the till and of course her husband is missing, along with his mobile and wallet.'

'Poor woman.'

'Indeed' Sarah said, 'I'm surprised she managed to tell me as much as she did through the tears to be honest.'

'It's awful to hear what has happened, and I don't want to seem callous, but we still have a TV show to make and therefore need to get another contestant in.'

'Yes, we have already identified a good fit in that regard' she said.

'And who is that?'

Again, referring to her notes she said, 'His name is Ashley White, similar age to Simon and from the same city in Wales, which helps us maintain the geographical mix on the show.'

'Very good' Mike sighed, 'And you'll be telling him the good news today?'

'Yes, I'll give him a call personally once we have finished here.'

'Thanks for that Sarah. Such awful circumstances to be picked for the show though.'

'Yes' she said replied.

'Well, I've seen reserve contestants win loads of shows before. Let us see if our Mr White can repeat that trick' Mike said with a glint in his eye.

Chapter 70

'Previously we spoke about your childhood, do you mind if we return to that theme Ashley?'

I was back in the office of Dr Sharma, talking about things I would rather leave unsaid, things that I felt needed to be kept in the past.

Saying all that I still replied, 'If we must.'

The doctor smiled before continuing, 'Last time we spoke about the difficult relationship you had with your father; can we now move on to your relationship with your mother?'

I could not even remember telling her all that, it was something I rarely spoke about, not even to Sadie.

'Not much to tell I'm afraid.'

'You were clearly much closer to her than your father though, would you not agree?'

'Aren't all sons' though?'

The doctor did not reply directly to that, instead she said, 'Did you feel suffocated by her at times?'

'What do you mean by that?' I snapped back. 'I loved my mother.'

'Sorry, wrong choice of phrase on my part' she replied. 'I'm just trying to attain how you felt about the relationship you had.'

I remained silence for a moment, unsure what to say next.

'Maybe it was a bit stifling at times' I finally admitted. 'I was her baby, with my brother being twelve years older. I felt like an only child for most of my childhood if I am being honest. Then my Dad got ill, and I was her only constant thing in life.

'It must have been hard?' Dr Sharma said.

'It was at times' I said quite tearfully. 'I often remember my friends calling and me making excuses not to go out so I could keep my Mum company.'

I was saying far too much, stuff I had not even told Sadie, stuff that I had bottled up for far too long.

'Did you ever talk to her about the way you felt?'

'How could I? She needed support and I felt I was the only one there for her.'

'You did need a life too though Ashley? the doctor replied. 'You were young, you needed company your own age.'

I said nothing in reply. I knew she was right of course.

Noting my reluctance to reply she continued, 'It was not your fault your Father began ill Ashley. It was not all down to you to look after your Mother.'

She was right again. All she was saying was bloody right. It was all in the past though and had nothing to do with the present.

'It was though' I finally said.

'What about your Brother?' she said.

'He had left home, was enjoying university too much to care about his family.'

'Did you resent him for that?'

'Yes, I did' I replied rather too quickly. I could detect the venom in my voice and was fairly sure Dr Sharma had as well.

'For deserting you?' she replied.

'Yes, I guess. He was off enjoying himself while I was stuck at home.'

'You were much younger though Ashley?'

'I know, it still felt like he was deserting me at the time though.'

The alarm on the phone next to her suddenly went off.

'We will leave it there for today Ashley' she said, turning the alarm off. 'I believe we are making great progress in trying to understand your depression and anxiety, with you opening up like this giving me a much better insight into why you feel like you do.'

Whilst being very reluctant to come to these sessions initially, I now had to admit they were beginning to help with the dark periods I often felt. Yes, I did not really want to talk about my childhood or my family relationships, especially to a stranger, but I had to admit they were helping. Talking about pent up emotions that had laid dormant for years was liberating and cathartic, and I left that room after these sessions feeling more like a normal human being. A feeling that I had not felt for many years.

There were some things that could never be spoken about of course. The things I had done over the last four days had to remain inside my head, and my head only. Yes, it had been four days since those events and there was still no news from the show. Had all my efforts been in vain. Had I committed those awful things for nothing?

A heavy downpour had started as I stepped out onto the pavement, and I ran quickly back to the car to avoid getting drenched.

Sitting in the car, the rain now bouncing off the roof I switched back on my mobile, which had remained off whilst I had my session with Dr Sharma.

As the phone started its rebooting, I squeezed my forehead as I felt the first pangs of a headache forming. The headache was quickly forgotten though as the rebooted phone next to me beeped to indicate an answerphone message.

I looked at the phone and checked the two missed calls I had received.

They were both from a number I had saved recently. They were both from the production team on *'The Duel.'*

Chapter 71

I ended the call.

With shaking hands, I put the phone down, a massive grin forming on my face.

YES, YES, YES!! I screamed.

I had done it; I had got on the show. The awful things I had done had been worth it, the end-result that I craved had indeed happened.

'You really think it was all worth it?' a voice behind me said.

I looked in the rear-view mirror, too scared to turn around and look.

The bloodied face of Simon Tucker looked back at me.

'You're not real' I shouted, 'This is just my imagination playing tricks.'

'Is it Ashley? Is it really?' Simon said in reply. 'Or is the guilt and shame for what you did to me the reason I'm here talking to you now?'

'I'm sorry for what I did Simon, I truly am. I was desperate, I needed to be on this show.'

'Nothing is worth killing for Ashley, and I mean nothing.'

'Maybe your right' I said, 'but have you ever been so desperate in your life that you would do anything to improve your situation? I am broke, my house is under threat of repossession and my wife knows nothing about it all. I needed to get on this show, I needed a way out of all this mess I am in.'

'And you think this show will provide all that?' he chuckled. 'You will be up against some of the best quizzing minds in the country. You really think you stand any chance of winning?'

'Yes, I do' I shouted back, 'I'm bright and good at quizzes. I have as much chance as anyone else on that show.'

'Your hardly in the same league though' Simon mocked. 'You can delude yourself all you like Ashley, you can dream all you like about *winning that show, but we both know it just is not going to happen. All this is for nothing and you KNOW IT!'*

'NO' I shouted back as I turned my head to look at the back seat.

There was no one there. No sign of the bloodied face of Simon looking back at me.

Shaking, and with my face as white as a sheet I turned around and started the engine. On the drive home I constantly kept looking in the rear view, expecting to see the image of Simon Tucker suddenly to reappear. Thankfully though it did not.

'How's it going?' I said, as I entered the living room, giving Sadie a quick peck on the cheek before taking a seat on the couch.

'Stressful' she said, 'this assignment has to be in next week and I'm no way near finishing it.'

'You will babe' I reassured her. 'I have total faith in you.'

'Thanks, you are very biased though' she laughed.

'I've got something to tell you' I said, 'it's probably something I should have told you before now.'

'What?' she replied, concern in her voice. 'It's not your Mum, is it?'

'No, it's nothing like that. It's really good news in fact.'

'Promotion?' she said excitedly.

'No, it's nothing to do with work either. Remember that new quiz show I applied for a while back?'

'Yes of course I remember.'

'Well, I've got on' I just blurted out.

'Got on?' she said rather perplexed. 'I thought you said you never heard back after applying?'

'I just did not want to tempt fate. When they rang me up and I went for the audition it all seemed so surreal. I never expected it to lead anywhere and did not want to burden you with it all, especially after Jenny ....'

'You're not joking, are you?'

'No, I'm not. I literally just had a call to say I'm on the show next week.'

'Next week' she exclaimed.

'Yes, so I had better get revising.'

She got up from her seat and joined me on the couch.

'That's brilliant news Ashley, I'm so proud of you' she said before planting a big kiss on my lips. 'I just wish you had told me you were doing all this though.'

'I'm sorry. Like I said you had more important things on your mind and I really did not think it would come to anything.'

'Well, it has, and I could not be happier for you. I know how much you wanted this.'

'I have lots to do though. This show is going to have some of the best quizzers in the country and I have so many gaps in my knowledge to try and fill, and so little time to do it.'

'You will get through it and I'm here to help as well.'

'Your assignment though?'

'I'm sure I can get that done as well' she smiled, 'helping you win all that money sounds much more appealing though.'

'Let us not count our chicken's babe, it will be tough to win it.'

'Yes, it will be tough, but I believe in you, as you should yourself.'

She was right of course, as usual.

Suddenly an image appeared in the corner of the room, it was again the bloodied form of Simon Tucker.

'You will never win that show Ashley. You are nothing but a MURDERER!'

'Are you ok? Sadie said with a look of concern on her face, 'you have gone so pale.'

'I'm fine' I said as the image slowly disappeared.

Chapter 72

Round 1 – Ashley White V Alan Norman

I rubbed my eyes, the early morning sunlight streaming through the gap in the curtains as I struggled to get back to sleep.

I lay there for a few more minutes in the hope that once again sleep would envelope me, that maybe I could snatch a few more precious moments before I needed to get up.

It was useless though. I was too on edge to go back to sleep.

I got up and sat on the edge of the bed for a few moments before grabbing my glasses and phone from the bedside table.

It had just gone past 6, according to the clock on my phone. My alarm was due to go off in thirty minutes anyway, and whilst the extra half hour in bed would have been nice, it was just not going to happen.

I looked around the hotel room I had spent the night in, one of these functional hotels that had sprung up everywhere in the country over the last decade or so. Whilst it may have lacked charm, it was spotlessly clean, and the bed was deliciously comfy.

Today was the day. The day that had the potential to be the most important of my life.

The week of cramming, with all those facts floating inside my head would be severely tested today. I just hoped I could remember all those prime ministers, presidents, chemical elements, kings, queens, and wars that I had learnt. My biggest fear now being that too much information was going on up there, and how I was going to cope in remembering it all.

I went into the bathroom and looked at myself in the mirror. The long hair and scruffy beard I usually owned had now been replaced with a tidy haircut and a nicely trimmed beard. *'Looking smart, will help you think smart'* Sadie had said before I left for the train journey up here. I just hoped she was right.

Now, dressed in jeans and a light grey sweater after a leisurely shower I was ready. Ready to face the biggest challenge of my life. I picked up my suitcase with the selection of five shirts in it that were required for today and made my way downstairs to the reception.

Sitting there I checked my watch once more; ten minutes and I was due to be picked up and driven the short distance to the studio.

The receptionist smiled at me from her desk, most probably used to seeing many people sitting here waiting to be escorted off to the studio for their five minutes of fame.

A young woman opened the front door and entered the reception area.

'Ashley?' she said as she spotted me.

'Yes' I replied, getting up from my seat.

'Morning, I'm Alex, one of the production staff at *The Duel*' she said with a breezy smile, shaking my hand in welcome. 'I hope you are well; despite this early hour we have got you up.'

'I'm good thanks' I said, 'I'm used to early mornings, so this is fine.'

'Good stuff' she replied. 'The taxi is outside so we will make a move if that is ok?'

I nodded in agreement and followed her outside to the waiting taxi, wheeling my suitcase behind me as I did.

'So, have you been on TV before?' Alex said as the taxi moved off.

'No, it's my first time' I said, 'Applied for loads of shows, never been successful in getting on one though, until now.'

'Well, you've certainly picked the right one to get on' she smiled.

Within minutes we had arrived at a set of security gates with the words 'Elstree Studios' emblazoned on the wall next to them. The barrier slowly lifted, and the taxi drove in.

As it slowly passed through the many large buildings that occupied the complex, Alex turned to me and said, 'Did you know that all the original Star Wars films were made here, Indiana Jones ones too?'

'Never knew that' I lied. The truth was I loved films and was always reading up on them, these studios at Elstree were synonymous with those movies and the largest studio on the complex was even named after George Lucas. Why I hid this fact from Alex I did not really know, maybe I wanted to hide my geekiness from her.

The taxi stopped at a building with Studio 7 written on it as Alex turned to me and said, 'Well, this is us' as she got out.

I followed her through a set of double doors where I was signed in by the rather stern looking guard and issued with a security badge.

Alex led me into a room on the right which contained a couple of two-seater settees, a small table, a large screen TV on the wall and coffee making facilities in the corner.

'Please take a seat' Alex said as she motioned to one of the settees. 'Tea or coffee?'

'Coffee is fine' I replied.

She returned a few moments later with the coffee and a bacon roll. 'Sorry it's nothing more exciting' she laughed, 'Unfortunately our catering budget is not that high.'

I laughed and said it was fine.

'So just a quick overview of what will happen this morning' Alex continued as she took a seat opposite me. 'First of all, I will go through the gameplay of the show with you, as this is a new show, we want you to be entirely comfortable with the rules before the recording starts. Patrick will of course make the rules clear on set as well before the game starts. We will then take you through to the dressing room so you can change into your chosen outfit, which will be picked by our costume team from the five tops you brought with you. Then it will be on to make-up. On that note, could you lay your outfits out on the table please, so the guys can come in and see what is suitable.'

'Of course,' I said as I went over to my case and got out my tops. I had chosen an assortment of shirts with one thing in common, they were all outrageously bold and colourful.

'Nice and colourful is what we love' Alex said as she watched me lay them all out on the table.

I returned to my seat and Alex continued, 'So, once you have changed, we will take you onto the set where the floor manager will explain the layout and how the recording will work. Then it is back here for some admin stuff we need to go through and a little relaxation before going back on set for the actual recording. Do you have any questions regarding all that?'

'No' I replied, slightly fazed by it all.

'I know it's a lot to take in' she said, sensing my obvious bewilderment. 'If you do have any questions as we go on then please do shout.'

The door opened and in walked a man wearing a flowery shirt, skinny jeans, and white trainers.

'Hello Alex' he said rather flamboyantly. 'And I'm guessing this is Ashley, our next lamb to the slaughter.'

'Ignore Freddie' she laughed. 'This is Freddie by the way, our shy and retiring costume designer.'

'Hi Ashley, I do apologise for my awful sense of humour, now what do we have here' he said, looking at the shirts I had laid out. 'Very nice, I'm even tempted to take some of these for my wardrobe' he laughed before finally picking up a navy floral print shirt.

'This one ok?' he said as he lifted the shirt up to show me.

'That's fine.'

'Great, and you're wearing the same trousers' he said as he put the shirt onto a hanger.

'Yes.'

'No worries. We will give the shirt a quick iron and it will be all ready for you when you come down to the dressing room.'

And then he was gone, and Alex began her lowdown on the rules of *'The Duel.'*

'Is that all clear?' she said after finishing.

'Yes, I think so' I said. The rules seemed straightforward enough to me and I did not think they needed that much explaining.

'Like I said Patrick will be explaining all this again on set anyway.'

I nodded in acknowledgement.

'Right, let us get you down to the dressing rooms then' Alex said as she led me out of the green room and down a short flight of stairs towards the make-up and dressing rooms.

The shirt that Freddie picked out for me was hanging up as I entered the small dressing room, freshly ironed as promised. I quickly changed into it and looked at myself in the mirror, thinking I scrubbed up well for my first television appearance.

'Not what I would have picked myself, not a bad effort though' the image behind me smiled.

'Go away' I said.

'There is still time to end this charade Ashley, still time to come clean and admit to what you have done.'

I closed my eyes tight. When I opened them again the image of Simon Tucker had disappeared.

'Everything ok?' Alex smiled as I left the dressing room. 'You do look a bit ashen all of a sudden.'

'I'm fine' I said, 'Just a bit of nerves that's all.'

'No need to be' she smiled as she led through to the make-up room.

As I sat there being plastered with foundation the first signs of nerves did indeed begin to hit me. The butterflies that I had so far successfully controlled started fluttering in my stomach as I watched the make-up artist finish her work. Seeing that image of Simon moments ago did not help either. The woman tried her best at chit-chat but finally gave up after a few minutes, most probably annoyed at my brief answers to her questions.

'All done' she smiled as she took off the cape that she had put round me. I offered my thanks, glad that the ordeal of sitting there had not taken that long.

Within minutes of leaving the make-up room we were stood outside a set of black double doors with a sign saying Studio 7 at the top, the on-air light next to it being unlit.

Alex guided me through a maze of cables that littered the backstage area before we finally came to the studio set.

I had never been in a TV studio before and the sight before me left me in awe. I looked above me at the gigantic array of lights, which although not fully on still generated a lot of heat on the studio floor. The set had two raised platforms facing each other, which I presumed would be filled by me and my fellow competitor.

A tall man with a headset approached us from the area behind one of the camera operators.

'Hi both' he said with a strong west country accent, 'And you must be Ashley?'

I nodded in confirmation and we shook hands as he introduced himself as Martin Ashdown, the floor manager for the studio recordings of the show.

Martin then proceeded to tell me all I needed to know for the recording I would be facing in around thirty minutes time. Where I needed to sit when I was announced on stage, where I should look when speaking to the host, where I should look when not speaking to the host, the list seemed to go on forever.

And then it was back to the green room, the fast pace of the morning now beginning to dawn on me as I looked at the clock on the wall and could see it had just gone past 9.30.

With all the required forms filled in, I finally had the chance to think about the task that lay ahead of me in about thirty minutes time. The excitement of being here was now being replaced by a feeling of dread as doubts began to swirl in my head.

Was I good enough to be here? Did I have what it took to compete with the quizzing talent assembled here?

My thoughts were interrupted by a knock on the door and in walked a tall man, dressed in a navy suit and a open necked white shirt, a man I knew as Patrick Reed.

'And you must be Ashley?' he said, walking towards me with a hand outstretched.

'Yes' I replied as I rose from my seat and shook his hand.

'Very pleased to meet you, I am Patrick, the host of the show.'

'Good to meet you' I mumbled, suddenly starstruck at meeting such a famous person, someone I had grew up watching on TV.

'Just though I would say a quick hello and wish you luck for the show' he smiled, 'Can I detect a Welsh accent there?'

'Yes, I'm from Swansea.'

'Ah, I love Swansea' he enthused. 'Myself and my wife have spent many happy stays on The Gower, such a beautiful part of the world.'

'It certainly is' I replied.

'Well, good luck to you anyway. Will see you on set very soon' he said, before heading out of the room.

'Seems a nice guy' I said to Alex.

She just smiled and said nothing.

I just sat there for the next fifteen minutes, thinking positive thoughts, and trying hard to relax.

Just as I was beginning to finally get there the headset on Alex crackled into life. 'Yes, we will be right there' she said into it.

'They are ready for us' she smiled. 'Are you all set?'

'As ready as I will ever be' I smiled back.

'You will be fine; everybody enjoys the experience once the cameras start rolling.

I hoped she was right about that.

She locked the green room and we once again began our journey to the studio, this time when I stepped out onto the set it would be for real though.

We stopped at a set of curtains that were obscuring the studio set, behind which I could hear considerable noise and chatter, the result of the studio audience now being there I guessed.

The audience hushed slightly as I heard a voice begin a countdown from ten. As the voice reached zero the audience responded with complete silence.

The voice of Patrick Reed could now be heard behind the screen.

'Tonight, two more contestants will fight it out for the chance to win the biggest cash prize on television. Welcome to The Duel.'

Music then started playing, pleasant enough stuff which I presumed was the theme music that would open the show when it finally aired on TV.

'Not long now' Alex next to me.

The music stopped and the audience started clapping and cheering before Patrick continued. 'Good evening to everyone here in the audience, and to everyone at home as we play another first-round match of The Duel. Tonight, we will see another two players battle it out as they compete for the chance to win the biggest cash prize in quiz show history, a whopping two million pounds.'

The audience whopped and cheered at that announcement.

'So, let us get down to business and introduce tonight's' contestants. First we have joining us is Ashley White from Swansea.'

'You're on' said a floor assistant next to me as the curtain was drawn back and I was directed to the raised platform towards the left of the set. Alex giving me a thumbs up as I left.

It felt so surreal coming out here, with the audience's clapping ringing in my ears and the studio lights blazing down on me.

Patrick had now moved onto a platform in the middle, and this is from where he now greeted my arrival.

'Welcome to the show Ashley' he said with a smile, a smile that I felt was just that ever so cheesy.

I smiled back, slightly awkwardly I felt. *For god sake Ashley, just relax and try not to force it,* the voice inside me said.

'So, it says here that you are an IT analyst who enjoys ultra-marathons and a spot of bungee jumping' he said from the iPad he was holding. I'm finding just reading that out makes me tired.'

The audience roared with laughter.

'Yes, that's right. I have done several ultra-marathons both here and around the world' I replied with as much confidence as my lie allowed me to.

'Certainly, an extreme way to keep fit' Patrick said.

'It is a very addictive way to keep fit also' I laughed.

'Not sure I would get addictive to it though. An hour a day in the gym is plenty for me' he replied. 'Anyway, we will get to know a little more about you as the show goes on, for now though can we have a big round of applause for Ashley.'

The audience once again clapped on cue.

Patrick waited for the applause to die down before continuing, 'And now let us welcome our second contestant tonight, Alan Norman from Sheffield.'

From the other side of the studio, out stepped a man in his mid to late fifties, I guessed. As he got closer to the podium, I could see he sported a rather scruffy beard, glasses, and a green polo shirt.

'A definite quizzer' I thought as he sat down opposite me.

As Patrick began chatting to my opponent, my worst fears were indeed realised.

A finalist on both Mastermind and 15 to 1, his quizzing pedigree was enhanced by being a member of the English team at the European and World quizzing championships.

'What had I let myself in for?' I thought, as Patrick rattled off the rules. What chance did I have against someone of his ability?

'Are you both comfortable with the rules?' Patrick announced as he finished going through them.

We both nodded in affirmation, in truth though I had heard these rules so many times I could recite them.

'Excellent' he announced with a smile. 'So, without further ado, let us see the first category for tonight.'

Dramatic music played on and the studios lights dimmed slightly as the screen behind Patrick brought up the words *'Music.'*

I am ok with music I thought. Not my strongest subject admittedly, but it could have been a lot worst for an opening category.

'So, the first question on music will go to you Ashley' Patrick said as he turned to face me. 'Before you answer I will ask Alan to allocate you 5, 3, 2, 1 or 0 points by using his judgement on how he feels you will answer it. Is that clear?'

'Yes' I said, my heart now pounding.

'So, your first question is ....'

I could feel perspiration starting to drip from my forehead despite the makeup I was caked in. I resisted the temptation to wipe it off as I stared intently at Patrick as he continued with the question.

'Billy Corgan is the lead singer of which alternative rock band?'

I knew this, I bloody well knew it. I so wanted to blurt the answer out straight away and show everyone how good I really was. The format of the show did not allow for that unfortunately though, so I contained my urge.

'So, the power all lies with you now Alan' Patrick said as he turned to face my opponent. 'Do you think Ashley knows the answer or not?'

My opponent weighed up his options before saying, 'That's a tough question, not one I'm certain of myself. Ashley does not look like an alternative rock fan to me so I'm going to allocate him 3 points and hope he proves me right.'

How lucky was I that my opponent had such poor judgement at where my strengths lay?

Patrick repeated the question and I felt like the whole studio was looking at me with bated breath as they awaited my answer.

After a few seconds of thinking, just to make sure the answer inside my head was indeed right, I finally spoke the words that had been in my head ever since the question had first been asked.

'The answer is The Smashing Pumpkins' I said, full of confidence that the answer was indeed that.

'Smashing Pumpkins, you say' Patrick replied as a low hum of music started to play, increasing the already electric tension that was surrounding the studio.

I looked towards Alan, trying to see any hint in his expression that he was anxious about the answer I had given, his face gave nothing away though.

Patrick looked at the screen in front of him, and then back to me before saying, 'I can tell you Ashley that The Smashing Pumpkins is ....'

The required pause that you always got on shows like this.

'CORRECT' he exclaimed, 'And you begin tonight's contest with 3 points.'

Relief washed over me as the audience clapped politely. My first answer on TV was correct and I could feel my whole body instantly relax as the feeling of elation hit me.

Unfortunately, the rest of the match did not follow in quite the same way, as silly mistakes, and a complete lack of knowing the correct answers brought me crashing back down to earth. It was fortunate for me that Alan also failed to bring his 'A' game with him, and as he faced the final question of the contest, I held a narrow 2-point lead. The big problem for me was that the question carried 3 points with it, and a correct answer from Alan would see me leaving the competition.

'So, we come down to the final question of this very tight match. A correct answer from you here Alan will see you receive 3 points, and victory by the narrowest of margins.'

I stared downwards, praying that he would fluff his big moment.

The studio was a deathly hush as Patrick began asking the final question.

'So, Alan, here is your final question on TV and film. A question that is worth a vital 3 points to you.'

Please get it wrong, I silently chanted to myself.

'In the 2013 film, The Lone Ranger, can you name the actor who played him, alongside Johnny Depp as Tonto?'

Bloody hell, that is a tough one I thought.

Alan looked composed though as he heard the question, a look that told me that he was confident that he knew the answer.

Oh well, at least I have not disgraced myself, and being knocked out by the calibre of this quizzer was nothing to be ashamed of.

'Yes, I really enjoyed this film when I saw it' Alan announced with a degree of self-assurance. 'And I believe that the actor playing the Lone Ranger was Arnie Hammer.' He relaxed back in his seat, confident that the job was done, and he was assured of his place in the next round.

'Could you please repeat that?' Patrick asked him.

'Arnie Hammer' Alan repeated, this time without the air of cockiness that had been apparent a few seconds earlier.

'I can tell you that Arnie Hammer is ....' Once again, we had the dramatic pause as Patrick ratcheted up the tension, most probably from instructions coming down his earpiece.

I sat there, ready to accept my fate.

'Incorrect I'm afraid' Patrick continued. 'The answer is Armie Hammer', as he emphasised the first name to a shocked Alan.

'Surely that is what I said?' replied an exasperated Alan, not quite believing the answer he had given was wrong.

'I'm afraid you said Arnie Hammer, and whilst it may only sound slightly different, there is quite clearly a difference. You have been involved in a fantastic game though and should be immensely proud of your efforts tonight. Can we have a big round of applause for Alan please.'

Alan still looked shellshocked as the clapping died down and Patrick turned to face me.

'And I turn to our victor tonight. That was some contest to win Ashley and we look forward to welcoming you back for the next round. A round of applause for Ashely too please.'

I was in a complete daze, still not sure what had just happened. Had my opponent just lost for saying Arnie instead of Armie?

Before I knew it, Patrick had closed the show and now stood before me as the closing music played in the background.

'Very well played' he said as he shook my hand firmly. 'That's certainly the best contest I've seen so far and it's always good for the viewers to have that bit of drama at the end.'

'Thanks, I do feel a bit bad though. He was so close to the right answer at the end.'

'Don't be' Patrick said dismissively, 'These things happen, and I did ask him to repeat his answer so there can be no ambiguity there. Anyway, huge congratulations again and I will look forward to seeing you for your next match.'

And then he was gone. Off to congratulate, or I should say commiserate with my opponent who still looked visibly upset opposite me.

As Alex approached to offer her congratulations, I realised the enormity of what I had just achieved.

The dream of winning the two million pounds was off to a successful start, a phenomenally successful start indeed. The dream was alive and kicking.

Chapter 73

I slumped down onto the bed, the relief of dropping onto the comfy mattress washing over me after the events of the morning.

Despite the ongoing protestations of my opponent, the result of the match stood, and I had officially been declared the winner. Whilst I fully understood the frustrations of Alan in missing out on winning by the slightest of margins, his constant griping after the contest and lack of empathy towards me afterwards quickly changed my feelings. I was glad to beat such a bad loser and see him dumped out of the competition.

After winning the match I was taken back to the green room by Alex where I composed myself after the tension and high drama of the studio recording. She then explained once again that as I had won, I would need to record my second round match the next day, which necessitated another night at the hotel.

I was still on an immense high as my mobile started to ring next to me. Fully expecting to see the caller to be Sadie I picked it up from the bedside table. I was surprised to see the name of 'Dan Hedges' staring back at me on the display though.

'Hi mate' I said as I answered.

'Where have you been? I've been trying to get hold of you all morning.'

'Sorry, I've had to go away with work at the last minute' I lied. Only Sadie knew where I was today and I wanted to keep it like that, for the time being at least. 'What's up?' I continued.

'Have you seen the Evening Post this morning?'

'No' I said, as I felt the phone begin to tremble in my hand.

'Well, if you can't get hold of the paper, I would highly recommend looking on-line if you can.'

'Look at what?' I said, though I fully expected I knew what he was going to say next.

'Well, it seems that Simon has gone missing according to the article in the paper. He went missing from the club a few nights ago, the night we were there for the Champions League match.'

'Missing?' I said, with as much surprise as I could muster.

'Yes, his wife reported him missing when he failed to return home that night. Apparently, money was taken from the club, along with his phone and wallet.'

'No sign of Simon though?' I said.

'No, he's vanished into thin air.'

I did not say anything for a few seconds as my heart started to beat a little faster.

'That's awful news' I finally said. 'Look can we catch up later this week, I really need to get back to work.'

'Yes, that's fine mate. Not sure we will be playing snooker this week though.'

We planned to meet later in the week and then I ended the call.

I brought up the website of the local paper on my phone and scrolled down the list of articles in the news section, it did not take me long to find the story I was interested in.

SWANSEA SNOOKER CLUB OWNER MISSING

Police are growing increasingly concerned for the welfare of a Swansea snooker club owner who has been missing for the last seven days.

Simon Tucker, aged 38, has not been seen since his wife reported him missing when he failed to return home from work on the night of the 15th April.

A significant amount of money, along with his mobile phone and wallet were also found missing from the snooker club he owned in the city centre. A police spokesman also confirmed that his car was found abandoned at the premises and urged anyone with information to contact South Wales Police on 01792 458762.

As I finished reading the article, I put the phone down, trying to take in everything. Whilst I had expected this, seeing it in front of me in black and white was still hard to digest. After the euphoria of my win an hour or so earlier, I now had to face the reality of what I had done to get here again.

Clearly the police would investigate, they would delve into Simon's life whilst trying to piece together the events leading to his disappearance. I had been incredibly careful to cover my tracks and was as certain as I could be that they would fail to find any evidence that led them to me.

Was I being too confident though? I may have dropped something that night or inadvertently left a fingerprint, despite my meticulous planning. Surely if I had the police would have been in touch by now though?

My thoughts were interrupted by my phone pinging. I picked it up again and could see it was a text message from Sadie.

Have you finished yet? Please ring me as soon as you can, I am on pins waiting for some news. Love you. xx

I needed to forget Simon and what I had done for now. Today was great but it would all be for nothing if I failed tomorrow.

I could not fail, and I told myself, I would not fail.

Chapter 74

DCI Ian Evans sat in his office on the third floor of Swansea Central Police Station, already on his third cup of black coffee despite it only being just after nine in the morning. He was certainly glad that tonight would be his last day on-call after a run of fourteen days as he covered colleagues on leave. Whilst the extra money was very much appreciated, the sleepless night were certainly not.

The case he was currently working on was certainly a puzzling one, and as he looked down at the case notes in front of him, he was no closer to finding out what had happened.

It seemed the missing man had just disappeared into thin air, and so far, him and his team had no clue to where he had gone, or for what reason.

The lack of CCTV made their task even more difficult, as most crimes were solved at least in some part by this vital tool. According to his staff, the CCTV at the snooker club that Simon Tucker owned had been down for several weeks, with no sign of when it would finally be back on-line. With that path of finding out what had happened now blocked off, Ian and his team needed to find other avenues that would hopefully unlock this case.

He had ordered a complete list of all members who were in the club that night, so they could in theory interview them all as potential witnesses. This was proving far trickier than he envisaged though, as no cards were swiped as members visited the club, which meant they had no idea who was there that night. He was now weighing up whether to contact the whole membership list to ascertain their whereabouts that night, a task that would take a lot of time to get through and was complicated by the fact the club also took in guest members who paid on the night.

He looked down at the notes he had written, which showed the two theories he was working on in relation to what had happened to Simon.

    1. *He had been taken by force, or his body removed from the club.*

    2. *He had left voluntarily, and therefore by his own choice.*

He had all but ruled out option two, due to several factors. Firstly, Simon's car had been left abandoned in the car park. Surely, he would have taken his own vehicle if he had left of his own accord. Secondly, only money from the till was taken from the premises, whilst the considerable amount of money from the safe was left untouched. Would you really leave all that cash if you were running away? Plus, his bank cards had not been used and his phone had been switched off in the vicinity of the club around 23:30 that night. The interview with his distraught wife the next day suggested no marital problems or money worries, and he had a reasonably successful business that was growing despite the current financial climate that was affecting other businesses. No, the first option was the only viable line of enquiry he could see, and the one him and his team would now concentrate on.

He got out of his seat and moved towards the window, looking out as the rush hour traffic began to dissipate in the street below him.

Yes, the only logical conclusion was that Simon had been abducted, or his body removed. Him and his team had found no sign that any violent act had taken place, which suggested that the perpetrator had subdued him before removing him from the premises.

Why though? What was the motive to all this?

Robbery did seem the most likely explanation, though the decision not to ransack the safe did concern him regarding this motive. Surely, the contents of that safe would also have been taken, alongside the money in the till.

He looked at the clock on the wall and could see it was now approaching 9.30. The daily team brief would be taking place in fifteen minutes, where he hoped to hear positive news from members of this team on the lines of enquiries they had been tasked with.

As he returned to his seat, Ian knew it was vital they had a breakthrough soon. If not, he had an awfully bad feeling the outcome would not be good, an awfully bad feeling indeed.

Chapter 75

Round 2 – Ashley White V Savannah Monroe

'Sierra Leone' I said confidently.

The usual dramatic pause from Patrick was gone as he quickly said, 'That is the correct answer Ashley, and takes you through to the next round.'

The reason for the lack of tension being that the contest had ended a few questions earlier, as my opponent saw her good start crumble, and her chance of winning the match evaporate.

I had not played brilliantly; her meltdown was my good fortune though, and I was not going to argue with that sort of luck.

The customary congratulations were again offered by Patrick and then I was led off the set by Alex. The adrenaline was still pumping through me as I sat down in the green room as Alex explained the next steps to me. I would be required to return in ten days' time to film my quarter final match, and what I hoped would also be a semi-final, as my dream of reaching the final continued.

Had *'little old me'* really just won another match, as I moved tantalising close to all that money. Money that would solve all my problems in one fell swoop, money that would clear my debts and stop our house being taken from us. Could I hold my nerve for three more matches and claim the prize, especially with the quizzing talent I knew would most certainly be left in the competition.

'Your taxi back to the station should be here in 15 minutes' Alex said, 'Would you like a coffee while you wait?'

'I'm fine thanks' I said, 'I could do with freshening up before the journey home though.'

'Of course,' she smiled back.

I walked out of the green room and towards the toilets that were at the end of the corridor, my mind frazzled by everything that was currently happening to me.

I splashed my face with the cold water that flowed quickly from the tap, the icy coldness as it hit my face felt so good. I took my hands away from my face, water dripping slowly off it towards the sink as I looked up to face the mirror in front of me.

And there he was, right behind me. The unmistakable figure of Simon Tucker once again.

He was different this time though, the handsome features he usually possessed had begun to decay slightly, it was like I was looking at a living corpse behind me.

'Surprised to see me?' he grinned.

It was horrible to see his image like this, him standing there like that reminded me of the scenes in *'The American werewolf in London'* where the main character keeps being visited by his dead friend, in various stages of decay.

Sensing my revulsion at what I was seeing he said, 'Not a nice sight, am I?'

'You're not real' I replied, 'You're just in my head.'

He laughed, the rotting teeth in his mouth now clearly visible. 'Maybe I am in your head, ask yourself why that is though? Why you cannot stop thinking about what you have done. Why you cannot get me out of your head!'

'It was an accident, I never meant to kill you' I limply said back, after checking there was no one else here to eavesdrop.

'It was always going to end that way eventually. You needed to release me for it not to happen, and you were never going to do that.'

I said nothing. He was right of course, letting him live was not an option.

'And now you are here, the place I should rightfully be. The place I would have been if greed had not taken over you.'

'I'm sorry' I said, tears slowly starting to well in my eyes.

'If you are really sorry, then you will end this charade here and now. Confess to what you have done and accept the consequences.'

'I can't, it's all gone too far' I pleaded, just as the door opened and a young man entered.

'Are you ok?' he asked, with concern etched on his face.

I walked out of the toilet without replying, taking a quick look behind me before I did.

All I could see was the bemused man behind me, the figure of Simon was nowhere to be seen.

Chapter 76

Up in the production gallery Mike Phelps took the opportunity to relax for a moment whilst the studio was prepared for the next contest.

'So, our lucky contestant marches on' he said to Sarah Mills, who was seated beside him.

'He sure does' Sarah smiled. 'Good performances too.'

'Yes, had a bit of luck in that first match though.'

'Well, we all need a bit of luck occasionally, and like you said, he's lucky to be here in the first place, so maybe the quiz gods are looking down on him.'

'Maybe' Mike said as he lent back in his chair. 'Did we hear anything else in the end about the contestant he replaced?'

'Nothing, and I don't really like to ring his wife, especially with us replacing him like we did.'

'What choice did we have though Sarah? We are making a TV show here.'

'I know, just seems so harsh, considering the reason why he could not appear.'

'I know, let us hope he's been found safe and sound at least. We can always offer him another chance if we do all this again.'

Both knew the chances of making another series of this show were slim though. Only the kind generosity of Stephen Howard and his company made this show possible and they all believed it was unlikely they would find such a kind benefactor for any further series.

'Well, I wouldn't bet against our Ashley White winning the whole bloody thing now' Mike said as he took a sip of his now tepid coffee. 'Let us hope he gets the chance to thank the unfortunate ... What was his name again Sarah?'

'Simon Tucker.'

'Yes, let us hope he gets the chance to thank Simon Tucker if he does win the two million pounds.'

Chapter 77

Patrick Reed slumped into the leather chair, grateful for the chance to relax after another hectic day of filming.

The hotel bar was fairly quiet as he watched Lance chatting to the barmaid as he got the drinks in. Lance was also staying in this central London hotel that the production company had put them up in whilst filming the show. Whilst Patrick knew he was only here to keep a check on him, he was glad of his presence.

Lance returned with the drinks and sat down in the chair opposite him.

'Thanks' Patrick said, picking up his whisky.

'So, I had a chat with Mike and Sarah before we left tonight, they seem incredibly pleased with how the filming is going so far' Lance said.

'That's good news' Patrick replied as he felt the warm feeling of the whisky enter his exhausted body.

'Should be great ratings for it when it airs, definitely the moment you get to the top again.'

'Without you this time though?'

Lance left that comment hang in the air.

'Is that still what you Lance, to throw our partnership away?'

Lance puffed out his cheeks before answering, 'We have been through all this Patrick.'

'I know, just thought you might have changed your mind, especially after getting the buzz of all this again.'

'I think I'll be ok' Lance laughed back in reply. 'I do have other clients you know, clients that are far less maintenance than yourself and who I can trust to stay out of trouble.'

'I apologised for that.'

'It wasn't just what happened in Tenerife, you know that.'

Patrick said nothing. He knew he no defence for what Lance was telling him.

'You will have your pick of agents now anyway. The will all want to represent the host of the biggest quiz show in the world.'

Lance may well have been right in that regard as once the show aired the attention on him would be immense, as his profile shot up like he had never experienced before. He would need a good agent to manage that pressure, and whilst he desperately wanted it to remain Lance, he knew that his old friend was finally done with him once the show had completed its run.

Patrick worried that no one could protect him like Lance had done though, from himself and the women he hurt.

Chapter 78

The woman glared at the TV as she watched the same trailer air for the third time that evening.

The charm oozed out of him as he invited the viewers to join him in the search for the biggest quiz show winner the world had ever seen. It was this charm that had seduced her all those years ago, until the darkness descended over him on that fateful night.

She turned the TV off and stared for a few minutes at the empty void, still seeing his image ingrained on the empty box, despite it being switched off. An image of a man without a care in the world, a man who had gotten away with his heinous crimes and was now allowed to resume his life. She could not resume her life though, his attack on her had put paid to her dreams and ambitions.

She picked up her glass of diet coke and finished what was left in it. Whilst she missed the wine that often gave her the release to forget the memory of that night and its aftermath, she knew that a clear mind was required now as she planned what she needed to do next.

She looked at the scribbled notes she had taken, the plan she had been devising for the last month or so.

The revenge she was going to take was beginning to take shape.

Chapter 79

'I'm off to bed' Sadie said as she lifted herself off the sofa, 'Are you coming up babe?'

'Yes, I'll be up soon' I said, barely looking up from the book I was reading.

'Don't be too long' she said as she came over and give me a kiss, briefly making me look up from my reading.

'I won't' I promised.

'I'm so proud of you, you know that. My clever husband on his way to winning all that money.'

'Let us not count our chickens love, I've still got to win three more matches to win it, and I can only see the contest getting harder from now on in.'

'You will win it; I have every faith in you' she said as she left the lounge and headed upstairs. 'And don't be late up' she shouted as an afterthought.

I mumbled a response and went back to my book 'The A-Z of everything known to man', which was proving invaluable in my revision with its lists of almost everything. The amount of information to take in was so vast though, and my brain was literally being overloaded as I tried to retain at least some of it.

In three more days, I would be back in the studio again. Three more days of cramming until I played my quarter final match.

I read and took notes for another hour before my tired eyes told me it was time to call it a night.

Like always, when my head was not filled with facts, my thoughts returned to what I had done to get on the show.

It had been seven days since the local newspaper had reported the disappearance of Simon, and thankfully for me, despite my daily checks on all local media there had been no further reports on the case.

Had I got away with it, or was it far too early in the police investigation to think that?

Images of that night flooded back, had I done everything I could to cover my tracks, or had I left something at the scene that could lead the police to me. The more I thought, the more I was sure that had not been the case. The CCTV being down had been a big advantage, which would make the task of the police investigation even more difficult as they tried to piece together what had happened that night. My use of gloves and the disposal of the glass that was laced with sedatives would surely make the crime scene as clean as I could make it, the near perfect crime I hoped.

I rose tiredly from the sofa and made my way slowly upstairs to bed.

That night I slept soundly, the first night I had slept since the murder, without the images of Simon invading my mind.

Chapter 80

Quarter Final – Ashley White V Kevin Hall

Just ten days after leaving the scene of my greatest achievement in life, I was back to face another immense challenge, a challenge I had to win or face the near certainty of financial ruin.

I had prepared well and revised the knowledge gaps I knew were there after my first two matches. The standard was only going to get harder from now on, with only the best being still left in the tournament. How I was still here I did not know; I was though and now needed to take my chance.

'So, how have you been?' Alex said, as she led me into the green room once again.

'Good thanks' I said, as I put my suitcase down and took a seat.

She gave me a breezy smile and explained that once again I would be needed for filming the next day if I was fortunate enough to progress from my quarter final match later that morning.

I looked at the suitcase that lay at the door, hoping that when I left here with it in a few hours it would be to the local hotel, and not the train station.

Unlike before, the wait to the recording seemed a lot longer, and my nerves had started to build when Alex finally said.

'They are ready for us in the studio Ashley, are we all set for this once again?'

'I think so.'

'Come on Ashley, we want more positivity than that. Think of all that money that lies at the end of all this.'

'I'm ready' I said, with just a touch more positivity than before.

'That's more like it' she said, as we began the now familiar walk to the studio area.

As I waited behind the curtain, I heard my opponent being introduced.

'And our first opponent tonight is Kevin Hall from Salisbury' I heard Patrick announce to the audience, and the viewers at home.

As Patrick began his chat with Kevin, my nerves did not ease.

It turns out Kevin was a civil servant at the Department of Transport and an avid quizzer who had competed at British and European events with great success. His two silver and one bronze medal at those events, coupled with his love of chess and sudoku told me everything I needed to know. I was up against an exceptional opponent here and would need a miracle to overcome him.

Twenty-five minutes later that miracle did materialise, and I now stood there once again being congratulated by Patrick as the cameras rolled.

'Well done' he said as he firmly shook my hand, 'Very close to that prize now.'

'Think I got quite lucky again to be honest.'

'Don't put yourself down, you won and should be immensely proud of that achievement.'

He was right, of course. I still had to win, and win I just did. Yes, my opponent fell apart, with popular culture being a particular weakness of his, a weakness I took full advantage of.

I watched as Patrick moved across to offer his commiserations to Kevin. The poor chap looked distraught at the result and I genuinely felt sorry for him at that moment. It must be hard for someone of his knowledge and experience to take this loss, a loss he probably could never have imagined happening when he first took to the stage.

My dream lived on. I was one match away from the final.

Chapter 81

I polished off the last of the steak and sat back in my chair as I watched the world go around me in the busy restaurant.

After leaving the studio just after lunchtime, I rang Sadie from my hotel room to relay the good news. Naturally, she was overjoyed, telling me how proud she was of me and what I had achieved so far. Her confidence and pride in me lifted my spirits, as despite winning today I really felt I had been fortunate to win. Her words right then were a great comfort to me.

'Was everything ok sir?' the waitress said as she cleared my plate away.

'Yes, it was lovely, thank you.'

'Would you like to see the dessert menu' she smiled.

'Why not' I replied to her with a smile.

I checked the website of the local paper as I waited for the menu. Still the only article on the disappearance of Simon was the one that had been listed ten days earlier. Clearly his body had not been found or it would have been splashed all over the media by now. I knew the longer the police had no leads, the longer that the body lay undiscovered, the more chance there was that the crime would never be solved.

'Thanks' I said as the waitress returned with the menu.

I glanced at the list and quickly called the waitress back to order a Banoffee pie, memories of my Mum's homemade version flooding back into my head. I thought of my Mum sitting there in that nursing home, totally unaware of the world around her as her dementia got rapidly worse. I doubted she would even know her son was on the TV when the time came. Tears began to form in my eyes as I thought of this once strong and independent woman who now struggled to speak and feed herself.

The waitress returned with my dessert and I greedily tucked into the mixture of bananas, cream, and toffee before hitting the crunch of the biscuit base.

It was good, not as good as Mum's though.

Chapter 82

Semi Final – Ashley White V Mahesh Kohli

The train stopped again for what seemed like the umpteenth time. Signal problems further on were causing this delay apparently. At this rate I would not be home for at least another hour, despite being on the train for over three hours already.

Not that I really cared to be honest.

I was still on such a high after the events of earlier. Events that I could still not scarcely believe had happened.

A live final in six weeks' time, where only one person stood between me and all that money.

I really had to pinch myself to believe it. The grin that now reflected back at me from the train window had been stuck to my face ever since I had been victorious in my semi-final.

I felt the shackles had come off me for the first time during the match. Yes, I had won my previous matches but had never fully relaxed in them as my own insecurities made me believe that my opponents had lost them, rather than me winning them.

The semi-final against Mahesh was so different though as I kept a quote from one of my former colleagues in the memory bank for the whole match. *'Never let anyone change you'* he said, *'Live your life like you want to, and never worry about what others think.'*

With this in mind I did not worry about looking stupid with guesses that maybe were wide of the mark. I just totally relaxed and for the first time really enjoyed the experience, knowing it may have been my last time on that stage.

This new approach did not mean a different result thankfully. Whilst Mahesh was a top quizzer, I matched him toe to toe for all the whole match. Like a limpet I stuck to him as I made sure he could not take a grip on the game, and like Kevin in the quarter final before, he collapsed under that pressure. I was certainly beginning to realise that these top quizzers knew nothing about soap operas or modern music.

As I sat there in the green room with Alex, trying to digest the magnitude of what I had done, and what lay ahead of me, there was a knock on the door.

And that is when I first met the head honchos of the show. Now that I had reached the final my importance to them had significantly increased. They did the obligatory congratulations and then told me what to expect once the TV audience knew I was in the final. That revelation would come in around five weeks' time, Mike Phelps, the executive producer of the show relayed to me. That week before the final was expected to be manic as the press would want both finalists for interviews and photoshoots, as interest in the show was expected to hit a frenzy.

The thought of interviews with the press scared the hell out of me, which I must have instantly conveyed to Mike.

'Don't worry about all that Ashley' he said. *'We have staff here that will guide you through it all, and me and Sarah will always be on hand as well.'*

Sarah Mills smiled and nodded her head in confirmation.

Their reassurances did not make me feel any better though. The thought of the attention I would now receive filling me with dread after what I had done to get here.

My phone on the table started to ring and all thoughts from earlier were temporarily forgotten. I quickly picked it up and saw that a Swansea number flashed up on the screen. A number I did not recognise.

'Hello' I said as I answered it.

'Hello' said a female voice at the other hand, 'Is that Mr Ashley White?'

'Yes.'

'Hello sir, this is PC Lizzie Thomas from South Wales Police.'

My heart sank.

Chapter 83

My mouth froze.

No words could come.

'Hello, are you still there sir?'

'Yes' I replied with my voice quivering. 'Sorry about the delay, I'm on a train at the moment and the signal is not great.'

'I can ring back when it's more convenient for you?'

'No, now is fine' I said quietly, not wanting the whole carriage to hear this conversation. 'How can I help you?'

'I'm ringing about a missing persons inquiry we are currently investigating. The disappearance of a Mr Simon Tucker on the 15th April from the snooker club he owned, a club you are a member of I believe?'

'Yes, I am.'

'Did you know Mr Tucker was missing?'

'Yes, I saw it in the local paper, awful news.'

'Yes, it is' the policewoman said. 'We are currently going through the list of members to try and find out who was in the club that evening. Can you remember if you were there on the evening of the 15th April?'

I could not hesitate at this point, or indeed lie. If I did that it would just arouse her suspicions.

'Yes, I was there that night. I remember because the Champions League was on that evening.'

'And you stayed there all evening?'

'Yes, I played a few frames of snooker with my mate and then we stayed and watched the football. We left just before closing.'

'You left together sir?'

'Near enough. I finished off my pint and left a few minutes after.'

'And this was when sir?'

'Just after 11.'

'Were you the last to leave the club?'

'No, there were still a few others there when I left' I lied.

'And how did Mr Tucker seem that night?'

'He seemed fine, very chatty and friendly, as he always was' I said. As soon as I said it, I regretted talking about Simon in the past tense. I just hoped that the policewoman had not picked it up.

'And you saw nothing suspicious when you left, no one hanging around outside?'

'No, I saw nothing suspicious.'

She paused for a few seconds, before continuing. 'Well, that's all for now Mr White. If we do need any more details, we will be in touch. Is that ok?'

'Of course, I really do hope you find him safe and sound soon.'

And with that the policewoman ended the call.

I put down the phone. My face now a deathly white.

Chapter 84

'Great show Patrick' Mike said as he sat down in the chair opposite him.

Patrick who was now dressed in a casual shirt and jeans let out an enormous yawn before saying, 'Thanks, I'm bloody knackered now though.'

'Well, at least you have the next month or so off to enjoy your endeavours from the comfort of your own armchair' Mike laughed.

Patrick did not return with laughter of his own.

'Unfortunately, your driver has been stuck in awful traffic. Should be here in the next thirty minutes with any luck.'

And he could not get here quick enough for Patrick. Whilst he had enjoyed the studio recordings more than he thought he would, the endless treadmill of it all he certainly would not miss. And a sustained period in his own bed with Maria would be nice also.

'Good pair of finalists as well' Mike said, 'And always great to have a woman get to the final, shows quizzing is not all male dominated.'

'If you say so' Patrick grunted back.

'Good personalities as well, what do you think Patrick?'

'Sorry?' Patrick said.

'I said they both have good personalities as well.'

'Yes, I guess they do.'

'Is everything ok?' Mike said, 'You seem a little distracted if I may say so.'

'I'm fine, just a bit tired that's all.'

Mike hoped it was just that, the last thing he needed was having to deal with any issues linked to his star presenter.

Chapter 85

'How much longer Dad?' Rhys said, already bored of sitting with us and being away from his precious X-Box.

'It's on next' I replied.

'Why did we have to come down so early then?' Rhys protested.

'Isn't it nice just to spend some time together as a family Rhys?'

Rhys grunted a reply that was unintelligible and glared steely at the TV.

It had now just been over a week since I had returned home after my semi-final triumph, and tonight was the night my first-round match was going to air.

As the four of us gathered around the TV I felt butterflies rise in my stomach, despite the fact that I knew the outcome already. I felt it was more to do with what lay ahead though, rather than with what I was about to see.

Sadie had wanted her Mother here tonight to watch the show, I had tactically dissuaded her against that though as the last thing I wanted tonight was to be judged by my overpowering mother-in-law.

The faceless announcer on the screen gave a rundown of the programmes that the viewers could delight in tomorrow evening, before introducing another first-round game of *'The Duel.'*

The smiling figure of Patrick Reed then appeared on the screen.

'When are you on Dad?' Ellie shouted.

'In a few minutes Ellie' I laughed.

And as quickly as I responded to her, I then watched the screen as Patrick announced my name.

Despite it only being a few weeks ago, I was amazed at how much I had forgotten about that first show. The walk-on, the chat to Patrick and the actual match now seemed like a distant memory.

'Whoa, my Daddy is on the telly' Ellie shouted excitedly.

Even Rhys was watching, and from the look of him seemed mildly interested.

'My clever husband' Sadie said, as she grabbed my hand tightly.

As Patrick continued his chat with me, I could see both children giggling.

'What's so funny?' I asked.

'Come on Dad, marathons and bungee Jumping?', Ellie giggled.

Sadie also joined in the laughter.

'I know, I know' I said as I watched my opponent come onto the screen. 'Let us keep that white lie to ourselves, shall we?'

We then watched as the contest unfolded and the controversial ending that concluded it played out.

'Well done Daddy' Ellie said.

'Yeah, well done Dad' Rhys also grunted. 'Felt a bit sorry for the other guy at the end though.'

'Yes, me too son' I replied, thinking how bad I felt at the time at the way I had won. I now felt even worse as I watched it on screen.

'You were fab, and totally deserved to win babe' Sadie said, giving me a quick kiss on the lips.

'Gross' Ellie groaned.

It was then that my phone pinged with the first text message offering congratulations. It did not stop pinging for the rest of the evening.

Chapter 86

I drove slowly down the country road, light rain hitting the dashboard as I tried hard to get my bearings.

I had not been down this road since the night I dumped Simon's body, and I was still not sure if I was doing the right thing coming back here now. The call from the police had really spooked me, yes it seemed to be a general chat with all the members at the club but that did not make me any less nervous.

I bought the car to a near crawl as I neared the spot, the spot I was quite sure I had dumped the body. I so was tempted to stop the car and take a closer look, the urge to check that nothing had been disturbed at the site now a nagging pulse in my head ever since that call. I resisted that urge though, fearful of being seen and thus arousing suspicion. So, as I crept the car along, I just looked out of the passenger window, as certain as I could be that nothing had been disturbed in the undergrowth.

Passing the spot, and content with what I had seen, I picked up speed and left.

As I drove home so much was going through my head, I thought it would explode right there and then. The most pressing matter at the moment for me being the investigation regarding the disappearance of Simon. I had not been expecting that call, naivety I guess you could call it, or maybe stupidity, but that call had definitely been unexpected.

The more I thought about it, the more I thought it may have been a good thing though. I was now on a list of hundreds of club members that the police had spoken to, a tiny dot in a maze of names. A maze I could definitely be lost in. If they kept down the path of robbery, or Simon simply disappearing of his own accord then my chances of getting away with it would be greatly increased. If some smart arsed copper looked more closely into the show Simon was due to appear on, and who replaced him on it then I would be in serious trouble. The exposure I was going to get in the next few weeks could ignite that clever copper's grey cells, and that worried the hell out of me.

The rain was starting to get heavier and I put the windscreen wipers on full blast, anxious to be home before the weather got any worse. As I continued to pick up speed, the spray from the car in front of me hit the dashboard window.

It was then that I saw him.

Staring back at me through the rear-view mirror, skin now hideously flapping from his cheeks, was Simon.

'You won't get away with this' he laughed as a piece of skin dropped from his face.

I pushed down hard on the accelerator, shoved the mirror down and raced home as fast as I could.

Chapter 87

'Over 20 million viewers' Mike announced. 'That is a phenomenal figure guys, you can all be so proud of the work you have done.'

The assembled staff members who stood before him in the offices of Gem productions clapped and cheered this news.

'So, enjoy today' Mike continued, 'The hard work for the live final starts in earnest tomorrow.'

Mike watched as everybody got into the party spirit, sipping champagne and swigging bottles of beer whilst enjoying the vast array of buffet food that had been laid on.

It was good to see his staff enjoying themselves after all the work they had done to make the show such a success.

He walked back to his office, Sarah closely following him.

Sarah took a seat as he closed the door, the noise from the party atmosphere outside now more muffled.

'And now we can breathe for a few moments' he said as he took the seat opposite her. Raising his glass of champagne and clinking it against her glass he said, 'To the Duel, and its continued success.'

'Indeed' Sarah said as she took a sip of the champagne.

Mike leant back in his chair and took a few moments to fully take in what they had achieved. The biggest quiz show launch ever, even surpassing the ratings for the hugely successful *Who Wants to be a Millionaire*' went beyond even his expectations. The ratings meant happy network bosses, and Mike hoped they would still be happy as the show continued its run every weekday evening over the next six weeks.

'Have you spoken to Patrick?' Sarah said.

'Yes, I spoke to him earlier and gave him the good news. I had hoped he might have made an appearance today to celebrate with us all but could not persuade him.'

'That's maybe for the best Mike.'

'Now, come on Sarah' Mike said with a sigh. 'He's been on his best behaviour these last couple of months, and I'm sure that would continue if he were here today.'

'Maybe' she said, although she was far from convinced.

'I'm keeping my eye on him and you have to admit he comes across great as the host.'

'I was not, or never have criticised his presenting skills, and yes I have to agree he comes across very well on the show. Still gives me the creeps though.'

'Let us just enjoy today' Mike said. 'Celebrate a winning start and start the hard work again tomorrow. Still lots to do to get prepared for the live final.'

And Mike certainly was not wrong there, Sarah thought. Whilst the nation enjoyed watching the high and lows as the contest got whittled down to the finalists, it was her job, alongside her top team, to prepare them both for the media frenzy that would follow.

Ashley White and Priya Patel would be household names in less than six weeks' time.

Chapter 88

The cool air blew across my face as I pounded along the path, the sheer drop down to the beach below only a few feet away from where I was running.

I stopped and looked at the Fitbit that was attached to my wrist, which informed me that I had run 3 kilometres and burnt 400 calories over the last forty minutes. Not a bad effort from someone who hardly ran, I thought. The white lies I told on the show springing back into my head as I stood there wheezing and struggling to catch my breath, a smile crossing my face as I pictured what they would say if they could see me now.

A concrete bench stood a few yards ahead of me and I wearily made my way towards it, slumping gratefully into its clutches as I reached it. It had been a crazy week and I was glad for this chance to reflect on it on my own, without any distractions.

Over the last six weeks I had watched engrossed, like the rest of the country, as the biggest quiz show on TV aired. The only difference being that I was one of the stars of the show. As my progress continued, I had become somewhat of a mini celebrity, in the Swansea area at least. The local papers and TV wanted to talk to me, and I was suddenly the most popular person in work and nearly everybody stopped me in the street to shake my hand in congratulations at what I had achieved.

I was suddenly Mr popular, something I never dreamed I would be.

And whilst I was still nervous about all this high-profile attention, for obvious reasons, I had to admit I found all this attention quite flattering. Tomorrow morning, I would be making the trip up to London yet again, this time it would be for the biggest prize of all, a prize that was now within my grasp.

It had just been three days earlier that I was there last. A quick day visit for media interviews and a pep talk from the guys on the show who were looking after me and my opponent, an opponent whose name and face I now knew but had yet met face to face. That honour would not come until we finally locked horns tomorrow night.

The thought of the media interviews were terrifying, but with the help of Sarah and her team I managed to get through them unscathed, and again had to admit I rather enjoyed doing them in the end.

As I watched the serenity of the scene before me, with the remains of the cast-iron Whiteford lighthouse standing firmly in the calm waters, I enjoyed this moment of peace before the expected frenzy of the next few days hit. The exposure I was getting still worried me, although my daily checks of the local news had reassured me with its lack of any updates to the case, as did the lack of any follow up from the police.

It looked like my hope that the police would not spot the link between me and Simon's planned appearance on the show was still holding firm. His wife must not have mentioned the fact to them when he went missing, or were the police just incompetent? My guess was on the former.

My thoughts returned to my opponent for tomorrow, Priya Patel.

Watching her progress on the show and the ease in which she dispatched her opponents had left me in awe at her quizzing ability, and truly frightened that I would be blown away like all her other opponents tomorrow night. Did I really stand a chance against a child prodigy like Priya, who had completed all her GCSE's with top grades when she was 12, had appeared on that show *Child Genius* and had gone to both Oxford and Harvard.

Was my luck finally going to run out at the final hurdle.

Despite my misgivings, I had to stay confident. I had to believe there were many things I knew that Priya did not. I had to believe that my age and experience would prove useful against my younger opponent.

I had to believe.

'Ashley' I suddenly heard a voice behind me call out.

I turned around, surprised to hear my name being called out by anyone during this early morning run.

The smiling face of Paul stared back at me as he jogged down the path towards me.

'Paul' I said, rising from the bench to meet him. 'How are things mate?' I continued as I shook his hand.

'Good thanks' he said as he took a seat on the bench. I also resumed my seat next to him.

'I've never seen you out and about before on one of my morning runs' he laughed.

'Yes, just trying to clear my head before the … ' I left the rest of the sentence hang in the air.

'The show' he said, completing it for me.

'Sorry Paul, I should have told you all about it I know. It's just been so hectic these past couple of months and I've not had the chance.'

'No need to apologise Ashley.'

That did not make me feel any better though. I knew I had neglected Paul, and now felt awful as I realised I had not spoken or seen him since that day I had successfully unlocked Jenny's phone. With all that had been going on in my life I had forgotten about him, Jenny, and the baby …

'How have you been keeping?' I asked.

'I have my good and bad days, got to hold it together for the boys though.'

I nodded, not really sure what to say next.

For a few moments we sat in silence before Paul finally broke the impasse by saying, 'So do I need to book an appointment now you are a celebrity mate.'

'Would hardly call myself a celebrity' I laughed.

'Don't put yourself down, I think anyone I see more than a couple of times on TV is a celebrity and you have been on way more times than that now.'

Despite my denial at what he was saying, I guess in lots of ways he was right. I was a kind of celebrity now. Yes, it may have been a Z-List celebrity in most people's eyes but who cared about that.

'So, how are you feeling about the final, it is tomorrow night isn't it?'

'Nervous but excited at the same time.'

'I bet you are, it's definitely something I could never do.'

I was not too sure about that myself. With his arrogance and full-on personality, Paul would be an ideal candidate for TV shows.

'I still don't know' he suddenly blurted out.

'Sorry?'

'I still don't who he is, the man Jenny was seeing, the man who got her pregnant.'

I did not want to hear all this again. Not now, not when so many other things were in my head.

'Why are you putting yourself through all this?' I said. 'Won't it be best just to leave it, concentrate on the boys, you have to stay strong for them.'

'I can't help it' he replied with a touch of anger in his voice. 'I need to know who my wife was shagging behind my back, who was the father of that child.'

Paul looked so angry and I could see in his eyes the hatred he now had for his dead wife. The hatred and anger that he would have for me if he ever found out I was that man who had got his wife pregnant, the man that had betrayed him and Sadie.

'I'm sorry, I really need to get going' I said, desperate to get away from the situation I found myself in. The peace and tranquillity I sought now shattered by this conversation.

'Of course,' Paul said, disappointment evident in his voice that the conversation we were having had to end so prematurely. 'I am sorry to have kept you so long, you must have lots to organise today.'

'No worries mate, and I'm sorry for not keeping in touch recently. I promise we will go for a few beers when I get back.'

'I will hold you to that, and it will definitely be your round, especially if you win' he chuckled.

'Definitely, I could probably stretch to a bottle of Prosecco if that happens' I laughed back.

I then shook his hand again and began my jog back home.

Turning back up the path, I looked back towards the bench just before I lost sight of it. Looked back at the sobbing figure of Paul.

Chapter 89

The woman stepped out of the shower, feeling refreshed and wide awake despite the early hour.

As he dried herself, she looked in the bathroom mirror at the face staring back at her.

The bags under her eyes that normally faced her back were now gone, as was the blotchy skin, the noticeable effects of drastically reducing her alcohol intake and getting a good nights' sleep.

She needed to be fully focussed now, needed to be strong if she was going to succeed.

She went into the bedroom and quickly changed into jeans and a t-shirt before making her way into the small living room.

She sat down at the small table she had and turned on her laptop.

While she waited for it to log her in, a process that seemed to get longer and longer with his ancient bit of technology, she wandered into the kitchen to make herself a coffee.

It felt so good to be up this early and not think about having to rush out to go that ghastly place again. She had quit her job a few days earlier, the need for it now being redundant. Her manager did not seem to care either way though, there were plenty of other people he could pick off the conveyor belt to do this job, she was no great loss.

She took her coffee back to the table and was relieved to see the laptop had finally logged her in.

She checked her emails, focussing on two in particular.

The first was the train journey to London which she had been booked yesterday and had already collected the one-way ticket from the station for, a ticket which was now safely placed in her handbag.

The second was the most important though, the one she had not been guaranteed to get and was so fortunate to now possess.

She printed out the ticket and held the piece of paper tightly in her hand, like it was a winning lottery ticket she was desperate not to lose.

It was like a winning lottery ticket to her though, a ticket that was the final bit of the jigsaw in her plan

A plan that would soon be over, she hoped.

She was ready to enact her revenge.

Chapter 90

Present day ...
And now it was time.

Time for this final act in what had so far been an incredible journey.

To fail now would be heart-breaking. It was something I could not contemplate.

The text message I had received in the dressing room had really spooked me. The fact that someone out there knew what I did terrified me but there was nothing I could do about that now. The most important thing now was to win this show and all that money, the identity of who sent that text message could wait.

As the curtain opened and I walked out onto that stage I felt the weight of the world on my shoulders. The outcome of today would affect everything going forward. Fail and my whole world would probably collapse, with my lies and stupidity finally being revealed to those closest to me. If I succeeded then all that could be forgotten, no one would need to know, and our lives would be changed forever.

The audience seemed even louder tonight, and their cheering and clapping was literally ringing in my ears as I made my way towards my podium and the smiling figure of Patrick.

Everything about tonight was so much bigger as the show supersized for this important event in television history. From the bigger studio, the bigger audience, and the extended running time of 90 minutes to accommodate the extra rounds it really did feel like I was part of something special here.

As Patrick went through the pre-match chat my nerves started to abate somewhat. Even after doing this same thing a number of times now, the butterflies still flowed through me as I waited backstage and walked onto the stage. Thankfully though, these nearly always dissipated as soon as Patrick began chatting to me. I was also thankful that these chats had now moved away from those white lies on my application form, lies that had a lot of people that knew me chuckle over the last few weeks.

As Patrick ended our chat and began introducing my opponent, I quickly glanced towards the audience, hoping that I could maybe catch a glimpse of Sadie. Alas it was not to be though, it was far too dark in that direction and I had no idea where she was actually sitting.

Just knowing she was out there was giving me great comfort though, knowing she would be at my side whether I won or lost.

And then Priya walked onto the set as confident as ever as she walked purposely to her own podium. She had the air of a person who believed she had already won, that the man who faced her had no chance. It was that confidence I needed to knock down if I was going to win here this evening.

And before I knew it her chat to Patrick had also ended, and it was time to get down to the important business.

The light dimmed and the first category of the evening was displayed on the screen.

My face dropped as I looked at the word on the screen.

SCIENCE.

Not bloody science I thought, did we really have to start with my worst subject! The only plus point it had in my mind was that it took an awful category for me out of the game nice and early.

And minutes later as the round ended my initial fears were realised.

'So, after the first round, Ashley has three points and Priya ten' Patrick announced.

A shocking start and I counted myself lucky to even get those three points out of it.

Patrick then announced a commercial break which signalled the full lights coming on in the studio.

'Well played both' Patrick said as makeup artists swarmed onto the set to retouch makeup on all three of us.

As foundation was reapplied to my face I tried desperately to think positively after that disastrous start.

Remember it was your weakness subject and her strongest. Yes, you are seven points behind, but just tell yourself that her weaknesses are still to come. THINK POSTIVE.

'Any water?' the runner asked when the make-up woman had left.

'No thanks' I said as I saw Patrick approaching.

'Remember it's still early days' he smiled, 'Plenty of time to catch-up.'

I then watched as he walked across to Priya, no doubt to offer a similar sort of pep-talk.

The lights once again dimmed and everyone else left the stage, leaving the floor manager to countdown for Patrick to restart the show.

Slowly but surely, I managed to claw my way back into the contest over the next four rounds and as we went into round six, I was only four points behind.

Three rounds left and I still had not seen Sport or Film and TV appear, two of my strongest subjects.

You could actually feel the tension in the studio as everyone realised it was all to play for in these last three rounds. Three more rounds until the biggest quiz show winner in TV history was crowned.

And in answer to my prayers, Film and TV flashed for the next round.

My confidence in this subject was clearly misplaced though as by the end of it I remained four points behind.

It was then that we went to the final commercial break.

Chapter 91

In the front row of the audience, the woman shuffled uncomfortably in her seat.

She had never been to one of these TV show recordings before and did not quite realise how long she would have to sit here. It had been over two hours already, and she could see it lasting for quite a while yet. Why they had to sit through thirty minutes of a warm-up act she did not know, although she had to admit he was quite funny.

She was enjoying the actual show as well, it was just a shame that monster was presenting it. Seeing him in the flesh after all this time made her skin crawl and she had to resist the urge to leave her seat right there and then to confront him.

It was another commercial break, and the woman next to her decided this was a good time to give her nose a good blow, something she had done in all the previous breaks as well. At least she would not have to put up with her much longer.

She opened the handbag that lay on her lap and looked inside at the contents.

Small makeup bag, her glasses and a small bottle with *'Evian'* written on it were the only things inside. When she passed through security with it they had not batted an eyelid at what they found inside. Just as she suspected they would.

Her hand trembled as she closed the handbag shut. Ever since arriving in the studio the adrenaline she had flowing through her had kept the nerves at bay, but now this was the first time since she had sat down that she genuinely felt nervous. She thought about just getting out of her seat and telling them she felt ill and needed to get some air outside. She quickly banished that idea from her thoughts though, she had not come all this way to bottle out now.

The lady on the studio floor began her countdown from ten, to indicate to us all that the commercial break was about to end. The woman next to me finally ceased her excessive nose blowing after a steely glare from the lady as her countdown hit five.

As she reached zero, she signalled for everyone in the audience to clap and cheer as the viewers at home were returned to the studio

The woman settled back in her seat to enjoy the rest of the show, waiting for her moment to act.

Chapter 92

This was it. The final chapter was about to begin.

Two more rounds, and a four-point deficit to close.

It would be tough, I knew. I had to keep faith that it was possible though as to give up now would prove what a loser I ultimately was, despite my meteoric run to the final.

And the task got even tougher at the end of the History round that came straight after the break, as Priya extended her lead to five points.

The positivity that had run through me from the start of this process was slowly seeping away now. I looked across at Priya, the air of confidence that exuded from her was fully justified and I knew in my heart of hearts that there was no way she was going to let this advantage slip. She was like a dog with a bone, with me being the unfortunate bone in her clutches at this time, a bone she would not release until the game was won.

All I had done to get here had been for nothing. I had committed murder to be a runner-up. There was no prize for being a runner-up, no one remembered the loser, or indeed cared what happened to the loser.

Sport flashed up like I knew it would. My favourite category was coming too late to save me, Priya would not let a five-point lead slip.

I looked glumly at Patrick as he asked me the first question for zero points, a simple question which I easily answered correctly, which Priya knew I would answer, hence her allocating zero points to it.

We were both going through the motions, we both knew the end was nigh.

She answered the zero-point question I assigned to her; the match remained as it was.

And then something extraordinary happened.

Priya Patel literally had a meltdown.

From the moment I got a ridiculously hard question about the NBA correct for five points and she failed to do likewise on her five-pointer, the cracks began to show on a face that had been so impenetrable before that.

I really should have taken more advantage of the opportunity; an opportunity that was so unexpected that even I could not fully grasp it.

It meant that by the end of the match we were both hearing these words from Patrick.

'Well folks, I promised you drama tonight, and that's exactly what we have got. After eight gruelling rounds, we cannot separate these two outstanding contestants who finish the contest all square.'

That generated loud applause from the audience.

As the applause died down, Patrick continued. 'So that means we now go into a sudden death situation. Nominating points to your opponent is now void, and from now on this is a straight shootout where I will both ask you questions in turn. If your opponent gets a question wrong and you subsequently get yours right, then the contest will end, and we will have our two million pounds winner. Is that clear to both of you?'

Both Priya and I nodded in agreement.

'Excellent, so as Ashley started the game first, we will give you the option to go first or second Priya? Patrick said as he turned to face her.

'First please' Priya said with confidence.

And so, it began ...

And after five questions each we were still at stalemate.

'Well, I told you they were good folks. I'm hoping none of you had any plans for tonight as these two could be here some time.'

The audience laughed at that one.

'And so, we continue' Patrick said as he turned to face me.

'Ashley, here is your next question. What is the capital of South Sudan?'

'Juba' I said without hesitation. There was no point in adding to the tension, especially when I knew the answer.

'Juba, you say' Patrick responded in reply.

Yes, I said Juba, which I know for a fact is the correct answer. So just say it is quickly and ask Priya her bloody question.

Patrick did not seem to get the memo though and continued his painstakingly slow reply to confirm my answer was correct. Finally, he did say those magic words I was waiting for.

'Is the correct answer Ashley.'

Thank god for that. Now the pressure was all back on Priya.

'So Priya, you have to get this question right to keep the contest alive.'

I could see that the self-assured and confident Priya had well and truly left us now. This was a woman under huge pressure, and I could see it in her face.

'So, your question Priya is this. Tokelau, in the southern Pacific Ocean is a dependent territory of which country?'

That was tough I thought, as I watched Priya's reaction to the question. She clearly was not sure as she sat there deep in thought, making sure she used up the full fifteen seconds to answer.

Fifteen seconds that seemed a lifetime to me.

Eventually she answered.

'I believe that is Australia' she replied, sounding completely unsure of the answer she had given.

Please, please, please be wrong.

Patrick then went through the same process he had earlier by slowly drip feeding his response to whether the answer was right or wrong.

'Your answer of Tokelau is ...' Patrick started to say before the dramatic pause.

Hurry up.
And then he said it.

'Unfortunately, incorrect.'

It was like time had stood still. Had I just heard him correctly, had he really just said her answer was wrong.

The pained expression on Priya's face opposite me told me I was not dreaming.

'The answer was New Zealand I'm afraid, which means we now have our winner, Ashley White.'

From high above us ticker tape descended on my side of the studio as the audience erupted into claps and cheers, with most standing as I looked with bewilderment around me, still not quite sure this was really happening.

'Huge congratulations to you Ashley', Patrick continued through the sea of noise, before raising his hand to ask for some quiet from the audience.

As the audience noise died down, he continued. 'We do have to remember that this brilliant contest could not have been possible without our amazing runner-up who has brought so much to this competition over the last six weeks. So, can you please give you biggest cheer to Priya Patel.'

The audience responded in kind, cheering, and clapping as before, with again most standing in appreciation.

Priya stood to acknowledge their appreciation, though understandably she looked sad and deflated at the outcome of tonight. Patrick moved across to her podium to give her a hug, one that lasted slightly too long in my opinion.

He then moved down to the front of the set, asking me to join him there. I really wanted to go over to hug Priya myself, to offer my commiserations and to say what a great quizzer she was, unfortunately there was no chance to do that and I just watched as she was taken from the stage by one of the production staff.

No one remembered the runner-up.

As I moved down to join Patrick, more ticket tape descended, and the audience again rose in unison.

Patrick firmly shook my hand and hugged me, the noise in the studio now at such a level that my head was starting to spin.

'So, how does it feel to be the biggest quiz show winner ever Ashley?'

'I still can't quite believe it' I replied, stumped for anything else to say.

'Well, I can assure you it's definitely happened, and you are the recipient of a whopping two million pounds. Not bad for answering a few questions is it?'

This led to even more cheers from the audience.

I looked again towards them, trying to glimpse Sadie, and wondering when Patrick would get her down here to celebrate with me.

It was then that I saw a woman in the front row leap out of her seat towards us.

As she ran towards us, I could see she had a small bottle in her hand, it looked like a bottle of water to me. I also noticed the pure hatred on her face, a hatred that was directed solely at the man standing next to me.

As she reached a couple of feet from us, she threw the contents of the bottle towards Patrick.

It felt like everything was in slow motion once the woman threw that liquid. As she did, I instinctively moved away from Patrick, sensing the danger of what was in that bottle.

And I was very correct in that assumption.

The liquid hit Patrick full in the face, with the anguish of pain that followed being something I would never forget.

Two burly security men rushed from the wings, finally catching up with the woman and bundling her to the ground. Patrick continued to hold his hands to his face, the screaming from his mouth becoming even more frenzied.

I began to walk back towards him, to try and offer some assistance. As I got closer, I could see steam rising from the gaps in the fingers that covered his face, steam that was coming from his face.

I could also smell burning flesh.

Chapter 93

'What the hell is happening down there?' Mike Phelps shouted into his headset from the control room.

As the events unfolded down on the studio floor, Mike knew he was witnessing something profoundly serious.

'Cut to a bloody commercial break' he boomed as he took off his headset and headed out of the room, quickly followed by Sarah.

The scene that greeted them was one of chaos and confusion.

Patrick was lying on the floor, still screaming as studio medical staff attended to him.

Ashley was close by, looking visibly shocked as he was consoled by a number of members of the production crew.

Mike called over Martin Ashdown, the floor manager.

'What the hell happened here Martin?'

'I really don't know Mike. That woman, she just leapt from her seat and ran at Patrick, threw something in his face. God his poor face ....'

And then Martin started to cry uncontrollably in front of them.

'It's ok Martin' Sarah said, 'Why don't you take a seat in the control room, we can take care of things here.'

He nodded in agreement and Sarah called over one of the runners to take him up.

'Has anyone called an ambulance?' Mike shouted.

'Yes, and the police' one of the crew shouted back.

Mike could see the woman who had caused all this seated in the corner, smiling as two members of the security team stood either side of her.

Who was she and why had she just done this?

So pre-occupied with the scene that confronted him, Mike had completely forgotten that the audience were still in the studio. As he turned to look at them, he could see most were just sitting there in complete shock at what they had just witnessed, some though were crying, and a tiny minority were shouting abuse at the woman.

He really needed them out of here, though he realised that would be impossible until the police arrived. Everyone in this studio were now witnesses to an awful crime and would need clearance from the authorities before leaving.

Mike held his head in his hands, hoping that when he took them away all this would be a bad dream.

From what should have been the greatest night of his career, was now turning into his worst.

Chapter 94

Lance raced down the hospital corridor, desperate to get there after being stuck in the studio for hours whilst the police took initial statements from everyone.

He found Maria seated on a plastic chair, crying softly.

'Maria' he said.

She rose from the chair and they hugged tightly for a few seconds. 'I'm so sorry' he said gently.

They slowly came away from the embrace and both sat down.

'How is he?'

She took a few moments to respond as she composed herself, 'The doctors have had to put him in an induced coma, they said his face has received awful injuries Lance, they said it looked like some kind of acid. Why would someone do that Lance. WHY!' She started to cry again.

'I don't know Maria; I really don't know.'

At the back of his mind Lance did think of a reason why someone might have done this, he really hoped he was wrong though.

Chapter 95

What a night, what a goddamn awful night it had been.

I looked in the bathroom mirror, at the shell of the man looking back at me. A man who should have looked so overjoyed at winning all that money, only to see that enjoyment crushed by what I had witnessed minutes later.

The memories came flooding back into my mind. The awful screams coming from Patrick, the laughter from the woman as she was bundled to the ground and that pungent smell of burning flesh that still seemed to be in my nose.

'I told you it would not end well' the voice behind me said.

The voice of Simon Tucker, now almost unrecognisable as his corpse looked like it had literally turned into a skeleton.

'Go way, I really cannot take this now.'

'You should have pulled out, confessed to everything. If you had, then you would not have seen all that tonight.'

'Go away' I screamed.

Suddenly there was frantic knocking on the door, 'Are you alright in there love' Maria called out.

'I'm fine, I'll be out in a minute' I replied.

The image of Simon had disappeared.

It was just past seven in the morning. They had arrived back at the hotel around two that morning after being forced to stay in the studio for questioning by the police. Not that I could tell them much, all I saw was the woman leap from her seat and attack Patrick, the same as the whole country witnessed through their television sets.

I had tried my best to get some sleep, but the images of the evening were so fresh, so raw, that they would just not leave my thoughts. I should be thinking about my win, about the fantastic opportunities it would bring me, Sadie, and the kids, not the brutal attack on the host of the show that followed.

I unlocked the bathroom door and returned to the spacious bedroom, where I found Sadie lying on the bed.

'Shall we go down for some breakfast?' she asked.

'I'm not that hungry really' I said.

'You have to eat something Ashley, you haven't eaten since before the show started.'

She was right, I probably did need to eat something and there was no rush to leave the hotel this morning. The media interviews that had been planned had understandably been cancelled, as had the big after party celebration last night. The big plans that had been organised being abruptly cancelled as everyone tried to digest what had happened.

And why?

Mike Phelps, the CEO of the production company had come into the green room and spoken to him at length after the police had finished with him. He was struggling to fight back the tears as he offered his apologises to what had happened. He looked visibly drained as he explained that all the things they had planned after the show would now be put on hold, such as the round of media interviews I was due to participate in the next day.

He then addressed the white elephant in the room.

'And please don't worry about the integrity of your win here tonight Ashley. You have won this contest and what happened afterwards will have no bearing on that. The money will be in your account as promised in a few days.'

Sadie, who was seated next to me, squeezed my hand tightly.

'Thank you' I replied.

'No, thank you Ashley. You have been a wonderful contestant and I'm so sorry it's ended on such a tragic note.'

As Mike left us alone in the room, Sadie turned towards me and whispered, 'Well done my clever man, you have changed our lives forever.'

Chapter 96

It was just after ten in the morning and facing Mike Phelps in his office were Sarah and James Pullman, director of programmes for the network.

'So, can you explain to me what happened last night Mike? How someone could be allowed to do that?'

Mike had been dreading this meeting.

'I'm still trying to get the exact chain of events myself' Mike said rather blearily, the lack of sleep now affecting him. 'From chatting to the security on the studio floor it appears this woman just suddenly jumped from her seat on the front row, and before they knew it, she had reached Patrick and threw that substance towards his face.'

'Do we know what this substance was?' James said.

Mike hesitated for a second before replying. 'From chatting to everyone on set, and subsequently the police, it looks like it was a corrosive substance of some kind, most likely acid.'

'Acid?' James said, deeply alarmed at this new development.

Mike said nothing in reply.

'And can you please explain to me how this woman brought a bottle full of acid into a TV studio.'

'It was in a water bottle' Mike countered in his defence. 'Security had no reason to believe a water bottle in her handbag was anything to be concerned about.'

'Do we know who she was?' James said, not really having an argument against what Mike has just told him.

'Sarah?' Mike said as he turned to look at her.

'Yes' she responded, as she looked down at some notes on her desk. 'From the ticketing records we have her name down as Sophie Charles. She applied for her ticket online as per the normal procedure and gave an address that was registered to a flat in Paddington. We have given the police all these details.'

'Thanks Sarah. The question is why did she do it though?' James said.

'That's a job for the police to find out' Mike said, yawning as he did so.

'You both need to get some rest' James said, 'We can continue this discussion later.'

'I'm sorry James' Mike said, 'I really am.'

'We can begin the repercussions when we know exactly what has gone on.'

Mike and Sarah looked on forlornly as James spoke again, 'Do we have any update on how Patrick is?'

'He had been put into an induced coma when I last spoke to Lance. Seems he will be in it for a good while yet as the doctors assess him' Mike answered.

At this precise moment he just wanted the ground to swallow him up so he could escape this nightmare. He could not even begin to imagine what the repercussions of all this would be to him and his company. A company he had worked so hard to build up over the years, and one which was now widely respected in the industry. *Would all this fall apart after tonight?* He tried desperately to put this thought out of his mind and focus on the hope that everything would be ok in the end.

'I can confirm one good bit of news to come out of all this' James continued with a hint of a smile on his face. 'I've just found out thirty million viewers tuned into the end of the show last night.'

Whether it was said in jest or not, Mike thought that comment was in seriously bad taste.

Chapter 97

I looked at the phone for about the umpteenth time that morning.

At the messages had started a couple of days after the show, and the last one I had received yesterday.

Unknown – Awful thing to happen at the end of the show, I really do hope you are ok. Have you received the money yet? Oh, and I should say congratulations, that was some performance.

Me – Who is this?

Unknown – that does not matter for now. You will find out soon enough. Now answer the question.

Me – Yes, I have.

Unknown – that's good news. I was fearful of a delay after what happened. I will be in touch soon with further instructions.

And despite me sending numerous replies, I had not received another message until yesterday.

Unknown – Good afternoon Ashley, I hope you are well. I am guessing you are, with all that money in your bank account. I want you to meet me tomorrow at 3pm in Castle Square. Sit on the bench by the fountain, I will meet you there.

Me – Hold on a minute. I am not meeting anyone unless you tell me who you are.

Unknown – You do not call the shots here Ashley, I do. You will meet me tomorrow or the police will be getting an anonymous call regarding the disappearance of Simon Tucker.

They were right, I had no right to negotiate.

I read the final two messages.

Me – I will be there.

Unknown – Good, see you then Ashley.

I shuddered as I finished reading them. The thought of somebody being out there that knew everything sickened me. Despite thinking I had done everything right it was clear from these messages that had not been the case. My planning and execution at what I had done had clearly not been careful enough to hide my tracks. Someone knew and was now clearly trying to blackmail me in order to buy their silence.

Shit, shit, shit, I silently mouthed.

Life was so good and now all this. The money was in my bank account and all the debts had been cleared, without Sadie even knowing anything about them. And even the tragic events that followed had positives when I had looked at it in the cold light of day. With all the headlines focussed with the attack on Patrick and its aftermath, I had been largely side-lined by the media as they sought the story on the woman and why she attacked Patrick that night.

The winner of the biggest quiz show prize in history was an afterthought, and that was just the way I liked it. No massive media intrusion in my life meant no police officer's ear would prick up and potentially spot a link between me and Simon. Or so I hoped.

We had both promptly quit our jobs on our return, safe in the knowledge that the money was in the bank and our future was secure. Sadie was busily making plans for trips aboard, mainly to see archaeological ruins and sites that she thought would help with that history degree of hers.

I was in a happy place, we both were. And now this person was spoiling all that happiness, spoiling all the plans we had made.

I had no other option than to meet them though, to do what they asked.

Hours later, I watched as the enormous seagulls swooped down onto the scattered chips and bits of thrown away burgers that littered the concrete square in front of me, a common problem with the McDonalds being so close by.

I checked my watch, it was now 15:05 and still no one had joined me on the bench. I looked furtively around at everyone that was milling around the square, wondering if any of them would suddenly sit next to me and reveal themselves as my blackmailer.

It was as I was looking around me that a middle-aged woman in black trousers, boots and a light cream jacket came around behind me and sat down.

I was startled when I looked at her face, a look of shock and surprise descending across my features. 'Dr Sharma, what are you doing ...' I spluttered without completing the sentence, and then the penny dropped. 'It's you, you have been the one sending the messages?'

She smiled as she watched the colour drain from my face.

'You bitch, you bloody bitch' I said as I grabbed her arm.

She pushed it away forcibly. 'I would not do that if I were you Ashley, remember we are in a public place.'

I reluctantly took her advice.

'How did you find out?' I said, still perplexed at how she knew about Simon.

She laughed back at me before saying, 'You really don't know, do you?'

'I wouldn't ask you if I did' I replied sarcastically. 'Have you been following me, is that how you found out?'

'Now, why would I do that. No, I found out completely by accident.'

'Accident?'

'You have been coming to see me for quite a while now, haven't you Ashley?'

'Yes' I replied, still not quite understanding where this was leading.

'And you have opened up to me, told me about your childhood, about your relationship with your parents and brother, how those early memories could have been the catalyst for the depression and anxiety you were feeling.'

Keeping my voice low, bearing in mind that a lot of people were milling about in the square, I said, 'And of course I tell you I've killed someone as part of these cosy chats, come on Doctor, I'm not an idiot.'

'You did tell me though Ashley, you told me everything.'

'And why would I do that?'

She looked at me with those kind and caring eyes she had, a look I had seen many times during our sessions. 'When we started our sessions, you were very uptight and reluctant to talk about these things, so I decided on another technique to get you to open up.'

'Technique?'

'Yes, we agreed that the use of hypnotherapy would be beneficial in progressing your treatment, and it was during these hypnotherapy sessions that you revealed your awful secret.'

'You hypnotised me' I shouted rather too loudly, before lowering my voice. 'You did that without my consent?'

'Oh, I had your consent Ashley. You can see the form you signed back at my office if you do not believe me. Why you do not remember agreeing is a mystery to me, maybe I took you under slightly more than I intended.'

I went as white as a sheet. All my work to cover my tracks had been for nothing. I had been exposed by something so ridiculous, it would have been a great plotline in one of those crime novels I loved.

'Why did you not go straight to the police?'

'I just did not believe any of it at first. It seemed that what you were saying was so farfetched that there was no way it could be true. It was only when I read the newspapers that a light switch flicked on in my head.

'So, why did you not go to the police then?' I asked, still uneasy to be talking like this in such a public place.

'Oh, I've picked up the phone many times since then, with the very intention of telling them everything I knew. Each time I hung up though, not sure where to begin, not even sure they would believe me.'

'I'm sure they would have believed an eminent psychiatrist like yourself' I sneered at her.

'Probably, but then I watched your progress on the show with great interest Ashley, deciding I could benefit much more if I kept my secret to myself, for the time being at least.'

'So, what do you want' I asked, sure I knew the answer but still wanting to hear the response from her.

'250,000 pounds in my bank account by the end of this week, otherwise the police get a helpful tip-off regarding the Simon Tucker case' she said in a matter-of-fact way.

'250,000' I said in disbelief.

'A small price to pay I feel, considering what I know.'

I said nothing back, she had all the cards and we both knew it.

'I will text you the bank details where I want the money to be transferred later today' she said as she prepared to stand up.

'How can I trust you? How can I know you won't be back for more money?'

'You can't, you just have to trust that I won't.'

Trust was not something I was good at, and I really did not trust Dr Amita Sharma one bit.

'Oh Ashley, there was just one more thing' she said as she turned to leave. 'I think we better cancel our sessions from now on. I think I've taken them as far as I can.'

And then she was gone, leaving me once again alone on the bench as the anger boiled up inside me.

Chapter 98

Lance hesitated at the door, as ever unsure whether to grab the handle and cross the threshold into the room.

After some moments he opened the door and entered the gloomy room where he found the unconscious figure of Patrick lying, his body illuminated by the tiny glow of a nightlight in the room.

As he took the seat next to the bed, Lance felt himself welling up to see his friend in such an awful state. With a tube coming from his mouth to the ventilator that was helping him breathe and various other tubes attached to his arm, it felt like he was never going to wake from the medically induced coma he was placed into a couple of weeks earlier.

It was his face that Lance was drawn to though, a face that was covered in bandages except for his eyes and mouth. Bandages that hid the horrific injuries that had been inflicted on his face that night.

The doctors were still hopeful that he would survive, though the damage to his body would be life changing. As well as the partial and full thickness burns to his face, they had also confirmed that Patrick had lost the sight in his left eye, the damage to his right one was still being assessed. Then there was the added complication of damage to his throat and lungs which had been caused by swallowing some of the acid.

These injuries would be devastating to anyone, more so to a man who relied on his looks and voice for work.

Lance cleared his throat before saying, 'Hi Patrick, it's Lance here. Sorry it is just me tonight, but Maria had to take care of some things back home. She promises to be back here first thing in the morning though.'

In truth he had told Maria to go home. She had been here constantly in the two weeks that had passed since the attack and was in desperate need of rest and a change of environment.

At first Lance really struggled to find what to say as he sat here for hours on end. The doctors could not be sure Patrick could hear anything whilst in the coma, but they said it would help to have familiar voices around him. And so that is what him and Maria did, sitting here for hours in the hope that Patrick could hear them, that hearing their voices gave him some comfort.

Lance spoke of the good times they had together; the fun they had as they planned his meteoric rise from radio to TV stardom together. It was always about the good times, no mention of the dark periods that regularly took hold of him. The dark periods which had ultimately led to where he was now.

Lance had his own theory about the woman and what she had done that night, a theory which had been proven to be frightenedly accurate as the exact details emerged.

The media had reported that the attacker was a 32-year-old woman, who they named as Sophie Charles. As the days passed it was reported that Sophie had been one of the many women that had come forward against Patrick, one of the many that were due to testify against him until the court case had collapsed. It had appeared that Sophie's life had gone into freefall after she was attacked by Patrick. She left her promising career at a law firm and started to move frequently between low paid supermarket jobs, unable to forget what had happened to her.

This drifting through life had continued until she joined the avalanche of women to report the attacks on them by Patrick. The papers quoted her family and friends who said her demeanour was much more upbeat as the court case approached, and that she was relishing the opportunity to tell her story and see her attacker pay for his crimes.

And then the case collapsed, and Sophie's world once again spiralled downwards. It was believed that she had been plotting her revenge ever since, finally enacting it on that fateful evening two weeks ago.

He looked at Patrick and said with tears in his eyes, 'You were lucky the last time old friend, but now your past has really caught up with you.'

Chapter 99

I opened the door and released Riley from his lead, the dog eagerly running into the kitchen where he greedily started to eat the food from his bowl.

'How was the walk?' Sadie shouted from the lounge.

'Good thanks' I said as I popped my head around the door. 'What are you up to?'

'Trying to find us a new home' she said, as I noticed a rather large, detached house on the laptop screen.

'Very nice, but can we afford it?'

'Very funny' she laughed.

As I started to make my way upstairs for a shower, I suddenly heard Sadie calling up to me, 'Ashley, come back down here for a minute.'

'What is it?' I shouted back, desperate for a shower after my exertions with Riley.

'Just come back in here.'

Reluctantly, I made my way back downstairs and into the lounge.

Sadie has paused the local news, with a familiar face now staring back at me on that frozen screen.

'Isn't that your therapist?' Sadie said, her face ashen.

'Yes, it is' I responded in surprise. 'What is she doing on the TV?'

Sadie said nothing and just began to rewind the programme back, before hitting play when she reached the start of the item, 'Listen' she said.

I watched as a news reporter stood outside a large, detached house, in what looked like an affluent area. A policeman could be seen at the front of the property.

The reporter started to talk to the camera.

'It was yesterday lunchtime that the body of Dr Amita Sharma was found at the detached property behind me. She was found with multiple stab wounds by a concerned colleague after falling to turn up at the psychiatry practice she ran on the outskirts of Swansea. Police have launched a murder inquiry and have asked anyone that saw anything suspicious in the area between Wednesday evening and yesterday lunchtime to contact them.'

The reporter then handed back to the studio.

'How awful' Sadie said.

I stood motionless, still staring at the TV even though the story had finished.

'Are you ok?' Sadie said, concern on her face.

'Yes, just really shocked' I replied in a trance like state.

'When did you see her last?'

'Before I went on the show, she was really pleased with my progress at the time, even suggested the sessions could end.'

'You never told me that?'

'I completely forgot with all that has been going on.'

'Well, it looks like they have definitely ended now' she said sadly.

'Yes, shocking to think I won't see her again.'

She smiled at me before rising from the settee and giving me a big hug.

'I know love, let us hope they find whoever has done it quickly.'

I nodded and slowly left her embrace, making my way back upstairs for the shower I definitely now needed.

As I looked in the bathroom mirror, the sadness in my face suddenly turned into a grin.

I could not leave her live now, could I?

How could I trust her to keep quiet once I had given her the 250K? The truth was I could not, so I needed to take matters into my own hands before she could blackmail me even more.

I ran the tap and splashed cold water on my face, the events of that night flashing back into my mind.

The hours I spent outside her practice, waiting for her to finish work. And then the drive as I followed her to the house she lived in on the outskirts of the city, the large, detached house in the affluent area. The house I had just seen on the TV.

I waited in the car for nearly an hour before I made my way towards her front door, still apprehensive in what I was about to do. Still not sure I should be doing it at all.

Dr Sharma was shocked as she answered the door, unable to comprehend how I could be facing her on her own doorstep. Before she had the chance to shut the door in my face, I lunged at her, making her stumble back into the hallway before closing the door quickly behind me.

'You madman' she screamed as she got quickly to her feet in a desperate attempt to flee my attack.

It was a fruitless attempt though as I quickly caught up with her and pinned her against the floor. As she attempted to scream again, I put my left hand over her face whilst quickly reaching into my coat pocket with my right.

Pulling the razor-sharp kitchen knife out, I looked down at the terrified face of the doctor. Looked at eyes that pleaded with me to see sense, to stop this madness before it was too late.

There was no going back though, I had come here to finish all this and that was what I intended to do.

In a robotic fashion I plunged the knife again and again into her chest, before moving to her neck to inflict more damage. Blood poured out furiously from the wounds, splattering the carpet and walls as well as me.

I only stopped my frenzied attack when I was sure Dr Sharma was dead, in truth she was probably dead much earlier. All my further blows did was cause more mess in the hallway as even more blood poured from the new wounds.

I stood over her body for quite a while afterwards, not the best thing to do I later thought as once a crime has been committed the perpetrator should leave the scene as quickly as possible to avoid detection. I was so shocked though by my own brutality that I just looked at her lifeless, blood splattered body. The killing of Simon had been an accident, this was cold blooded murder though.

I snapped out of my trance like state eventually and looked at my clothes, feeling lucky that most of the blood had splattered onto the thick coat I wore, a coat I could easily dispose of later. I looked at myself in the hall mirror, at the ashen face that was had spots of blood covering it.

And then I ran from that house, slamming the door behind me as I left the body of Dr Sharma behind me.

The same ashen face now looked back at me in the bathroom mirror.

I was not a bad person, but I had to do bad things to protect me and those close to me. I would have been constantly on edge if Dr Sharma had been allowed to live, not knowing from one day to the next if she would reappear in my life to demand more from me in exchange for her silence.

Her death meant I could get on and enjoy my life. A life that would be so different with all that money to spend. Money that the unfortunate Doctor would now never lay her hands on.

I laughed as I got into the shower.

Singing away to my favourite Robbie Williams song as I let the warm water cascade down my body.

Knowing I had done a good job, an incredibly good job indeed.

Chapter 100

DCI Ian Evans winced as he took a sip of his now tepid coffee, not quite sure how long it had been there as the evening sunshine quickly turned into darkness.

He looked at the clock on his office wall.

It had just gone past 21:30.

So much for an early finish, he thought.

Ian cut a frustrated figure as he hovered over his desk, with case notes and witness statements scattered all around. Documents that said little really, certainly nothing that was going to solve the case.

The disappearance of Simon Tucker was as much a mystery now as it was when he first found it in his in-tray. With no CCTV, no forensic evidence and no witnesses, the hope of finding a breakthrough was becoming less likely. And to top it all off he had now lost most of his team as focus shifted to the murder of that doctor a few days earlier.

That was why Ian had to make an incredibly difficult decision at this moment.

With no leads, he had reluctantly come to the decision that the case could not go on unless new information came to light.

Like all coppers he wanted to solve all the cases he led, sometimes he had to admit that was not always possible though.

He picked up the file on Simon Tucker and with a heavy heart put it on the tray on his desk labelled *'Inactive cases.'*

Epilogue

1 year later...

Kerion Hughes would be glad to finish for the day. After a day of sitting in his mini digger he was ready for home, just one more section left of the trench to dig and he could finally jump out and stretch his legs.

The incessant rain that had started a few hours ago was still falling and Kerion was thankful that he at least had shelter sitting here in his cab. His colleague Mark Francis was less fortunate as he directed his path from the outside, his luminous yellow jacket, and trousers clearly visible in the gloomy conditions.

This stretch of road had been susceptible to flooding for years, and now finally the council had provided funding for new sewerage measures to be implemented along its length.

As Kerion got ready to dig another section of the trench, he suddenly saw Mark wildly wave his arms in his direction.

'Keiron, stop digging!!' he heard his colleague shout.

Keiron stopped the digger and got out of the cab to join Mark.

As he got closer, he could see his friend had gone a deathly pale as he looked into the ditch that Keiron was moments ago going to dig into.

Mark said nothing, just pointed into the ditch, urging Keiron to look.

Keiron flinched as he saw what had made Mark stop him digging.

Lying in the ditch were the near skeletal remains of a human body.

The door slammed shut behind her, leaving the woman to lay there in near darkness, with the only light coming from the soft glow of the lamp on the small table next to her bed.

It often took her a few hours to get to sleep, the clattering of doors and whispered voices from others reverberating around the prison long after the cell doors had been closed for the night.

She had been inside this small cell for a year now and knew it would be at least another seven years before she would finally taste freedom again. Not that she really cared, she had felt like a prisoner ever since the attack anyway, so actually being physically incarcerated now did not feel much different.

Her trial had been held under a media frenzy, with a packed court room everyday as the events of that night and the reasoning behind them were played out.

Patrick Reed had survived the attack, something which pleased her very much as she had never wanted to kill him, only wanting to destroy his life, like he had done to hers.

Against the wishes of her legal team, from an awfully expensive firm which had been paid for by her parents, the woman bravely took to the stand to explain her actions. She wanted that courtroom to hear the pain and suffering Patrick had inflicted on her, how he had literally destroyed her life that night. She wanted them to understand why she had done what she had, wanted them to feel her pain in some way. This was the testimony of Sophie Charles that the court did not hear in that first aborted trial of Patrick Reed, the testimony she had waited so long to give.

She had received fifteen years for the attempted murder of Patrick, not that the man himself saw her go down, apparently still too ill to attend the trial. It was a shame as she really wanted to see his face as she stood on the stand, or what was left of his face.

The memories of that night came flooding back, the anger that had built up for years finally being released as she ran at him, the satisfaction on her face as the toxic liquid struck his face.

As she slowly drifted off to sleep, the woman finally felt like a huge weight had been lifted from her. She finally felt like Sophie Charles again.

She had finally got her REVENGE!

Patrick used to love visiting this garden, with its potent smells and visions of colour it had always been his little piece of paradise, a place he could escape to and forget about all his troubles.

Not anymore though.

Now it just represented misery in his eyes, of the things he could not do, of the things he could not see as well now.

'I'm heading in' he said to Maria, who was sitting next to him with a bagel and cup of tea as they enjoyed their breakfast in the early morning sunshine.

If you could call anything he did now as enjoyment.

'Me too.'

'No, you stay out here and finish your breakfast' Patrick said as he rose from the wicker chair he had been seated in, 'Enjoy the sunshine.'

She seemed reluctant to let him leave on his own but did not argue.

Patrick slowly made his way back into the house, careful as always as his sight was now limited to one eye. Still wearing the baseball cap and face covering he had on, he went straight up to his study.

Sinking into the leather chair, Patrick remembered the happy times he had enjoyed in this room. The phone calls, the meetings; all the plans for his career had been instigated in his room. A career that had now shuddered to a halt once again.

He could remember extraordinarily little of that night when he finally woke up from the induced coma nearly a month later. He could remember small amounts of the actual show but not the attack from that woman. The bitch that had ruined his life by throwing the contents of that innocuous bottle into his face.

He hoped she was rotting away in whatever prison they had sent her to, hoped her life was every bit as miserable as it was before she attacked him.

Lance had stayed with him after the attack, the threat of ending their partnership now unspoken. Not that there was much for him to do now, as with a face like Freddy Krueger's and fresh revelations surfacing during the trial of that woman, his career was all but finished.

He slowly took off his cap and then the face covering, something he only did in private, not wanting the world to see the mess the woman had inflicted on him.

He gingerly walked over to the mirror, closing his eyes tightly shut as he got closer, knowing he had to look but resisting the urge for as long as possible.

And then he opened them.

Looked at the grotesque face that stared back at him, at the scarred skin that would never properly heal. All looked at by the one good eye he still had.

He closed them shut again, moving away from the mirror and back to his chair.

Whilst the physical scars could be seen, it was the unseen mental scars that were just as hard to deal with.

Patrick had barely left the house since he had been discharged from hospital, preferring to hide away here than let the public see him. He even refused to go to the trial, refusing all pleas from the prosecution to attend. They had wanted him there so the jury could see the effects of the attack on him first-hand, although Patrick doubted his appearance would make any difference to the final verdict. Millions had seen what had happened and a conviction was all but assured.

Whilst she had indeed been convicted, the punishment was no way harsh enough in Patrick's opinion, and it had felt that he had been on trial just as much as her.

The reopening of old wounds and bringing back into the public domain all the things he had hoped had been laid to rest.

And then the phone call yesterday from his lawyer to confirm that the CPS were going to charge him with fresh offences. The trial being the catalyst for more women to come forward.

He sat there for a few moments, enjoying the peace and quiet of the house, thinking of the wonderful memories he and Maria had made here.

He was still reminiscing as he pulled open the desk drawer and lifted the gun from it.

Still thinking of those wonderful memories as he put the barrel inside his mouth and pulled the trigger.

This was the life.

The life I had always dreamed of. The life I was now living.

I picked up my glass of Rioja as I watched the kids play in the swimming pool. Both enjoying this new life we were now living.

'This is the life' I said to Sadie, who was sitting on the sun lounger next to me.

'Indeed, it is, and all thanks to my clever husband.'

It had now been a year since I had won, and our lives had changed so much in that time. A new five-bedroom house back home was complemented by this beautiful luxury villa we had bought in the countryside of Majorca, a place we tried to visit every few months for some much-needed sunshine. Sadie was now volunteering in a local museum, whilst still working hard on finishing her history degree. Free from work, I had started write a novel, something I had always wanted to do and now had the freedom to do.

Life was good.

I had pushed the memories of what I had done to the back of my mind, and that is where they had successfully stayed. I had seen nothing relating to the disappearance of Simon in the media since that first newspaper article, and it looked like the investigation into Dr Sharma's murder had stalled with no positive updates being reported.

I smiled as I took another mouthful of Rioja.

I had got away with it all.

And with nearly all the focus being on Patrick and the woman that had attacked him, the media interest in me had been diminished. Yes, there had been the odd interview but not the avalanche I had been expecting. For obvious reasons I had become the invisible winner for the most part.

Not that it bothered me one bit. With less attention on me, it meant there was less chance for an eager copper to delve deeper.

As I watched Ellie and Rhys dive into the pool again, I heard my phone go off next to me.

I picked it up and looked at the new message on the screen.

My heart sank as I did.

'*Dr Sharma was not the only one who knew what you did Ashley. You may have dealt with her, but I am still around. I will be back in touch very soon.*

I dropped the phone and started to cry ...

Printed in Great Britain
by Amazon